THE RIGHT WRONG MATCH

A SWEET, SMALL TOWN ROMANTIC COMEDY

LOVE IN MIRROR VALLEY
BOOK 2

SARA JANE WOODLEY

Daisy & Luke art by
VECTORSMARKET

 ELEVENTH AVENUE
PUBLISHING

1

DAISY

Going to your best friend's wedding with a blind date as your plus one might *sound* like a fun, quirky idea...

Until said plus one drinks a little too much red wine and proceeds to roll a huge, sloppy meatball right off his plate and onto your blush pink bridesmaid's dress.

"He's just so excited for the happy couple," I offer cheerfully as an explanation to the table of stunned bridesmaids and their dates while subtly dabbing at the stain on my lap. Lucky for me, by the time I found Eddie wandering around the garden and sat him down for dinner, the food was already cold. No chance of getting a meatball-shaped burn on my upper thigh.

It's the little things.

"Do you need help, Dais?" Val, one of the bridesmaids, holds a napkin aloft with a sympathetic expression.

I give her a bright smile in return. "I'm okay, thanks."

Val goes back to chatting happily with her husband Ethan, and I continue scrubbing at the red splotch. This is what I get for asking to be set up: a lap full of tomato sauce and a date who spends a suspicious amount of time lingering by bushes.

But maybe I'm not being fair to Eddie. The guy seems about as shady as a ladybug and he's repeated—more than a few times—that he normally doesn't drink. He's probably just as nervous as I am about this blind date business.

I decide to brush it off, lighten the mood. "I'm sure I can work this into my maid of honor speech. Something about *Lady and the Tramp*, maybe. Right, Ed...?"

I trail off. My date has, once again, disappeared. It's an impressive feat, to be honest. The hundreds of fairy lights strung up in the trees, around the gazebo, and along the paths of the Brookrose Garden—not to mention the flickering candles on the tables—flood the garden with light. A dreamy, enchanting light... but lots of it nonetheless.

"Excuse me." I rise to a stand in what I hope is a graceful, elegant, poised kind of way. Val and Ethan thankfully don't spare me much of a glance, so I think I've done an okay job cleaning myself up and retaining some shred of dignity.

Until I turn around. A couple of guests at the table behind us—Courtney from the hair salon, and her date Shane (of the infamous "Dude Crew" as I call them, and a pretty surprising plus one for the sweet, mild-mannered girl, if you ask me)—both look at me with a certain amount of surprise. Courtney politely averts her gaze, but Shane isn't quite so tactful and instead points directly at the comet-shaped stain on my dress with his mouth open like he's about to say something.

This would normally be time to come up with something smart and sarcastic. Channel my inner Lorelai Gilmore and knock everyone's socks off with my quick wit. Instead, I hold my hands up in surrender. "Gotta love spaghetti!"

And with that brilliant remark, I skitter away to find Eddie.

Literally. While rounding the table, I slip and narrowly avoid face-planting on the grass.

I curse my white ballet flats. I'm usually happy when my height gets me out of wearing heels, but these flats have about as much grip as flip-flops on an ice skating rink.

I make my way to the edge of the garden closest to the creek, passing by the bride and groom's table. I shoot a look at my best friend and forever-single—or so we both believed—life partner, Ivy Brooks. Currently known as "the girl I won't be talking to ever again since she was the one who set me up with Eddie, the meatball-roller."

What was she thinking? Pairing me up with a guy who would make me one half of "Daddie".

Or "Eisy". Which sounds like a medical condition.

I got on the celebrity couple name bandwagon around the time "Bennifer" started making the rounds, and I've never looked back. Because surely the principle *has* to apply to us commoners as well, right?

It just further reinforces that Eddie and I are *not* a good match.

Luckily, what my best friend lacks in matchmaking skills, she makes up for in wedding prep. The ceremony was heart-achingly beautiful, and the reception is no different. Ivy and her now-husband, James Weston, planned the entire event themselves in the manicured garden of her family's inn. The enchanting lighting and string music coming from the gazebo only add to the romantic atmosphere.

Most impressively though, she's stayed relaxed about the whole thing. Excited, even. A far cry from the anxiously perfectionist Ivy Brooks I used to know.

Seeing her laugh and stare into James's eyes now, with this soft smile and her eyes basically shooting out cartoon hearts, I couldn't be happier for her. She and James were the last to see what everyone else in Mirror Valley knew since the two were in high school. They could act like they hated each other 'til the cows came home, but it took Ivy's brother's wedding last year to bring them together for good.

Well, Ivy's brother's *almost* wedding. But that's a whole other story.

"Psst. Daisy!"

The whisper-shout wrenches my attention towards a cluster of white roses in the one shaded part of the garden.

"Eddie?" I ask with a tinge of annoyance. "What're you doing?"

I finally spot him crouched behind the bush like some sort of creeping meerkat. He waves me forward with so much gusto, *he* almost face-plants. "I need your help."

I raise an eyebrow, staying put for the time being. "With what?"

"I have to get her back. I *will* get her back," he mutters determinedly, clutching a delicate bloom in one hand and a silver object in the other. He sticks his tongue out the side of his mouth as he places the silver object around the stem...

A fork. He's trying to cut a rose with a fork.

"Get who back?" I walk towards him, holding out a hand to help him up and ideally out of rose-harming territory.

"Courtney."

My brows raise in surprise and I point towards the girl at the table behind ours. "Like, that Courtney? The one who is currently on a date with Shane?"

"Yup." Eddie abandons the fork-sawing and stares wistfully over my shoulder. I follow his gaze to where Courtney is now laughing at something Shane said, shaking her head so her light brown hair falls down her back. I like Courtney —she's shy and quiet but has a real sparkle when it comes to her job as a hairstylist. Or her cat, Jeff.

At that moment, her gaze slices our way, meeting Eddie's and lingering for a second too long.

I nod. "You dated."

"For two and a quarter years. We broke up three months ago. She said I wasn't around enough for her and Jeff. I should have fought for her. For them."

The poor guy's shoulders slump and he looks so down-trodden that my heart goes out to him. I place a reassuring hand on his elbow and give a squeeze of sympathy, but I'd be lying if I said I didn't also feel relieved. At least I'm not the only one who knows this blind date isn't going anywhere. And helping ol' Eddie here win back his ex definitely sounds like something I can help with. "Have you talked to her about how you feel?"

Eddie shakes his head, then collapses onto the ground next to the bush, propping his chin on his palm. With the short brown hair fuzzing over his head, his coal-black eyes and his small nose, he really does look like a meerkat. A sad meerkat who's just watched his meerkat girlfriend waddle away for good. "What would I even say?"

I sit with him, tucking my dress beneath me. The cool grass tickles the undersides of my legs and branches from the rosebush poke my bare back. "You could start by being honest," I say gently. "If you want to get her back, you have to start from a place of truth and love."

"I do love her," he says passionately, raising his fork in the air.

I place a hand on his arm to lower it. "Let's go back to our table, and we can talk about it. Talk about what you'll say to her." I see a fiery determination in his eyes and quickly tack on, "Tomorrow. After the wedding. When you've sobered—um, had time to think."

And haven't spent an evening trying to cut flowers with a fork.

Eddie's eyes are still on Courtney, then he shoots to a stand. "Gotta pee."

Before I can say anything, he stalks off in the direction of the Brookrose Inn and I utter a heavy sigh. What a disaster—for both Eddie and me. Ivy can't have known that she was setting me up with a man who is clearly hung up on another woman.

The good news is that my evening just got a lot more interesting. Helping Eddie plan how he's going to approach Courtney should be a fun project. I love a good second-chance love story.

And besides, their couple name would be "Court-Ed". How perfect is that?

I head back to my table and take a seat in front of my cold spaghetti with veggie meatballs. The band is coming off their break and instrumental music ebbs and flows from the gazebo. My table empties as people make their way to the dance floor to join Ivy and James, who are swaying with their eyes closed, heads bowed together, and looking so in love, my heart aches.

"Almost makes you sick, doesn't it?"

The cheerful comment is followed by the scrape of Eddie's chair on the wood flooring, but it's certainly not Eddie. I'd recognize that voice anywhere—deep and gravelly but with a richness that's hard to describe. Like dark chocolate, if it had a voice.

Luke Brooks takes a seat next to me, his eyes on the happy couple.

I chuckle. "Spoken like the best best man."

"You know I'm happy for them. I couldn't imagine anyone better for my baby sister than my best friend," he says dryly as he undoes the middle button of his navy suit jacket and sits back. "Don't tell them that, obviously. Can't have Ivy tearing up and ruining her makeup."

"I would never." I let my eyes return to the newlyweds. "But what kind of best friend would I be if seeing Ivy happy made me sick?"

"What kind of best friend is she to set you up with a guy who's in love with someone else?"

"You noticed."

Luke's eyes meet mine and the dark hazel is like tempting, melted caramel in the flickering candlelight. *No, Daisy. We don't go there anymore, remember?* "I noticed," he says. "That's the guy she picked for you, huh?"

"That's the one. But I can't blame her. I asked for it."

"You wanted to be set up with Ed?"

"I asked her to find me a blind date," I clarify. "I thought it might be fun."

"Hm." Luke grunts like he doubts the concept of "fun" as a whole.

I peer at him for a long moment. I haven't seen much of Luke tonight, but I can understand why he's laying low. I'm mostly curious as to why he's sitting here with me now. Why he's bringing up my date with Eddie.

Luke and I have an interesting friendship. If I had to classify us, I'd call us life-long friends with the closeness of gym buddies. In fact, I mostly see him at the Valley Fitness center these days, when I'm working at the front desk, and he comes in for his daily workout. Of course, with him being Ivy's big brother, we often see each other in passing or at family and friend events. But we don't talk about this type of stuff—dating, relationships. And ever since what happened with his ex-fiancée Eleanor Wilkes last year, that boundary's been even more set in my mind.

But we're already on the subject with Eddie (ish). Not to mention I've had half a glass of wine and am feeling a little bold. "What about you?" I ask. "Did you come with anyone tonight?"

7

Luke leans further back in his chair, clasping his big hands in his lap. "If the town had anything to say about it, I would be here with someone," he grumbles. "With the way people are looking at me, I almost wish I'd caved and brought a date."

He looks around with barely veiled irritation, and I press my lips together. Luke's had a tough go with the Mirror Valley rumor mill over the last year and a half. His runaway bride is all anyone talks about, even now.

Which is why I usually steer clear from dating-related topics with him. Luke's the kind of guy who doesn't like prying, doesn't like his private life to be public.

If he wants you to know something, he makes sure you know it.

I gesture half-heartedly at my dress. "Well, on the bright side, you've gotten to enjoy your meal tonight instead of having it on your lap."

This pulls a smirk out of him, and he leans forward to take a look at the stupid stain. His cologne fills the air between us, and it does *not* remind me of a peaceful, manly forest after rain. If there's such a thing as a manly forest.

Maybe one with those really big trees, and fog to make it a little mysterious, and it would smell earthy and rugged and warm all at the same time...

"You've got a winner there, Dais." Luke's dark eyes rise to meet mine again.

I give my head a shake, still half-caught in my forest contemplation. "I will definitely be crossing 'blind date' off my list," I mutter to myself.

Unfortunately, Luke has the hearing of a freaking bat.

"What list?" he asks. Oh so curiously.

My cheeks start to heat. Why did I say that out loud? I should have buttoned my lips right up and kept that comment where it belonged—in my head. My list has

CIA-level top secret clearance. Even Ivy doesn't know about it.

But Luke is looking at me all imploringly, and I am *not* feeling anything for him, and so therefore, I should be able to tell him about my list.

He probably won't care anyway. Luke's been single for a year and a half now and has shown zero interest in dating.

"It's this new thing I'm trying," I concede with a shrug. "I made a list of romance tropes from movies and books to try and find my own version of them. See if anything clicks."

To my surprise, Luke seems invested. "What do you mean?"

I furrow a brow. Then, for some reason unbeknownst to me, I shuffle through my clutch until I take hold of my pen-streaked napkin. I started putting together my list of tropes after a particularly awful date a couple of weeks ago. I met the guy at a speed dating event at the senior center (to be clear, *he* was not a senior; the event was just hosted there), but when we sat down at McGarry's…

Let's just say that it took the time for the waitress to come over for me to remember why I stopped going to those events.

The napkin looks comically small in Luke's hands. He frowns as he skims the list. "Gym crush, blind date, workplace romance…" He glances up at me. "Which workplace? You have, like, eleven jobs."

"Eight," I shoot back. "The vet no longer needs an assistant, so I have free time on my hands."

"I've never known you to have free time."

"Maybe free time is another new thing I'll try."

Luke raises a brow. "You'll be pretty busy if you're going to be dating all these people."

I scrunch my nose at his tone. "Not at the same time, weirdo. Besides, some of them are unavailable or unattainable. Like that one." I point at the top of the list, where a stern red line crosses out a name. "My childhood friend—and kindergarten husband, actually—was Cody McLaren. Turns out, he's in jail now."

"No jail romance for you, then?"

"That's one line I'm drawing. And here's another." I grab a pen and hold Luke's hand steady beneath the napkin. Put a line through "blind date." I screw the lid back on with a firm nod.

"Wise choice."

Luke and I sit together for a little while longer, sometimes chatting, sometimes not. People crowd the dance floor but Luke doesn't make a move to dance, and I don't either. It's funny to consider that Past Daisy would've been foolishly hoping that he'd ask her to dance. But that crush is long, long over, and I'm happy for it.

"Want to play a game?" I eventually ask.

Luke turns that piercing gaze on me, and the soft glow of the candles sets his features alight, bringing out the darker streaks in his stubble and the shadows off his angular jawline. "What kind of game?"

"Friends, first date, or married."

One side of Luke's mouth tips up in a smirk. "Let's do it."

We first played this game at Valley Fitness sometime last year. I originally pitched it as a way to fill silence while he was standing by the front desk waiting for one of the squat racks to open up. It's since become a kind of inside joke for us.

My eyes scour the crowd. "What about them?" I point to two people swaying together awkwardly on the edge of the dance floor.

"First date," he says immediately.

"What? How can you tell?"

"He keeps looking at her, and he's turned close to her, like he wants to take her hand. Definitely interested." He frowns. "Jury's out on her, though."

"She's into him. Look at how she's tucking her hair behind her ears, shyly meeting his gaze. She's waiting for him to make a move."

"She'll be waiting awhile."

"Patience. Patience." I continue looking over the crowd and spot my next target. "What about them?"

Luke squints to see the couple. They're dancing quickly, doing a bizarre shuffle across the floor so fast that even I can't see their faces properly right now. The girl's head is thrown back in laughter at something the guy said. "Friends... Or married."

I laugh, surprised by his answer. "Friends. Definitely friends."

"How do you know?"

"Because it's Noah and Dee."

My little sister Diandra—goes by "Dee"—has been best friends with Noah Jackson since they were in diapers. Nothing romantic has ever happened between them; Luke and I both know that.

"Cheater," he says. Then, he leans close again and nods towards the far end of the crowd. "What about them?"

I follow his gaze to Eddie, who is now standing near the gazebo. He's looking straight at Courtney, who's gazing longingly back at him. They seem lost in their own world. "Exes," I say confidently. "Exes who want to be more."

I cut my gaze away, not wanting to intrude on their moment.

Luke doesn't do the same. "Looks like your date's got an idea," he says.

I turn in my seat to see Eddie climbing the stairs into the gazebo and grabbing the microphone.

2

DAISY

Oh, no. Oh, nooooo.

My palms are pressed to my cheeks, and my eyes are wide and unblinking as I watch the slow-motion car crash happen right in front of me. Eddie trips a little as he grasps the mic, his face flushed. There's a desperation in his eyes that no longer screams "sad meerkat" but "trash-hungry raccoon."

"Hello, good evening, howdy doo!" he starts off. "How's everyone doing tonight?"

Silence.

"My name's Edgar—Eddie, if anyone doesn't know me. I'm friends with the bride's grandma's pet groomer." He pauses as though waiting for applause.

I can't physically move my body.

It's bad. So bad.

"Anyway. I am so excited to be here on this special night. Ivy and John..." *John? Please stop, Eddie.* "Are the best of people, and just the sweetest couple. Their love is inspiring." He takes a breath, becoming all the more serious. "I would know, because I was in love. True love."

Oh, no. This is somehow *worse*.

12

"I lost it. But you know what? It's okay, because tonight, I met someone awesome. Met someone who changed my whole perspective. Daisy Griffiths, get on up here!"

Curses. He's pointing at *me*!

There might as well be a big, bright, shining spotlight pointed directly on my face. Which is on fire, by the way.

I manage to shake my head jerkily as a few people look my way. "No, thanks," I squeak.

"Okay, fine." Eddie pauses again, and I wonder if he's finally realized what a terrible idea this is. I'm all for a grand gesture, but an alcohol-fueled declaration of love at another couple's wedding is not generally the way to go. He clears his throat. "Anyway, Daisy gave me the brilliant advice that I come up here and say what I need to say." *I said WHAT now?* "I have to speak from a place of truth and love. So here goes…"

He inhales a deep breath, closes his eyes and sways backwards slightly on his heels.

"Courtney," he says, emotion flooding his voice. "I love you, have always loved you. Jeff, too. Despite the fact that he attacks my ankles every time I walk into the kitchen for orange juice. Oh, I would love some orange juice. Could I get orange juice up here?"

Please. Stop saying "orange juice."

I manage to break my gaze from the gazebo to look at Courtney, standing in the crowd a few paces away. Her face is ashen, her expression appalled. And it's clear as day that this is *not* the right move. This is not what she wants.

Her shock is enough to kick me into gear, and I rise from the table. I start to make my way towards the gazebo.

"Whether we're baking bread together, or watching *Real Housewives* with that eggplant dip you love, or I'm massaging your feet while you play Wordle, I know that we're meant to be together," Eddie drones on. "Our love is the stuff of movies and books. And I know this isn't the end. It can't be over. They say love hurts but..."

He wouldn't.

He does.

Eddie closes his eyes and starts bellowing "Love Hurts" by Nazareth.

Finally, I'm at the gazebo. "Eddie!" I hiss. "Eddie, this is not what I mea—"

"Oh!" he exclaims, delighted. "Daisy, you're here. Come up, everyone wants to see the person who gave me the courage to do this."

Before I can say or do anything—like run far, far away, never to show my face in civilized society again—Eddie grabs my arm and tugs me up the gazebo stairs. He holds up my hand like I'm a million-dollar lotto winner.

My face is surely bright enough to stop traffic miles away. I offer the most feeble of smiles to the audience of alarmed wedding guests before forcefully lowering my arm to my side. Unfortunately, Eddie doesn't let go, so it looks like we're doing a bizarre robot dance or something.

"This isn't a good idea," I whisper.

"But this is what you told me to do," he whispers back. Into the microphone.

I wish the ground would open up and suck me into another dimension.

"Ed, I think we're done here."

The firm voice surprises us both, and Eddie and I spin around to see Luke standing at the bottom of the stairs, one hand in the pocket of his suit pants, the other clenched slightly by his side. The middle button on his jacket's done up again, and his strong jaw is set.

He's actually quite an imposing figure when he wants to be.

Now Eddie covers the microphone with his hand. "Just a minute. I have to say this one thing, I—"

"You want your girl back, I know. Come on, let's get you some orange juice, and we'll talk to her after."

"But I have to give a speech—"

"You did it. She knows how you feel. You know what the next move is? The next thing Daisy was going to tell you? You have to let *her* come to *you*."

Eddie stares at Luke skeptically for a half-second, but Luke holds his gaze. With the amount of confidence in his stare, even *I* believe that that was my next piece of advice. Eddie puffs out an exhale. "Really?"

"Absolutely," Luke says smoothly. "Let's go."

Finally, Eddie drops my hand, along with the mic, which clatters to the ground and emits a screech of feedback. He thunders down the stairs, and I hand the mic back to the band's singer with an apologetic grin before running out of the gazebo myself, my skin still burning.

The music gets back on track, and the dance floor fills with people again, like the drunken interruption never happened. I crane my neck around to look for Ivy and James, now feeling ill for an entirely different reason. It doesn't matter what people think about me or Eddie. I just hope that this whole drama—because of advice that *I* gave— didn't ruin their wonderful wedding.

"Dais!"

A ball of tulle and lace crashes into me, almost knocking me over. I steady Ivy, helping her stand upright. "I'm so sorry, Iv! That was completely…"

I trail off as I realize that Ivy's holding onto me tightly not because she tripped, but because she's laughing so hard, she can barely stand.

"That was… You… looked… That was *hilarious*!"

She doubles over with laughter, crinkling the beautiful princess-style wedding gown we found for her at Belle's Bridal. After a particularly scarring experience with a bridesmaid's dress last year, we made sure it was tailored to a comfortable size for her. No one should go hungry on their wedding day.

And yet...

"You'll have to excuse my wife. She hasn't had much to eat today," James says as he walks up behind Ivy, shrugging apologetically. He twirls her on her feet, and she collapses against his chest. "Let's get you some dinner, Brooks."

"I like when you call me that," she says sweetly, gazing up at him.

James tucks her hair behind her ear. "Brooks?" he asks, amused.

"No, your wife." She sighs, and her gaze zeroes back in on me. "Don't worry your pretty little head, Dais. I knew you and Ed weren't gonna work."

I blink. "You did? So why—?"

"CAKE BALLS!" Ivy takes off after a waiter holding a tray of colorful desserts. She's lost in the crowd before I even can wrap my head around what she said. And James simply gives me another apologetic smile before going after her.

I stand for a moment, biting my lip. Why on earth would my best friend set me up on a date she knew would be a bust?

Suddenly, a large, warm hand grasps my elbow. "You okay?"

Luke's standing behind me. Despite the fact that he spent the evening fielding questions about his past, avoiding the town gossips, and rescuing me from public humiliation, he seems as cool, calm, and collected as ever.

I tilt my head up and grin. "Of course. Everything's good."

"I sat Ed down with a pitcher of water and got some of the guys from my old soccer team to watch him. I've said my goodbyes to James and Ivy already, and I'm going to take him home, but I wanted to make sure you're alright. That was... really something."

"Never a dull moment at these Mirror Valley gatherings," I say cheerily, then peek around him. "How's Courtney? Is she okay?"

"Seems like it. She keeps looking over at him. I doubt she loved his speech, but I don't think he's completely destroyed his chances yet."

"Good to hear. That was a risky move on his part."

"What? Making a fool of himself for the love of his life?" Luke winks. "That was some advice you gave him."

I punch Luke in the arm. "That was *not* what I said. At all. My words were taken out of context."

"In context or not, you seem to be good at bringing people together."

Yes, bringing people together. That's what I do.

The one thing I can't do is bring someone to *me*.

"Anyway." Luke glances over his shoulder. "Got a drunk guy to load up with water and bring home, and then I'm sure Stella's missing me. So I'll see you later, Dais."

With that, he disappears through the crowd towards a group of tall, buff guys that I can now see hovering near the French doors of the Inn. Shane is part of the crowd, joking around and clearly unaffected by Eddie's proclamation of love to his date.

I watch Luke go with a half-smile on my face. Despite the drama of the evening, I had a good night.

I'm just glad I'm over my crush on Luke. At least I have that going for me.

3

LUKE

"Whoops!" Ed stumbles over a rock in the parking lot and almost keels over into a bush.

I let out a frustrated grunt before grabbing the guy's arm and reluctantly slinging it over my shoulder. He's been moping and dragging his feet through the parking lot, and my patience is quickly running out. If I'm helping him to the car, we can at least pick up the pace.

"Really did a number on yourself tonight, Ed," I grunt.

Ed hiccups—actually hiccups—in response. "I swear, I don't usually drink this much. It's just seeing Courtney... I didn't know how hard it would be. I ended up drinking *two* full glasses of wine."

He says this so gravely that I have to stifle a snort. I don't drink much myself, but when I was doing my master's program, some of the guys would have six beers for breakfast on event days. I personally don't see the point in doing such a thing. Polluting your body like that is irresponsible. Not to mention how hard it is to do a workout after a night at the bar.

We finally reach my car—a brand-new Genesis G70—and I open the passenger door. Ed falls into the seat, and I tug out the seatbelt and hand it to him. Helping a drunk dude put on his seatbelt is *not* within the scope of my generosity.

"Do you really think she might take me back?" Ed asks.

I try to keep my voice calm and level and not full of sarcastic exasperation, which is what I'm currently feeling. "Maybe. But you know what might help your case?"

"What?"

"Not getting sick in my new car." I fix him with a look. "If you don't feel well, let me know."

Ed fixates on my expression and gives this slow, wide-eyed nod. "Will do."

I leave Ed to sort out his seatbelt and walk to my side of the car. I take off my suit jacket, fold it, and lay it across the backseat, then I take a moment to close my eyes and situate myself.

I know I'm being short with Ed, but my patience has already been worn very, very thin by the pointed stares and whispers I've had to deal with all night. It's the first big Mirror Valley event I've come to in a year and a half, and I can see now that I made the right call lying low. The only reason I came tonight is because I was the best man at my sister's wedding to my oldest friend.

So, you know, kind of a big deal.

But now, I can't wait to get back to my condo. And to my rescue pup, Stella. I adopted her a year ago, and she's actually less of a pup than a sleepy old girl with droopy eyes, the loudest snore known to man, and an undying love of carrot sticks.

"Where am I taking you?" I ask as I slide into the driver's seat.

Ed gives me his address, then promptly rests his head on the passenger window with his eyes closed. With a sigh, I start the car.

"Dancing Queen" by ABBA blares through the speakers.

I hurriedly switch to the radio, my neck warm, but Ed doesn't even shift.

As I pull out of the parking lot of the Brookrose, I put down my window and rest my elbow on the sill. A cool, fall breeze flows into my car, and I welcome it, along with the silence.

Mirror Valley's normally a quiet little place, except during big sporting events or any of its ritual monthly festivals, carnivals, fairs, etc. celebrating literally anything and everything. But it's late—a quick glance at my watch confirms that it's later than I expected, actually—and by now, it's a complete ghost town. The streets are empty, the restaurants and shops closed down and locked for the night. Only the glare of the street lamps and the lone, annoying stoplight at the end of Main Street hints at the fact that this is, indeed, a liveable place.

Though to be fair, everyone's probably dancing the night away in the Inn's garden. Ivy and James are practically hometown sweethearts, and almost every person in town has been waiting years and years for tonight.

Including me.

In school, James got the most action of anyone on our soccer team. He was constantly going out on dates, bringing girls to games, or flirting with someone new. Far as I could tell, he didn't go around breaking hearts, but he dated. A lot. Polar opposite of me, really, given that I was with Eleanor for most of my high school years.

But for every girl he went out with, he never looked at her like he looked at Ivy. I was in denial for a long time, refused to accept it. I would've had to be an idiot not to see it, though.

When the two of them finally told me they were

together, I wasn't the least bit surprised. They balance each other out, and they're clearly so in love. The kind of love I envy in my grandparents, Richard and Maggie. The kind of love I thought I had...

Ed suddenly sits up in his seat, and I have a bad feeling that my one request of him might not be heeded. "So how d'you know the bride and groom?" he asks, words slurring slightly.

I give a humorless smirk. "Bride's my sister. Groom's my best friend."

"Ohhh! So you're..." Ed trails off, and I can almost hear the gears turning in his alcohol-fogged brain. "Hang on, you're Luke Brooks?!"

His tone is so flabbergasted that I almost start laughing. "Yes."

"So you know *exactly* what I'm going through with Courtney."

He leans in close, too close. I tense up my arm so my elbow pokes into his chest as a blocker. "How do you mean?" I ask, but I already know the answer.

"Eleanor Wilkes left you at the altar, like, a year and a half ago. Remember?" Ed shakes his head. "Tough break, man."

The pity in his voice makes my stomach curdle and my jaw clench. It's everything I can do not to stop the car. "Yeah," I say with practiced nonchalance. My knuckles are white on the steering wheel. "I remember."

"I hope you can get her back," Ed says with a long sigh. "Just like I want to win back Courtney."

The tension in my body releases a little, and my hands unclench. I give my head a shake. "I don't want her back. Our relationship is dead."

And I mean it. Eleanor was my rock, my first love and girlfriend. We were together for so long and supported each other through so many things that, by the time I started noticing the ways that we were growing apart, I thought it was simply a matter of adapting myself to fit her lifestyle. But after what happened last year, I had to move on. I'm glad I did.

But I don't tell Ed any of this as it's not really his business. And he's no longer paying attention anyway. He's staring out the window wistfully, no doubt comparing Courtney to the stars in the sky or something.

I'm being grumpy. It's been a long night, and these constant reminders of Eleanor are grating. I wish people would get over it... over my broken engagement, but also over the idea that I'm *desperate* to date again. The amount of phone numbers and email addresses and names of "women about my age" that have been thrown my way over the past few months has been overwhelming. I appreciate everyone's concern, but the reminders of the past aren't exactly helping me move forward.

I've only buckled under the pressure once.

Over the summer, the guys from my high school soccer team—the "Dude Crew," according to Daisy and Ivy—got together for someone's 28th birthday barbecue. Against my better judgment, I went. And while there, each and every one of them pulled me aside to try and convince me to start dating again.

I'm not kidding. It went from birthday party to dating intervention *real* fast.

In the end, I downloaded a dating app to shut them up. "RightMatch", it's called. I put in zero effort—going by my middle name and using a photo of the back of my head.

When I stop the car in front of Ed's apartment building, he doesn't make a move to exit the car. I lean forward to see that his forehead is pressed against the window, eyes closed, and his mouth is open, fogging up the glass. In fact, he's about a second away from drooling.

I give his shoulder a quick shake. "Ed, we're here."

"Jeffy?!" he shifts awake, leaving a grease stain on the window. Fantastic. Then, seeing it's me, he frowns. "Oh. You."

I raise a brow. "Yup. Just me. The guy who gave you a free ride home."

"Thanks, man." Ed attempts to give me a fist bump but misses wildly and knocks his fist into the steering wheel instead. He opens his door and steps out of the car. Not in that order.

I reluctantly get out, too. "You going to be able to make it inside?"

I really, *really* don't want to have to walk this guy into his house. But Ed seems alert enough to grasp for his keys in his pocket. He gives me a salute. "Got it. Thanks again. 'Preciate it."

I grunt out a "sure". I would say *anytime*, but this is an event I'd rather not repeat. Ever.

"Say thanks to Daisy for me." Ed looks like he's about to turn around and finally go inside, but instead, he stops. Tilts his head pensively. "You know, that girl is a total knockout. She's got those long legs and crazy blue eyes... If Courtney wasn't the love of my life, I would've gone for her. She's just a bit too, I dunno..."

And I'm not sure if it's the long night finally wearing me down, or the fact that Ed's been basically drooling across my car, or that he's clearly about two seconds away from insulting probably the kindest person I've ever met—not to mention my little sister's best friend—but what happens next is an automatic reaction. Instinct.

I step up close to him, my muscles tensed, and I level him with a firm stare. "A bit too what, Ed?" I ask calmly, my

23

voice just a shade away from intimidating. "Too nice for stopping you embarrassing yourself? Too gracious for babysitting you all night? Because I'll tell you right now, you'll have a hard time finding someone else who wouldn't have punched you in the face after you made a complete fool of yourself. And her. You're in no position to say that Daisy is anything but wonderful."

Ed seems to sense—wisely—that he's treading close to a dangerous line, and he presses his lips together. "Never mind."

I turn on my heel and walk back to my car. "Have a good night."

I pull out and drive away, not bothering to see if Ed made it inside. Likely, he'll pass out in the lawn out front and wake up with a wicked hangover. Might teach him a thing or two.

I can't imagine what Ivy was thinking, setting Daisy up with a guy like that. Daisy deserves much better than a date who drinks himself stupid and makes declarations of love to another woman. When Ed dragged her up onto the gazebo, she kept her cool in a way that I couldn't or wouldn't have been able to.

Daisy's like that, though, even at the worst of times: sweet, unfailingly optimistic, and believing the best of every person and every situation.

I am none of those things.

I had to intervene, had to help her. And I'm glad I did. Because honestly, I wouldn't have stayed so long tonight if she hadn't been there. I loathe small talk with every fiber of my being, and I dreaded having to do it all night. Daisy's probably one of the only people with whom I find it bearable. She's the type of person who calms the environment around her, who creates light wherever she goes. Like one of those self-illuminating deep sea fish.

But cuter. And less, you know... toothy.

This is stupid. I need to call it a night. I can already picture Stella curled up and snoring on my sofa, leaving black hairs everywhere, while the plush dog bed I got for her sits abandoned in the corner.

I smirk ruefully. For months, I trained her to sleep in her bed, but her will is stronger than mine.

As I make my way towards home, my mind drifts from Stella back to Daisy. I'll admit that I'm curious about her little romance list thing. Daisy and I never talk about dating —in fact, she's one of the only people who doesn't harp on about Eleanor anytime we see each other. But this experiment of hers intrigues me.

Sounds like the kinda thing I would do. If and when I decide to date again.

I let out a grumble and put the thought far, far out of my mind. Instead, I switch on the specialized cassette player I had installed in the car—I've always been a sucker for old-timey cassettes—and enjoy the sounds of *ABBA's Greatest Hits* as I relax into my seat and drive home.

4

DAISY

"England!" Dee cackles as she takes a sip of her large black coffee. The handle of the mug is slightly chipped, but what else is new for the coffee shop at the community center. "Of course, Ivy and James are in England."

"Where else would they go?" I smile dreamily, swirling my own mug with remnants of hot cocoa with extra whipped cream. "Imagine... a honeymoon in the English countryside. I'm so, so happy for them."

And not jealous.

Nope. Not at all.

"Look at you." Dee smirks over the rim of her mug. "You wish *you* were exploring the English countryside with some noble gentleman."

Curses. I forgot that my sister can see right through me.

I tilt my nose up in an exaggerated sniff. "Doesn't everyone?"

"I don't." Dee tucks her left leg under her and leans back in her chair. "I'm more of a sunny Southern California girl myself."

I let out a huge, very unladylike snort. I gesture at her outfit, consisting of a black ball cap, a baggy band shirt and dark jeans despite the unseasonably warm fall weather. She's gathered her blonde hair into a wispy ponytail. "Southern California, huh? You sure look ready to hit the beach."

Dee sticks her tongue out at me. My sister is many things, but I would never peg her for a beach bum. She's far too practical and sand-averse for that. Not to mention she doesn't have the… sunniest of dispositions. Dee has an edge to her and can be a "little testy at times" (her words, not mine). Her walls are up so high that sometimes even *I* can't see over them. But she had to be tough to get where she is today.

"Did you have fun at their wedding the other night?" I ask as I put down my mug and fiddle with a napkin instead. The Mirror Valley Community Center logo is splashed across it—a rare show of modernity for the public building. The logo itself looks like it was designed sometime in the 50s.

"I did, actually." Dee takes another sip of her coffee. "Noah brought Lauren so I thought I'd be bored senseless and would have to hang around with the volleyball team all night, but he ended up spending a lot of time with us."

"Yeah. What on earth was that weird shuffle you guys were doing?"

"Noah asked me to dance when Lauren went to the restroom," she offers with a shrug. "I think he was trying to make me feel better for not having a date. Not that he needs to worry about me. I like being on my own."

She really does. Dee is impressively independent and self-sufficient. Like one of those robust Jeep Wranglers in a car commercial. Or an asexually-reproducing sweet potato (don't ask how I know about those). She doesn't need anyone else to live her best life. She's alone and prefers it that way.

"Part of me wishes I'd gone solo," I say, and then grin.

"But then Eddie wouldn't have had his moment in the spotlight."

Dee lets out a quick laugh and covers her mouth. "Now *that* had to be the highlight of my night. Bless his heart."

"The guy wants to win Courtney back so badly."

"Do you think it worked?"

"The speech? No, not at all. But I don't think it's over yet. For either of them." I pause. "Eddie *seems* like a good guy underneath it all... I think he just lost his way."

"Let me guess. You're going to meddle your way into getting them back together."

I place a hand over my heart and feign surprise. "Dee, whatever do you mean? I would never *meddle*."

She raises a brow skeptically.

"Okay, fine. Sometimes I meddle a teeny, tiny bit. But with Ivy and James, it worked out wonderfully, didn't it? It's tougher with Courtney and Eddie, but if the opportunity presents itself to get them to talk, I'll *have* to take it."

"Or not. You could leave it alone. Like you've done Noah and me."

Ugh. I used to have such hope for those two.

If only Dee could see how perfect they would be together. These days, I wouldn't touch the Dee-Noah relationship with a ten-foot pole. Dee has made it abundantly clear that she would impale me with said pole if I tried.

"Yeah, you're right," I say. "It's time I hang up my matchmaking gloves for good."

"Look at you, bursting with boxing lingo."

"Thought I'd use words you understand."

Dee gives me her trademark dry, sarcastic smile. "I saw you chatting with Luke for awhile. How was that?"

"It was good. Fun." I finger the rim of my mug. "We've become closer friends since he started coming to Valley Fitness every day during my shift."

"Sure seems like it." Dee is carefully composed. "He spent the whole evening dodging people, but he was happy to seek you out."

"Probably because I'm the only one who doesn't ask him endless questions about Eleanor."

"And why is that, sister of mine?" Dee's voice is light and innocent, but I'm not falling for it. I never told Dee about my schoolgirl crush on Luke, but she seems particularly pointed whenever she asks me about him. As if there was, in some iteration of the universe, a possibility of Luke and me.

Which there isn't and could never be. For a myriad of reasons, one of the main ones being that the best friend I've ever had is his sister. I don't think Ivy ever noticed the crush I had on Luke, but then again, there are a few things I don't think she realizes when it comes to her big brother. Like the fact that he's inarguably, objectively handsome. In an almost intimidating kind of way. He might be an accountant, but he could easily moonlight as a rugged, sculpted fireman in one of those saucy calendars Fran likes.

You know... if you could ever get Luke to do a job like that without scowling.

"It's none of my business," I say with a tone indicating that this conversation is over. "And speaking of dating, how's the job?"

Dee shifts in her seat and sighs. "Fine. The person in my position before me made a real mess of the code. It's like they didn't know the difference between Python and..." She trails off as my eyes glaze over. Lets out a short chuckle. "Let's just say that there's a ton of cleaning up to do."

She takes a last swig of her coffee, and exhales with satisfaction. I'm filled with a mixture of awe and pride for my little sister. Of the two of us, Dee definitely got the brains. She's been into coding and programming since we were teens, and far as I can tell, she's become *very* good at it. At 25, she's two years younger than me and has been out of her Master's program for only a year, but she's already one of the lead developers at her tech company. It's based in LA but her job is remote, which means that she gets to stay right here in Mirror Valley.

Dee takes out her phone—the latest state-of-the-art smartphone, of course—and swipes across the screen. "I wanted to ask how you're liking the app. Do you have any feedback? Any suggestions to make it better?"

I laugh. "I see how it is. I'm the guinea pig."

"You're not just *any* guinea pig, Dais. You're a guinea pig with unrivaled experience on dating apps." Dee smirks, and it's my turn to stick my tongue out at her. "So do you like it?"

I take out my phone and open my RightMatch app. "I've enjoyed it so far. Your team has created something fun, light-hearted, and casual while users search for a relationship. It's exactly what dating's supposed to be."

Okay, maybe RightMatch isn't *exactly* like dating.

For one thing, I've never had a dating experience in which points are so heavily involved...

On the app, you match with someone based on a couple key conversation starters and one photo. The more you speak with the person, the more points you get, and the more information you "uncover" about them. First, you get access to additional photos, followed by a playlist if they uploaded one. Eventually, with enough points, you're encouraged to share your phone numbers, and then you're prompted to meet in person.

RightMatch's mission is to be the first dating app to encourage a slow burn romance instead of the instant gratification of other apps. It's like that Netflix reality show, *Love is Blind*... the app version.

As I click through my profile, Dee's jaw clenches. Compared to how she types and swipes, I move at a turtle's pace. In all honesty though, I haven't used the app much yet; I've been more preoccupied with my trope list. But I want to offer something constructive. "One thing I like is that you don't know where your match is from right away."

"That won't be a forever thing," she says. I can tell she's forcing herself to sit back and not take my phone right out of my hands. "This is the beta, and it's only available in a few towns across Colorado, Nevada and California. Once it fully launches, it'll show you the profiles of people closest to you, no matter where you are, just like other apps."

"Smart."

I finally put Dee out of her misery and give her my phone. She jumps on it hungrily, scrolling through my account. As one of the coders and not a user herself, she likes having someone else's profile to click through.

Within moments, she pauses. "You're only talking to one person."

"He's the only one who's really captured my interest." Then, I hurriedly tack on, "So far."

"Aaron." Dee frowns as she scrolls through his, albeit limited, profile. "He doesn't have any photos of himself. How do you know if he's cute?"

"The back of his head is cute enough. Hopefully the front is, too."

"Risky."

I cover a smile with my palm. I can't fault the guy for only having a photo of the back of his head; I'm not exactly forthcoming either. In fact, I'm not even using my real name. I go by "Sisi" on the app—my grandmother's nickname for me before she passed away—and my profile photo is of an animated cactus—my favorite plant. "Looks aren't everything, Dee. You'd know that if you dated

31

more. Or didn't have an exceptionally gorgeous best friend."

"Is he gorgeous? Gee, I hadn't noticed," she quips. Dee's been subject to more than a few of Noah's fangirls over the years, appealing to her as a way to get to him. "Anyway, I should probably tell you that we discovered a glitch with the messaging feature this morning. My team's crafting up a warning to let users know."

"What kind of glitch?" I ask, mildly disappointed. Aaron messaged me last night, and I haven't had time to get back to him this morning. I was going to respond right after my coffee with Dee.

"We're not exactly sure, but best not to message anyone, just in case. We should have it fixed by this evening. That's why I could only do coffee today and not lunch." Her expression becomes suddenly vulnerable. My sister may be rough around the edges, but our weekly lunch means as much to her as it does to me. With our parents living in different states, Dee and I are the only family we have left in Mirror Valley, and it's made us very close over the years.

I put my hand on hers. "No problem. Glad you could make it."

She clears her throat and removes her hand to check her watchless wrist—an inside joke she shares with Noah that's somehow spilled over to me. "I should get going though. Apps to develop, bugs to fix, fires to put out."

"Sounds like a blast."

I give my sister a hug, and she extends an arm around me, patting me on the back. "I'll see you later. And don't worry, Aaron can wait. Leave him wanting more or whatever they say in those cheesy movies you like."

I roll my eyes. We both know that she likes those movies, too. "Bye, Dee."

She holds up two fingers in a peace sign, then leaves the

coffee shop. I take our empty mugs back to the counter for Ricky, the barista. He barely spares me a glance from behind his comic book. Not that I can blame him for doing such a thing on his shift—the coffee shop is lucky to get a handful of visitors in a day. Ricky's a certified introvert, and I've wondered before if he wanted this job purely because he knew he wouldn't have to talk to people.

I head back to the front desk and remove the "Back in 15" sign, ready to get to work. I was recently promoted from front desk worker to Marketing Manager. It was a position I begged the town council to give me. And, okay, a position I named myself given that we needed someone to do *some* semblance of marketing.

And yes, I do still work at the front desk... but given how quiet the desk is these days, marketing will likely be taking up much more of my time.

Like the logo, the community center hasn't had a facelift in decades—both in terms of its physical appearance and its image. The center is a staple of Mirror Valley, a crown jewel tucked away from Main Street that desperately needs to be polished and refurbished so that it can shine again. I plan to find a way to bring in more customers so that we can make improvements to the facilities and give it new life.

I'll admit that it's a bit of a personal mission for me. Dee and I spent a huge chunk of our childhoods here—this was where we came when our parents were working, attending some event, or engaged in a heated debate about our house, our taxes, their schedules or whatever else was on the agenda that week. We played sports in the on-site gymnasium, went to summer camps on the grounds outside, and attended after-school programs in the meeting room. We studied in the tiny, worn library and swam in the indoor pool back when it was functional and not indefinitely closed.

Realistically though, for all the dreams and aspirations I have for this place, I simply don't have the time right now to throw my all into it. I've never been good at saying no when someone needs help, and so I've amassed more than a few jobs/volunteer positions in the last few months. I may no longer have to work at the vet's office, but my days are still chaotic.

Ivy often says that I need to find my "main character energy". To which I say that I *do* have main character energy... if my main character is Bugs Bunny on a hot cocoa sugar high.

I double-click the mouse on the front desk's ancient computer, and it buzzes to life. While waiting for the screen to come on, I open RightMatch again and reread Aaron's last message.

Aaron: You've got great taste. I love 80s music.

I smile as I bite my pinky fingernail. No, I haven't used RightMatch a lot, but I started talking to Aaron before making my romance trope list, and he's now a solid contender for the "online date" option.

In fact, he's quickly and unexpectedly become someone I look forward to talking to on a daily basis. Aaron is interesting, and smart, and passionate, and he has this dry wit that makes me laugh. It's effortless with him.

Sure, I might've once been interested in Luke Brooks—head over heels, some might say. But I moved on a long time ago, and I'm ready to find my happily-ever-after.

And maybe RightMatch has it right. Instead of falling for someone based on how handsome they are, or how they speak to you, or make you laugh, or, let's say, care for you after unintentionally kicking a ball into your face, there's a beauty in getting to know someone anonymously. Having conversations and peeling back each others' layers, one by one, while your identities are still kept a secret.

But you know what isn't a secret?

How much of a machine hog Sid Rossleigh can be.

Every day at 12:05pm, Sid comes into Valley Fitness and proceeds to do a series of reps on either the bench press or the leg extension machine while grunting loudly like he's the only one in the entire building. Then, he spends thirty minutes sitting on either machine, preventing another gym-goer from using it while he posts photos of himself on social media with captions like "Don't complain, enjoy the pain" or "leg day is best day" or "#swol".

I suspect he doesn't like me either given the amount of times I've asked him to move along and share the equipment. There also that time that I was cleaning the machines and accidentally took a couple of his towels to put into the laundry.

Poor Sid only had two towels for the rest of his workout sesh, and he let me know how much of an inconvenience that was.

But as annoying as I find Sid, I also recognize that this is a valuable opportunity for me to cross another thing off my trope list... the classic enemies-to-more. If movies and books are any indication, the fact that I can't stand him *must* mean that he's a perfect match for me. Right?

And that is why, as soon as my shift at the community center comes to an end, I race to the fitness center, change into my uniform, and slide into the desk chair for 12:05pm.

As scheduled, Sid ambles through the door and comes straight to the front desk to scan his key card. *It's showtime!*

I lean back and cross my arms in what I hope is a casual, carefree, attractive sort of way. "Back again, Sid?"

Sid startles like I interrupted him mid-thought and looks

at me blankly. His eyes are fairly small and mole-like, but they're a lovely green color. He also has a prominent brow ridge that casts a shadow over his face, but I don't think that's a bad thing. "Huh?"

"I said that I'm surprised to see you here," I deadpan. "You never come to Valley Fitness at this hour."

I wait for him to crack a smile, raise a brow, make a sarcastic comment back... *something*. Instead, he stares at me. "Do I know you?"

Hm. So maybe it's not that Sid dislikes me but that he doesn't even know I exist.

Great start.

But I'm not ready to give up on my mission yet. I lean forward, moving closer to him. It's a careful balance, this flirtatious fighting thing. "We only see each other basically every day. Or have you been too busy oiling your abs to notice?"

Sid's frown deepens. "I don't oil my abs."

"Sure you don't." I wink flirtily. "Weirdo."

He raises a hand to his head and scrubs his buzzcut hair so his sizeable bicep pops. I flinch back instinctively, like the muscle somehow developed a mind of its own and tried to whack me in the face.

Seriously. The guy's arm is bigger than my head.

"Uh," he says. "I think you have me confused with someone else, ma'am."

Ma'am?!

I let out an indignant squeak. Everyone in Mirror Valley knows that you reserve the respectful "ma'am" for people visibly over the age of 45. I'm only 27. But before I can react to Sid's very incorrect assumption, he lumbers off towards the machines.

I glare after him.

This is good. Really good. My dislike of Sid is heightening by the hour.

Now I just have to get him to notice me, and then hate me back...

"Anyone ever tell you how charming you are?"

The voice sends an electric shock down my spine, and I whirl around to see Luke standing at the other end of the desk. His lips are tilted in a smirk, and his hazel eyes meet mine without an ounce of embarrassment for his shameless eavesdropping.

I smooth down my uniform and paste on a smile, trying to hide how ruffled I'm feeling. "'Charm' is my middle name."

It isn't. Luke knows that.

He lets my comment slide, then scans his keycard and signs in his license plate. I take a moment to gather myself. It's a little difficult given that Luke is wearing the gray athletic shirt that shows off his toned biceps. Biceps which are neither too big, nor too small, but that I would characterize as being "just right".

To be fair, if anyone's going to know how to optimize the attractiveness of his muscles, it would be Luke Brooks. He probably has spreadsheets for it. He could call them his "mu-xcel spreadsheets".

"That guy on your dating list?" Luke interrupts my rambling internal monologue, standing straight so I get the full force of his serious, nonplussed expression. I don't miss the playful spark in his eyes, though.

"Romance trope list," I correct. Uselessly. "And yes. Yes he is."

"Well. Don't hold out on me. What's his trope?"

I clear my throat, look away briefly. "You sure you want to know? We don't usually talk about this... stuff."

Luke's lips tip up. It's not a sarcastic or arrogant smile

but one of his rare, genuine ones. He seems to shine it on me whenever I've said something that surprises him. "Ivy always said you had the best dating stories. And it looks like your future fiancé is using my machine, so I've got time."

He places his bag on the floor and runs a hand through his hair, filling my airspace with that manly forest scent once again.

Wow. That's not even cologne, he just *smells* like that.

"I'm gonna guess..." He bites his very lovely lower lip. Lovely from a purely objective standpoint, of course. "Gym crush."

I give my head a shake. "Nemesis."

Truth be told, I crossed "gym crush" off my list a couple days ago. Luke doesn't need to know that the closest I have to a gym crush is... well, him. Mr. Wilhelm is next on the list, and as sweet as the 47-year-old divorcé can be, there is *no way* I'm going there.

"Hm." He grunts, and the little crease between his eyebrows reappears. Whenever he frowns like that, I have an almost unstoppable urge to press my thumb into the crease and smooth it out. It's stupid.

"What?" I ask.

"Do you like the guy?"

"No, but that's the point. We're meant to hate each other."

"Sure, on the surface. But think of Ivy and James—they 'hated' one another, but it didn't take much to see that they were totally into each other."

I look over at Sid. He's taken his shirt off so his pecs are on full display. We both watch as he flexes his arms in the mirror.

Plants a kiss on his left bicep.

My mouth turns down in a grimace. "I might like him. Someday."

Luke's skeptical gaze returns to mine, and I'm grateful to have something nicer to look at than Sid's self-adoration. "It seems to me that if hate turns into love, there has to be something there to begin with. Thin line between the two and all. Assuming you feel strongly about him."

I pop out my lower lip, thinking. Truth is, I don't feel *anything* very strongly for Sid.

Curses. Did I just call him a weirdo for no reason?

"Sorry, Sid," I mutter under my breath.

Luke frowns again. "What?"

"Nothing." I lean against the back counter with a sigh. "Just thinking that, for someone who is on a dating hiatus, you're pretty smart."

Luke's face remains impassive. "I learned a lot after what happened with Eleanor. I won't make the same mistakes when or if I choose to date again."

I nod, caught slightly off guard by his casual mention of Eleanor. But I understand where he's coming from, and I understand why he isn't dating. It must be hard to come back from having your fiancée leave you at the altar without an explanation—without even a proper apology. Far as I know, she hasn't been in touch at all since that day.

Luke's handled it well, or so it appears. He moved out of his house and adopted a rescue, but aside from that, nothing's changed. He's just kept on living his life. Which is actually very Luke of him—the guy has never been particularly fond of change as a whole and prefers more of a slow, calculated approach to things. If I were him, I don't think I'd be in a rush to rejoin the dating pool either.

"He's finally leaving," Luke grumbles as Sid heads to the squat rack. "So I'll see you in a bit... *ma'am.*"

With a final smirk in my direction, Luke strides off to the locker room to put his bag away.

I take one last long look at Sid as he sets himself up for

squats, then settle back into my desk chair with a sigh. So much for my enemies-to-more romance. Back to the drawing board... also known as my flimsy napkin-list.

One of the romance tropes has to be for me, right?

I give my head a quick shake and decide to put a pause on my romantic woes for now. After the failed flirting, it's high time I get to work.

I'm making my way through the fitness center's voice-mail messages when the front door slams open. "This will be helpful, I know it will," a familiar voice says.

"What was it Jane Fonda used to say?" another voice asks. "Sweat it out?"

"I don't think Jane Fonda said that," a third person replies. "Also I think that has to do with something the kids call 'binge drinking.'"

"Which kids?"

"I dunno. The ones on that tree hill show."

I stand from behind the desk. "Hey, ladies."

Fran Bellamy, Gloria Perez, and Dora Mae Movis look over at me with identical bright smiles. The three older ladies come in every week for the senior pilates class... and to catch up on gossip. I look forward to these days because you never know what Fran's going to wear. Last week, it was tight, bright, 80s athletic gear a la Olivia Newton John in her "Physical" video (RIP). This week, it's a white tennis skirt over black leggings and a red polo shirt, complete with a matching red sweatband.

Next to Fran, Gloria and Dora Mae look frighteningly normal in their leggings-and-top ensembles.

"Hello, Daisy dear," Fran cheers, signing into class with big, swooping letters. "You're looking well. Any news from that Edgar fellow?"

"Nothing, but no surprises there," I say with a grin.

"Indeed. We could hardly believe it when he took the

microphone at James and Ivy's wedding like that. Professing his love to sweet Courtney in that way..." Fran tuts. "But then again, when you know, you know."

I give a shrug. "Onto greener pastures."

"That's the spirit." Dora Mae nods, her short brown hair bobbing with the movement.

"Yes, don't you worry, dearie," Gloria adds. "Your prince will be along shortly!"

My smile doesn't falter as I change the subject. "Excited for class today? Flo's got a great playlist lined up for you."

"Very excited," Fran exclaims. "We were just saying that we need a good sweat to brainstorm a solution to a town issue."

Yes, a *town* issue.

Because it makes total sense that Fran—ex-administrator at the police and fire department, ex-boudoir photographer, ex-motorcycle mechanic, ex-many-other-things—is now a Mirror Valley town councilor. Fran is easily in her seventies and is our town's most eccentric character by far. Her wardrobe choices are the tip of the iceberg.

She joined Gloria and Dora Mae on the town council earlier this year, and I'd say our town is in very good hands with those three in the mix. Gloria used to be a teacher and now has two of the sweetest French bulldogs on the planet. Dora Mae, on the other hand, is a relatively new addition to Mirror Valley. She moved here from the East Coast a couple of years ago and has extensive experience in public service, which got her voted onto council in no time.

"What kind of issue?" I'm only half-listening for the answer as I alert Flo that everyone's arrived for class.

The ladies go silent... uncharacteristically silent. And suddenly, I'm paying attention. The three exchange loaded glances, and there's a seriousness in the air that feels completely foreign.

"You can keep a secret, can't you, Daisy?" Fran asks, her voice low.

"Of course," I reply, matching her tone.

"Well, the truth is..." Gloria looks around, her voice a whisper. "The town is absolutely *hemorrhaging* money."

My eyes widen. "Hemorr—"

"That's a bit extreme." Fran tuts, shaking her head at Gloria. "We've simply found some... financial irregularities."

"What kinds of irregularities?" I ask.

"Let's just say that there's an unexplained gap in our public funds."

I frown, confused. "A *gap*? I thought we had the busiest summer on record what with the Brookrose bringing in tons of guests, and—"

"Yes, yes," Dora Mae cuts in, raising a manicured hand. "The Brookrose has been wonderful for tourism."

"Regardless, something is irregular," Gloria finishes.

"But how is this possible?"

"We're not sure yet," Fran replies. "We've given our finances to Argent Accounting to help us investigate the cause of these irregularities. But don't you worry, dear. We'll sort it all out."

"Hashtag Council-Is-On-It." Gloria pulls out her phone. "I'm gonna get us trending on the app... ah, what's it called? With the dancing? Ooh! Maybe Flo can choreograph a dance for us, and all the celebrities will see it!"

Fran delicately lowers Gloria's hand to the desk. "Let's save that for the young'uns like Daisy, shall we?"

Take that, Sid!

Though in all honesty, my social media know-how likely isn't much better than Gloria's... Social media marketing is one of the things I will be working on in my role as self-appointed Community Center Marketing Manager.

I give the ladies a reassuring smile. "It'll work out, I know it will. Argent is Luke's firm; I'm sure they're going to be a big help."

The three nod in agreement before bustling away to join Flo and the others in class. As soon as the door shuts behind them and the upbeat, poppy music begins, I sink back in my chair with an uneasy feeling rolling in my stomach, despite what I said. What on earth could be causing "financial irregularities" in our town?

My eyes land absently on Luke across the room. He's got his headphones in—probably blaring ABBA, not that he'd ever admit it—and is doing bicep curls. He's got a sheen of sweat across his forehead and down his muscular shoulders and arms, giving his tanned skin a glow. His full lips move slightly as he counts his reps, brows drawn together in concentration.

Probably thinking about his mu-xcel spreadsheets, perfecting a formula for those arms of his...

I snap myself out of it and pick up my phone. I might as well draft a message to Aaron. The messaging feature might be down at the moment, but better I think about writing to him than watch Luke do his sweaty, intense, muscly workout.

5

LUKE

I don't usually drive to the fitness center. Driving is time wasted.

The Valley Fitness center is a 20 minute and 18 second brisk walk from my office, give or take depending on traffic and snowfall in the winter. Which means that it's the perfect distance for a warm-up and a cool-down. I've figured out how to maximize my workout breaks, and I don't coo the point in deviating from something so efficient and carefully timed.

But today is an exception, because our firm's new intern started this morning, and that's thrown off my entire schedule. After explaining how our filing system works and setting him up with a company laptop, I only had 10 minutes to change and make it to Valley Fitness.

I don't do exceptions. They stress me out.

Although seeing sweet, kind-hearted Daisy accidentally insult our resident gym bro did cheer me up a little.

"How was the workout?" Noah asks when I walk into my office—our office, for today and today only. The small "intern nook" down the hall is currently filled with boxes that will be cleared out by tomorrow morning. I will make sure of it.

I drop my bag into the wardrobe near the door and walk to my desk, shaking out my damp hair. I ran out of shampoo mid-shower and have to make a note to pick up more.

"Fine," I offer as a reply. Then, reminding myself to be nice, I add, "You grab lunch?"

"Sure did. Burger, fries, and this smoothie, because a well-balanced diet is important, Luke," he mock-scolds me as he holds up a cup of disgusting purple/green sludge. "Spinach and berry. Looks nasty, tastes delicious."

I blow past that bold statement. Clasp my hands on top of my desk. "What do you think of Argent so far?"

Noah leans back in his chair and fiddles with his black-and-white squiggly tie. I'd bet money Dee got that for him.

When Noah asked if he could intern with my accounting firm, I was skeptical. Not only is the guy comfortably out of college—you know, the age at which most people choose to intern—he's also a jock. Big into sports, wears backwards ball caps, laughs loudly, and uses words like "man" and "dude" religiously.

He's not the kinda guy you'd catch wearing a suit, and his business casual look leaves much to be desired... the charcoal gray jacket is a couple sizes too big while his dress shirt underneath strains around the buttons. Plus, he's wearing pinstripe blue slacks. And the ensemble is topped off with a solid layer of cat hair.

It's a whole, fuzzy mismatch, but I hold back from pointing it out. If he was anyone else, I'd say something, but the guy is Daisy's younger sister's best friend, and I've learned not to get involved when it comes to the Griffiths sisters. Chances are Daisy would want to talk about any perceived insults at Valley Fitness tomorrow, which would offset my timing all over again.

"It's alright." Noah runs a hand over his short black hair. "Mr. Argent is an uptight little dude, isn't he?"

"Kenneth isn't known for his sense of humor."

"All I did was hand him the salt instead of the sugar to put into his coffee this morning. Classic first day prank. I was gonna tell him the truth, but he poured in half a cup of the stuff before I could say anything. Poor guy was gagging for, like, an hour."

"Pranks aren't really a thing around here."

Noah passes a hand over his hair again. He seems put off by the lack of ball cap on his head. I'm just surprised it was hiding *that* much hair. But the guy clearly needs to fidget, and if he's going to fidget, he might as well do something productive with it.

I reach into my drawer and take out a lint roller. "Use this."

Noah frowns as he takes the roller. "For what?"

I don't reply, just give a wave indicating a particularly large clump of gray hair on his pant leg.

He raises a dark brow at me, then looks down at himself as though he hadn't realized that he'd basically brought an entire pet with him to work. With a bright, beaming smile, he stands and starts rolling his jacket and pants.

"Sorry, man, must've missed this when I was getting dressed this morning. I went by Dee and Daisy's place last night to show Dee my awesome suit and Bruce decided that my pants were the perfect place for a nap." He rolls his eyes, clucking like an old hen.

"Bruce?" I ask distractedly while I open my Notes app and type in "shampoo" along with a few other food items for myself and Stella.

"Dee's cat. Mangy furball, that one, but he sure can be cute when he wants to be." He holds out his arms and does a spin. "Better?"

I glance up from my phone. "Much."

"Thanks." Noah throws the lint roller back to me. "I don't think Lauren would be thrilled to see me rocking Bruce's hair on my pants."

"Hm."

"Then again, maybe that wouldn't be such a bad thing. Things between us lately have been... rocky."

I can't say this news surprises me. For obvious reasons, I make an active effort not to listen to the Mirror Valley rumor mill, but even *I* know that Noah's got a heartbreaker reputation around town. I'd bet that he's dated almost every eligible woman in the county at this stage.

But Noah and I aren't exactly close—I really only know him through Daisy—so I choose not to reply. Instead, I start up my computer to get to work. When I hear him let out a sigh, I glance over.

"Something isn't right," he says. For some reason. "With Lauren, I mean. Like when I brought her to the wedding. She was pouting all night."

I'm momentarily thrown. It's rare to see Noah serious like this, which is one of the reasons I was hesitant about asking Mr. Argent if he could intern here. It wasn't until Daisy stalked me around Valley Fitness going on and on about Noah's optimistic spirit and positivity and how he might be a breath of fresh air in our "stale and gray office environment" that I changed my mind.

"I wanted for us to hang out with the team, but she wasn't thrilled about that. Plus, there was the whole 'we both ordered chicken, but she wanted fish' situation. Then, I danced with Dee for a minute, and she *really* didn't like that. I tried to explain that I only did it because Dee was there alone, but Lauren wouldn't hear it. It took her a couple days to calm down, but I don't see how I can move forward with her."

"Then don't." My voice is a little sharper than intended, and I soften it with a shrug. "No sense leading someone on."

Noah looks at me, and his eyes clear. "True. I don't want to hurt her, but it's best to be honest."

"Great idea. So this afternoon, we're going to cover—"

"What about you? No plus one at the wedding. Are you seeing anyone?"

My nostrils flare slightly. *This* is what being nice gets you: chatty, curious people who want to know your business. How does Daisy do it? "We should get to work," I say.

"Come on, Luke. I told you about Lauren and me, what's happening with you? Maybe with a certain blue-eyed blonde who really likes meatballs?"

My lips seal even more firmly together. I don't know what he's alluding to, but he's crazy if he thinks anything is happening between Daisy and me. Sure, she's beautiful in that girl-next-door kinda way that's a perfect mix of cute and sexy. And yeah, she's got a heart of gold that could rival Mother Teresa's. And she makes me laugh more than anyone else ever has...

Daisy is incredible. One of a kind. The type of girl that any guy would be lucky to call his. And even though she's notorious for going on first dates but never seconds, there's a man out there worthy of her. I've no doubt.

But it's not me.

For one thing, she's Ivy's best and oldest friend. On top of that, I shouldn't be dating *anyone* right now. We all know how things ended with Eleanor. After time and reflection, I know how I messed up: I was committing to her for the wrong reasons—out of a sense of duty and loyalty. Relationships work when both people are committed to loving each other. I was committed to being committed. There's a difference.

When and if I commit again, it'll be for the *right*

48

reasons. It'll be for love. But it won't happen overnight; it'll take time, effort, patience, and work.

Sexy, right?

"Daisy and I are a no-go," I say briskly to nip this conversation in the bud. "Anyway, let's move onto—"

"Really? 'Cuz I could swear there's a little spark between you two. Every time you look at each other, you both seem sucked into your own little world. Like planet..." Noah taps his chin. "Duke."

I roll my eyes with an agitated sigh. "Don't tell me you're into this couple name thing, too."

"Couple names? Don't know what you're talking about. It's a Dee thing."

"... That she got from Daisy."

Noah's eyes go wide, and he points a finger directly into my face. "See? Look at you! You've been a stodgy, straight-faced accountant all morning, and now you're *smiling*."

I force my lips back into a line. "Enough. Let's get to work."

Noah leans forward obediently, but his eyes are still dancing in this annoying, smug way. "What's next on the ol' training agenda?"

I walk Noah through his project for the afternoon: getting the town council's finances organized for the book-keepers. Then, I start on my own project. The fiscal year-end is coming up for Clear Reflections—the cleaning company owned by that guy Ivy used to like. Cam something or other. I think the guy's engaged now. I try not to know anything about peoples' personal lives past what I need for tax purposes.

But as I stare at the spreadsheet on my screen, my focus is elsewhere. Noah's got it wrong when it comes to Daisy, but I'll admit that the woman I'm speaking to on Right-Match has caught me by surprise. I'm not saying I'm changing my mind about relationships, but there's something about her. She's refreshing. Whip-smart, and funny, and so easy to talk to. We move between joking and more in-depth, introspective talks seamlessly.

I reflexively check my phone again, but there's still no response. She hasn't messaged all day, and the disappointment that fills my chest surprises me.

This distance is good. I like that we're talking online without knowing who the other person is. For all I know, she lives in rural Nevada. It's low risk.

Noah clears his throat, pulling me back to the moment. "Hey... uh, I think you should see this."

He pushes his laptop towards me, and I scan through the spreadsheet on his screen. It details the money made on the community center.

Actually, the *lack* of money from the community center.

"Wow." I do a low whistle, sitting back. "That is really interesting."

"Agreed." Noah also sits back and steeples his fingers in what I realize is a perfect imitation of me. Until he goes too far and pouts his lips so he looks like that guy from that ridiculous movie about male models.

I place my hands on the desk. "We haven't even started digging into the finances yet, but we should talk to town council about this. They've had some concerns with money, and there might be an opportunity here for them to make some changes right away."

Noah blinks, his brow furrowing. "What kinds of changes? Because I'm pretty sure we know a couple people who might be upset if something happens with the community center."

He's right. Daisy works at the community center, and I guess Dee must be attached to it as well. "I'm sure nothing drastic will happen. They may just want to tone down on their spending, or reduce their hours of operation, or something." I give a nod. "This is a good find, Noah. You might have a future as an accountant yet."

His face freezes for a second before he smiles again. "Thanks, dude."

Sisi: Sorry for the late reply, the message feature was down.

Aaron: I saw that. At first, I thought my confession about 80s pop music put you off.

Sisi: No. It wasn't the 80s pop that did it.

Aaron: Aren't you charming

Sisi: I get that a lot. So what do you do when you're not listening to old-timey music then?

Aaron: Um, I guess you could say I'm a money guy.

Sisi: That makes sense, you seem like a knowledgeable, financially savvy kinda person.

Aaron: Yes. I suppose....

Sisi: Okay let's see if you can put your money where your mouth is (pun intended). What are your best money saving ideas?

Aaron: Don't tell me you're one of those people who calls those numbers on TV to find out their credit score.

Sisi: Nope, I'm totally asking for a friend. Or, more like a group of friends. A community.

Aaron: Is this your way of telling me you're in a cult?

Sisi: Maybe

Aaron: Well every community—or cult—is probably doing its best to save money. So my advice is always to trim where you can, make calculated decisions about what's best for everyone and go from there. Start small and work up.

Sisi: I like it :) And for the record, it's not a cult. It's a town.

Aaron: Ah. Can I assume that you also live in a small town?

Sisi: I do and I love it. Most of the time.

Aaron: Same. Most of the time.

Sisi: Do you ever think about leaving?

Aaron: I have. I did. Last year, my life changed a lot, and I considered moving to a big city. Problem is I have a house and a dog, my job's here, my family's here.

Sisi: I get it. Well, not exactly. My family's spread around different cities. But I get wanting to start fresh. Must be nice to have a house all your own, though.

Aaron: It's alright. Except when my best friend and sister used to come over for barbecues. They always insisted on playing soccer and it totally messed up the yard.

Sisi: Haha my best friend's like that too.

Aaron: From what we've talked about, I feel like your best friend and my best friend would get along... you know, if we all met. I think we'd get along too.

Sisi: Agreed :)

6

DAISY

RightMatch: Congratulations, Aaron and Sisi. Time to meet in person!

I read the text over again, then put my phone screen-down on the desk.

Knee bouncing, I clasp my hands, unclasp them. Poke the adorable potted cactus I brought in for decoration, then stand and walk around the desk. The community center is totally deserted, so no one's around to see my pacing.

The prompt came through in my message thread with Aaron last night, and since then, neither of us have said anything.

I feel like I'm back in high school, waiting for my SAT results with tense shoulders and wide eyes. Which one of us is going to speak first? Will I cave and say something, or will it be Aaron? Will we finally cross the barrier from "text flirters" to "in person daters"?

The voice in my head—which sounds alarmingly like the voiceover from *The Bachelor*—continues to throw questions at me left and right.

Dee may have been teasing last week when she said that not answering Aaron would leave him wanting more, but her little premonition apparently came true. After getting the all-clear that the message feature was back up and running, I finally sent him a text, and we've been messaging nonstop since.

I'll admit that I can be a chatty Cathy, but this is something different. Aaron has this dry and sarcastic wit that's totally sucked me in. Though we've only ever met through a phone screen, I feel like I know him. Like he knows everything about me. I even put a pause on my trope list search for the moment.

In any case, all of our conversations made us gain enough points to blow past the prompts to share our playlists, more photos, and our phone numbers. Nothing could stop us...until this prompt came through.

I've enjoyed anonymously getting to know Aaron over the last few days, but the next logical step *is* to meet in person. And if he is, in fact, the person I'm meant to spend the rest of my life with... well, what is there to be afraid of? Aside from catfishers, kidnappers, Tinder Swindlers, Craigslist creeps, etc.

But surely it isn't possible for Aaron to catfish me if I don't know what he looks like. Right?

In all seriousness though, Aaron's never given me the slightest inkling that he has bad intentions. He might come across a bit rough around the edges at first, but I've been pleasantly surprised by his genuine kindness and caring.

Those are my favorite kinds of people—the ones who aren't what you expect.

"Come on, Dais. It just takes one second..." I mutter my mantra to myself.

Before I can lose my nerve, I walk back to the desk, pick up my phone, and type out a message. Think of a nice, neutral location that's close to home, and cross my fingers that he won't have to drive too far.

Sisi: Well, look at that, the RightMatch gods have spoken. How would you feel about meeting for drinks this weekend? Maybe at a bar called McGarry's in Mirror Valley? It's not too far from where I live.

I pause. *Just one second...*

I squeeze an eye shut.

Press send.

Adrenaline pumps through my body. All my limbs feel like they're buzzing, and my hands shake.

There's no immediate response—which makes logical sense—but that doesn't stop me from glancing at my phone screen every two seconds.

Until the door to the community center bursts open, and I leap back in my chair like I've been caught doing something bad.

You don't even know if this guy wants to meet you. Why are you blushing?!

"What are we going to do?" Gloria's voice rings out. "We can't let this happen."

"We'll figure it out," Fran responds calmly. Her long mauve skirt swishes across the linoleum floor as the two walk towards the coffee shop. "This doesn't have to mean the end."

"End of what?" I ask before I can stop myself. Because I'm a Mirror Valley girl, and "nosy" is basically a given here.

Gloria and Fran both whirl around in surprise. "Daisy!" Fran holds a hand to her chest. "You frightened me! I thought you were a ghost."

"Sorry." I give a sheepish shrug. There's a shelf above the front desk that is my exact height when I'm seated, so people usually can't see me when they walk in. Years ago, the admin would be standing to man the desk as there would always be something to do, someone to check in or chat to. But the community center isn't quite the happening spot it used to be, and I'm the only one haunting this place most days. Pun intended.

"Don't be sorry, dear," Gloria says as she strides towards me with Fran hot on her heels. "It's fortuitous that we ran into you, in fact."

I furrow my brow. Gloria Perez is retired now, but every once in awhile, her English teacher ways reveal themselves. "How fort—forit—fortunoitus," I agree.

Fran peers at me over her red spectacles. "Yes, how *are* all the marketing whatsits and gadgets going?"

"Good. I created an Instagram and a TikTok account for the center." I haven't had time to do much more than that... yet. "What brings you ladies in today?"

"We thought we'd pop into the coffee shop, grab a hot drink," Gloria says. "Morning Bell is simply *awash* with people, so we decided that this was the perfect backup."

"Backup" is right. I enjoy the community center coffee shop myself, but the only decent drink you can get there is black coffee. Or the syrupy hot cocoa from the machine, if you're like me. Even the tea tastes funny. "Great. I think Ricky's at the counter, he'll be happy to help you. And I can let Dora Mae know when she gets here."

"Oh, she won't be joining us today, she's absolutely swamped at the moment. And we have important matters to discuss." Fran pauses. "Matters about the community center, actually..."

She trails off into silence, and I hold my tongue this time, pasting on an innocent expression. I don't want to be rude and pry again, even though I'm bursting with curiosity.

But lucky for me, Gloria leans towards Fran. "Should we tell her?"

"I don't see why not," Fran mutters. "She's technically management now."

I hold back a smile—Fran and Gloria aren't exactly

known for their secret-keeping. As I hoped, the ladies pause for a beat, exchange another glance, then turn to me. "You remember what we said about the town hemorrhaging money?" Gloria asks quietly.

"I believe you said 'absolutely hemorrhaging,'" I add cheerfully. Immediately regret my tone.

Not the time, Daisy.

Gloria blows past it. "We know what the problem is."

"One of the *potential* problems that *may* be contributing to these financial irregularities," Fran clarifies.

"In any case, there is a problem area, and it's here." Gloria punctuates her statement by tapping her ruby red index fingernail on the front desk.

"Here." I match her tone. "On the desk."

"No, my dear. I'm afraid the problem is the whole building."

"The community center? How can that be a problem?"

"It's a publicly funded building," Fran explains. "And those still cost money. Money that comes from the town council's coffers. We've had meetings over the last few days, and while we still can't identify the root cause of these irregularities, we are needing to come up with some solutions. The community center has been considered as a potential... quick fix."

"Quick fix?" I don't like the sound of that one bit.

"Yes." Fran lays a hand on top of mine sympathetically. Her rings are cool against my skin. "There is talk of potentially scaling back on hours, scaling back on staff... that kind of thing."

"Scaling back," I repeat, mulling over her words.

"It's a money issue, and as you can see..." Gloria trails off, gesturing around. Her words echo around my brain. Or maybe it's just her voice echoing around the empty lobby. "There's no money coming in here. Everyone goes to the community center in Summer Lakes these days, even though it's a drive away." Gloria leans in close. "Did you hear that they have a *jacuzzi?*"

"So why don't *we* get a jacuzzi?"

"Because we'd need money for a jacuzzi. But a jacuzzi would bring in money... you see the issue."

Fran shakes her head. "It's a real chicken-crossing-the-road kind of situation."

"Chicken and egg," Gloria corrects.

"We can't just scale it all back," I say quietly.

"Daisy, girl. You always look on the bright side, what if this is a blessing in disguise? You already have so much on your plate."

"I like having lots on my plate. The more, the better. Full plates are the best plates." Fran and Gloria exchange a slightly concerned glance, but I give my head a shake. Shoot to a stand once again. "The community center isn't going anywhere. This is a fun, safe space for our kids and our entire community. We can and will make sure that this place stays open, even if I have to raise money for it myself. Hashtag Save-The-Center!"

My impassioned speech is met with raised eyebrows and dubiously pursed lips.

"You ladies leave it with me," I say with a confidence I'm not sure I feel. "I'll find a way."

"Alright, my dear," Fran says. "We trust you, and we know you have our town's best interests at heart. Best of luck to you. *Bon courage!*"

With a wave, Fran and Gloria head off to the coffee shop, chatting like our world-tilting conversation never happened.

Meanwhile, I place my head in my hands.

Do I know anything about how to "save" a public building? No.

Do I know how to raise money for a cause like this? Absolutely not.

Am I in way over my head and may have bitten off more than I can chew?

Yes. It certainly looks that way.

At that moment, my phone dings. The bright side of this ridiculous situation is that I'm too emotionally wrung-out to be nervous about Aaron's response to my text asking him out. I'm grabbing my phone when it dings again. And again.

I check the screen and see that I've received not three messages, but closer to ten. All from RightMatch.

Sure. I'd love to meet you!... I had no idea we made it this far, but I'm free that day... Happy to drive out to Mirror Valley to meet for drinks... You seem great. I'll be there.

What in the flippity flip-flop is going on?

I open RightMatch, and my stomach twists violently.

The message intended only for Aaron sent to every one of my matches.

Every. Single. One.

Even the ones I'd barely talked to. Even the ones with whom I hadn't gained any points at all.

I need to find Dee. Now.

I somehow, accidentally, unintentionally have twenty dates lined up for the exact same time and place this Saturday night.

7

LUKE

What am I doing? This is the stupidest, least thought-out thing I've ever done in my life.

And yet, here I am.

I stick my hands deep into the pockets of my blue jeans as I stride down Main Street. It's just before sunset on Saturday night, and people crowd the street. Warm, savory scents waft from restaurants, and shop windows reflect the colors of the sky, painting the town gold. I offer a nod to people I know, but I'm too preoccupied to stop and chat. I'm in no mood to waste my limited small talk abilities before I go on what will likely be a disappointing date with Sisi.

Sounds pessimistic, I know. But I work off statistics and probabilities, and there is a pretty good chance that this date will not go as planned. First off because, though we've had many lengthy conversations, I have no idea what she'll be like in person, or what she expects from our interactions. For all I know, she's an elderly lady simply looking for someone to chat with.

Which would be fine, really. Not for dating, obviously, but my grandma Maggie is one of my favorite people on the entire planet. I have a soft spot for kind old ladies.

There are just so many ways that this could go off the rails. Maybe Sisi isn't as easy to talk to when we're face to face, or maybe she's not as genuine as she appears to be. Maybe she's a circus performer who has two heads, who knows. Or maybe she's one of those toxic positive, sunshiney types who casts an all-too-bright glow on everything. Daisy is the only exception to my dislike of overly positive people. With Daisy, it never feels false or performative.

And why am I thinking about Daisy Griffiths right now?! I'm going on my first first date in over a decade.

When I got Sisi's message this past week about meeting for drinks, my gut instinct was to shut it down. Things between us were so natural, so organic, and I didn't want to jeopardize that. Didn't want to change that.

But I'd be lying if I said that there wasn't a part of me that wants to meet her. Wants to see her in person and hear her voice, hear her laugh...

I'm still not sure I'm gonna do it.

I might be walking towards McGarry's, but that doesn't mean I have to go in. It doesn't mean that I have to look around for a girl who's looking for a guy called "Aaron." I could just sit at the bar, grab a Coke, and see if anyone interesting shows.

I only responded to her this morning during a rare bout of reckless optimism with an "OK". She hasn't responded or confirmed, so it's possible she won't be there anyway.

I'm not sure whether I feel good or bad about that.

Too soon, I'm standing in front of McGarry's. Teetering back and forth between walking in or going home.

But it turns out that what I want doesn't matter. Because a group of guys I've never seen before shove past me into the bar, and I'm dragged in with them.

"Watch it," I growl the warning, but it's lost beneath the literal roar of conversation and laughter in McGarry's.

Seriously, I don't think I've ever seen the bar this busy. There are people crowded across the floor, every booth is taken. Servers and bartenders zip around, looking more than a little frazzled. I can hardly hear my own thoughts, let alone the shouts being exchanged all around me.

What on earth is happening here?

I come to my senses and crank my mouth shut, gazing around with a very, very firm certainty that there are a thousand places I'd rather be than this crammed bar that smells of spilled beer and perfume.

I knew I shouldn't have left my cozy spot on the couch next to Stella.

I turn on my heel and am about to walk right back out the door when I hear a familiar light, breathy voice.

"Luke!"

I freeze in surprise, then half-turn towards the voice. "What are—"

"Thank goodness you're here!" Daisy grasps my arm and uses it as an anchor to pull herself through the crowd. She bumps into a couple of couples speaking with their heads bent close together and throws a "sorry!" over her shoulder.

As she's about to reach me, she trips and falls forward. I manage to catch her, pulling her close to help her stand upright. Her long, blonde hair brushes my arm, and the familiar, floral smell of her shampoo reminds me of a calm meadow. It's an instant relief, and my shoulders relax a bit as I hold onto her, shielding her from the crowd.

"What's going on?" I demand.

"It's a long story." She stands away from me and brushes off the front of her dress—a silky black one that skates down her body and goes to her mid-thigh. For some reason, my breath catches. I usually see Daisy in athletic wear or one of her various work uniforms. But after seeing her in that pink bridesmaid's dress at Ivy's wedding, and now in this elegant black dress, I have to admit that she cleans up nicely.

"This some kind of event?" I ask.

Daisy's silent for a beat as she looks around the bar, her brows pulled together. "Sure looks like it..."

I follow her gaze, and at that moment, I realize something.

The couples that Daisy crashed into aren't the only ones at McGarry's. In fact, there are couples all across the room.

It's like a freaking Noah's Ark in here.

My shoulders tense up. "Dais. Is this what I think it is?"

Surprise flashes in her eyes. "What do you think it is?"

"A singles event." I bristle. "And don't tell me it's one of those ludicrous fundraising ones where they play a cheesy video at the end of the night." I give my head an abrupt shake. "I feel like I'm about to be forced onto a boat destined for a new world."

Daisy snorts that funny little snort she does sometimes. "You think this is a singles event," she says innocently.

Too innocently.

"I'm outta here." I turn back towards the door.

"No, please." Daisy grasps my arm again, her slim fingers not quite circling my bicep. I stop. "Please stay, Luke. This is all... I didn't... Well, it's kinda my fault."

That's enough to get my attention. "How is this *your* fault?"

Daisy grins up at me, and the crystal blue of her eyes dance like waves on a lake's surface. Her expression is sweet, almost a little vulnerable, and I soften a little. "If you stay, I'll tell you." She leans in close so her calm meadow smell surrounds me. "And I promise it's a good story."

I clear my throat but don't step away. I'll admit I'm curious. And besides, Sisi might be here, lost in the crowd of couples somewhere. It can't hurt to stay a little longer.

"One drink," I grumble. "Then I'm out."

8

DAISY

We swing by the bar to get a guilty-pleasure Shirley Temple for me and a Coke with a slice of lemon for Luke. The bar is completely packed, and Luke and I were pushed against each other more than a few times. I wish I could say that I didn't notice the way his arms would circle me absentmindedly when someone pushed past us, the way his firm front felt against my back, the way his hand rested on my arm when we were standing at the bar.

When we finally get to the seating area, drinks in hand, I spot Isobel, a care worker I know from the senior center with curly red hair and the cutest button nose, vacating a corner booth with a man I've never met but who looks vaguely familiar.

I give them a wave as they head towards the bar, trying not to be too sheepish, then slide into their booth. My bare thighs squeak and squawk against the vinyl.

Ugh. Whoever put vinyl booths at McGarry's wasn't thinking straight. Our town is filled with the kind of people who wear shorts year-round, and these booths have a sticky reputation. They're almost as infamous as the useless stoplight at the far end of Main Street.

My hands circle the cool glass, which drips with condensation, as Luke takes off his brown suede jacket. He places it on the hanger next to the booth, and slides in easily because his thighs aren't moonlighting as scotch tape.

As he settles in, I can't help but notice the way his clean, white T-shirt sets off his year-round tan. The way the sleeves cut across his arms, somehow amping their muscle definition by a factor of a thousand.

Is it possible for a shirt to make you look *more* muscular?

My cheeks get warm all of a sudden, and I look down at the menu though I have no intention of ordering anything. I've barely eaten today, but I feel too apprehensive to even read the Starters section.

Luke places his elbows on the table, leaning in. I risk a glance up to meet his eyes, which happen to be squarely on me. I was pleasantly surprised to see him come into the bar earlier, but now, I'm not sure what to say. How am I supposed to even start explaining how this whole evening came about?

So, I reach for an easier subject. "How's Stella?" I ask conversationally.

"Good. Sleepy. The usual." Luke goes silent, which isn't a surprise given his feelings towards small talk.

His gaze swings around the bar again, and I take the opportunity to appraise him. His scruff is nicely trimmed, and his hair carefully styled. Yup, Luke Brooks is definitely bringing his A game tonight. And most nights, if I'm honest, but tonight, it's like he actually tried.

But why...?

"You're staring," Luke says without even a glance in my direction.

I startle, and my cheeks get warm. I try to play it off with a shrug. "You just look... okay."

Now, Luke turns to me. Gives me that lopsided smirk of his. "Okay, huh? That a good or bad thing?"

"Good," I respond before I can stop myself. *Wow. I am the opposite of smooth and subtle.* I clear my throat. "You look *nice*."

"You look surprised."

"I'm just not used to seeing you not in a suit. Or athletic wear."

"I could say the same for you. I've gotten used to your work uniforms." His eyes give off that rare, teasing spark that makes my stomach flutter in a way that it has no business doing. "Or those camo leggings."

I scrunch my nose at the memory, fluttering stomach aside. "When are you going to let that go? I told you, I lost a bet with Dee and had to wear those leggings for a week. A *week!* Do you know how many 'I can't see Daisy' jokes I heard?" I shake my head. "Bernie even sat on me once."

Luke coughs out a laugh. "Like 65-year-old Bernie with the motorcycle."

"Yup. Leather chaps and all." I give a shiver.

Luke chuckles just as a server somehow squeezes up next to our table. She looks more than a little stressed, and strands of wispy brown hair are coming loose from her ponytail. "Can I get you guys anything to eat?"

"Sure," Luke says. He runs a finger down the menu, then looks at me. "You're vegetarian, right Dais? Do you like cauliflower wings?"

"Uh... I don't need anything. I'm happy with my drink."

"Don't be ridiculous." Luke keeps his eyes on the menu. "I heard your stomach growling the moment I walked in."

The server keeps looking around anxiously. "I'm fine," I insist. "Really."

"Okay. I'll get the wings, and you can help yourself." He gives me a little smirk, then turns to the server. "We'll get the cauliflower wings and a slice of chocolate cake." His gaze briefly drops to her nametag. "And don't worry if there's a wait, Cindy. It's busy."

Cindy smiles appreciatively at Luke, no doubt caught in the snare of his hazel eyes. A blush creeps up her neck as she mumbles "thanks" before running back through the crowd.

I sit back in the booth with a grin. "I think she likes you."

"I think she's the only one on the floor and probably likes anyone who treats her like a human." Luke's jaw clicks. "I'd be absolutely miserable if I had to work around all these people."

I laugh and catch a breath of his manly forest scent again. There's something else in there too... a subtle spicy cologne? He raises one of his hands from the table to rub the scruff along his jawline.

Yup. Can now confirm that the T-shirt just goes to make him look *more* toned than even his workout clothes do. Luke is tall, but not Sasquatch-level, and he's muscular, but a lean sort of muscular that aligns him more with a long-distance runner than a weightlifter. There's something about him that screams larger than life.

He just seems... powerful.

Where are you going with this line of thought, Dais??

"So, chocolate cake?" I ask, my voice cracking on the last word.

"What's wrong with chocolate cake?"

"Nothing. Just thought cake wasn't allowed in your 'strict diet and exercise regimen'. Not to mention cauliflower wings."

"I can let loose sometimes."

I raise a brow. "I don't think I've ever seen that side of you."

Luke smirks at me, his eyes sparking again. "I don't think you could handle it."

Something in his words, in his tone of voice, makes my cheeks heat up to entirely new levels, though I'm sure he meant them innocently enough. Just the thought of a big, strong and silent type like Luke "letting loose" makes my head spin.

I shift in the booth. Luke gazes around once more, and I suddenly get the sense that he's looking for someone. Before I can ask, he turns back to me. "So, you planning on telling me this story or what?"

"Right. The story." I pull my white scrunchie off my wrist—it doubles as both a hair piece and a decorative bracelet. And, for the time being, the thing I fiddle with. "I don't know where to start."

"How about with your claim that this is 'your fault'?"

I take a deep breath, now feeling warm for an entirely different reason. What is Luke going to think about me being on a dating app? This blows entirely past our boundary of not talking about dating, and I wonder if we cross that line, whether we can ever go back. Whether I'd *want* to go back.

But it's a fair question, and I did promise him a story.

"The thing is," I start, staring down at my scrunchie and choosing my words carefully. "I might have brought these people together tonight. Unintentionally."

"You know everyone here?"

"Not exactly. I know most of the women from Valley Fitness, the senior center staff, the vet clinic... They're all single."

"So this *is* a singles event." Luke's jaw sets.

"An accidental one," I say hurriedly as my scrunchie-fiddling intensifies. "And one that the town council probably shouldn't hear about. I can't imagine what the Mayor, or Fran, or Gloria would say if they knew this was happening tonight."

He nods once, and I take it as my cue to go on.

"In any case, the guys are from a dating app." I swallow thickly. "Dee's dating app. Have you heard of RightMatch? These guys were all my matches on the app."

Luke goes still, his lips slightly more pursed than usual. "You're on RightMatch?"

It's not the first question I thought he'd ask—to be honest, I doubted Luke knew about any dating apps at all. Plus, there's a tone in his voice I can't quite place. He must just be surprised.

"Yeah." And then, maybe because the silence feels too loud, or because I'm nervous about Luke's reaction, or because my mouth likes to develops a mind of its own at times, I start rattling off everything I know about Right-Match. "The way it works is that you gain points and uncover more information about someone the longer you speak with them. At a certain point, you're able to meet. But there's been a few glitches with the messaging feature lately, and so when I sent a message asking someone out, the text ended up going to everyone I'd ever matched with."

There's a beat of silence, and I sit on my sweaty palms. They certainly don't help the scotch-tape-thigh situation.

Luke's full-on staring at me now. "You sent a message to someone asking them to meet you here?"

I shrug a shoulder helplessly. "I intended for the invite to go to just one guy. He's the only one I was speaking to seriously, the only one I was interested in. And now... well." I gesture around the bar. "Everyone else is here, and I have no clue who this guy could be."

"Do you know the guy's name?" Luke's hazel eyes are lasering into mine.

"I'm not telling you that."

"Why not?"

"Because what if you know him? Or what if you meet him someday, and you bring up this crazy night before I can talk to him about it? It's not exactly romantic to be like, 'oh hey, the first time we met, we were in a bar surrounded by *all* of my matches on a dating app. Love ya!'"

Luke chuckles. "I won't. Promise."

I bite the inside of my cheek, debating. It really isn't *that* big a deal. Even if Luke knows Aaron, it won't change anything. He only just got back to me this morning; I truly thought he was a lost cause and my one second of foolishness had scared him away for good while simultaneously triggering an absurd dating disaster.

But who knows if he'll even show tonight. And if he does, fingers crossed that I recognize him by the back of his head.

"Okay, fine." I exhale a breath. "His name's Aaron."

"Cauliflower wings with a side of ranch," Cindy sings as she reappears next to our table.

I take the dish, my stomach emitting a loud growl. "Ooh, thank you!"

"No problem." Cindy turns to Luke, which is fine as my full attention is on the cauliflower at this point. I sense her pause, and then turn back my way. "Would you like sharing plates?"

When I look up, Luke hasn't even acknowledged Cindy. He's staring over my shoulder with the darkest expression on his face, like he's calculating some impossible equation. I snap my fingers in his line of view. "Luke? Do you want sharing plates?"

His eyes meet mine, and there's something weighted and swirling in his gaze. He turns to the server. "Uh... yes please, Cindy."

"Great." She disappears back into the crowd.

I take a big bite of cauliflower wing and lick the ranch dressing that dribbles onto my fingers. "You okay? You look like someone told you the government shut down its tax branch."

Luke clears his throat. I'm expecting one of his usual quick, dry replies, but he seems uncertain. Which is very unusual for Luke Brooks. "Yeah."

"Seriously?"

Luke shifts and drops his gaze to the table. "I'm fine. Sorry. I think I was just... caught off guard by the dating app stuff. I can't imagine a bunch of strangers showing up at a bar to meet me."

"That's the thing." A smile crosses my lips. "None of them know who I am. On the app, I go by a different name and I don't have any photos of myself. Anyway, as soon as the mass message went out, I went to find Dee so we could rectify the situation—shut down my account, or at the very least, cancel on everyone. But I was getting messages every few minutes. It was overwhelming."

"You must have a solid profile to have all these guys wanting to meet you without even a photo," Luke says, sounding more like his old self.

"Well, like I said, I haven't spoken to many of them. Maybe they were as curious as I was about this glitch because we shouldn't have been able to meet. In any case, Dee pointed out that the damage had been done. I could either cancel on every single person, or go through with the dates. She's the one who suggested I invite my single girl-friends and see where the night goes."

"Sounds like something Dee would say."

"Noah was all for it too, of course. In fact, he was suggesting that we reschedule so the dates would happen *sooner*."

Luke casts another glance around the bar. "Well, everyone seems to be having a good time."

"That's a fluke and a half if I ever heard of one." I chuckle. Luke shifts again so I get another whiff of his spicy cologne, and I suddenly remember my earlier question. "Hang on. Why are *you* here tonight?"

He runs a hand through his thick, dark blond hair. It's longer these days, almost shaggy but in this neat, groomed kind of way. His Adam's apple bobs as he swallows. "Came to play pool."

"On a Saturday? I thought you hated coming out on Saturday nights because of the—and I quote—'rowdy crowds and drunken hooligans'."

"You've got me pegged, Dais."

I smirk, but then, the air between us changes. Just a little, just subtly. But Luke goes serious, and his eyes are intent when they meet mine. For a moment, it almost feels like he's seeing me for the first time. His lips twitch the smallest amount, and he raises a shoulder in a shrug.

"Guess I made an exception."

His husky voice washes over my skin, and paired with the unexpected intensity of the moment, I feel a little breathless. I have to take a quick, heady sip of my Shirley Temple.

I don't know what's going on with me tonight, but I'm extra aware of Luke Brooks. Aware in a way that I really shouldn't be.

I sit back to put some physical distance between us. "Now you know the full story. So what—"

"Excuse me," a tinkling voice says from behind my shoulder. I turn to see Flo, the pilates instructor and one of the single ladies I invited tonight. But she's not looking at me; her gaze is zeroed in on Luke. "This might be *so* forward of me, but you look familiar. Have we met before?"

I press my lips together. I happen to know that Flo has definitely seen Luke before, and that she has a crush on him. I've overheard her talking to her friends at Valley Fitness while he was working out.

Luke tilts his head. "Nope, don't think so." He extends a hand. "Luke Brooks."

"Floriana, but you can call me Flo." She laughs a sweet, sing-songy laugh. "Wow, you look fit."

Luke, as always, is carefully composed. Meanwhile, I have to hold back an unintentional giggle. Flo seems to realize how that sounded, and she backtracks quickly. "I mean—sorry, no. I mean that you look like you workout. Maybe at the fitness center here in Mirror Valley...?"

Flo continues rambling, and I feel bad for the girl. I sit up in my seat. "Yeah, Luke comes into Valley Fitness often. You probably saw him there."

Her eyes swing over to me for the first time, and her cheeks turn even more red. "Daisy! I didn't see you."

"It's okay." I smile. "These booths have really tall backs."

"They do."

Flo's blushing more than ever, but of course her blush is this sweet, petal pink flush that makes her look like a naughty baby deer or something. Far from my own traffic-light level of blushing. She looks at Luke again, and he nods. "It's nice to meet you, Floriana. I'm sure I'll see you around."

There's a note of gentle finality in his voice, and Flo gives him a shy, flirty smile before walking away.

I bite my lip. "Sorry, Luke. If you want to chat with Flo, I can go."

"She seems sweet, but I don't want to lead her on."

"Right. Of course."

Because Luke doesn't want to date Flo right now. He doesn't want to date *anyone* right now.

"Sharing plates!" Cindy announces, returning to the table.

"Thanks, Cindy." Luke takes the plates and puts one in front of each of us. "Here's hoping I can grab some wings without losing my arm."

And so, because I'm me, and because Luke is not and will never be on my trope list, I make my goofiest face and pull the dish of cauliflower wings to my side of the table.

9

LUKE

"First date!"

Daisy's voice is full of excitement and cheer as she cups her hands around her empty glass.

"That's optimistic," I reply. "They've been talking for hours, but I don't see much flirting going on. I'm gonna say 'friends'."

"You always play it so safe, Luke." Daisy's blue eyes are playful when they meet mine. "You guessed 'friends' for Isobel and Mark over there, but they've been making moony eyes at each other all evening. And look!" she exclaims, pointing not-so-subtly towards the couple. "They're holding hands!"

"It's not enough to change my answer."

Our table is littered with empty glasses and a basket with a lone cauliflower wing. The chocolate cake is long gone, as are the veggie tacos I insisted we order when Daisy's stomach continued to growl like a feral cat.

It's been a strange and unusual evening, food-wise.

And overall-wise.

When I last checked my watch, it was 10pm. Which means that Daisy and I have been sitting in this booth for the past three hours, but it feels like no time has passed at all. Especially because we've been playing a variation of our "friends, first date, married" game on the singles. As in, guessing which couples would progress their relationships to any of those levels, or break up for good.

I have to admit that, while I have no real interest in other peoples' dating lives, I've always enjoyed playing this game with Daisy.

In fact, until this evening, I'd never realized how many of my rules I break for her. How many of my walls she manages to squeeze over. It's never once bothered me that she steals my snickerdoodles, or drags me into these dating-show type games, or teases me mercilessly.

I don't fully understand how she gets away with it.

Daisy turns to me suddenly, her mouth twisted in concern. "Hey, I meant to ask you, how're your grandparents doing managing the Brookrose with Ivy and James being gone for a month?"

"They're doing well. I think they're kind of happy to be temporarily back in charge."

"Well, if they ever need someone to cover reception for them or help out in any way, I've got some free time on my hands."

"Yes, tell me again." I lean forward, and I can hear the challenge in my own voice. It's almost... flirty. "How many jobs do you have now, Daisy?"

She blinks innocently and holds up both hands, counting down on her fingers. "Front desk at Valley Fitness, marketing at the community center, dogwalker, bike path maintenance worker, after-school program coordinator, senior center helper, event T-shirt creator, part-time wizard to cheer kids up at the hospital, and..." Daisy frowns. "That's it."

"Wow." I truly have no other words.

"Oh, wait. That *was* it. I did sort of accidentally end up offering to raise money to save the community center."

I frown. "Yeah, I'm sorry about that. My team came across that actually, we saw that the community center was losing money, and we noticed that it was a potential area that the council could scale back on if necessary."

Daisy nods. "Right. Scale back."

I meet her gaze. "I understand if you're upset, Dais, I know you work there. I just wanted to be upfront with you..."

"No, I'm not mad. I understand why you did it, of course. And now I get to be the one fundraising for it."

I press my lips together. Good for Daisy for offering to do such a thing. I might be a money guy, but fundraising is very comfortably outside of my wheelhouse. Good luck to her.

Daisy looks out around the bar again, but I'm finding it hard to look away this time. My gaze travels over her side profile, and I register her rosy cheeks on porcelain skin, her lips that form a perfect bow, even smiling. I notice the way her eyelashes brush her cheeks when she blinks and the way her nose is slightly crooked. She has these almost delicate features, but she exudes a strength and passion I can't really define.

At that moment, she catches me staring. I hurriedly look down, and she clears her throat. "Okay, I've had three Shirley Temples, and I think I might burst. I'm gonna run to the restrooms, and then I might call it a night. Have an early morning dog walk tomorrow."

She awkwardly shuffles out of the booth and stands, shimmying her body so I have to laugh. "You look ridiculous."

"I'll take that as a compliment." She gives me a wink before taking off towards the restrooms.

I watch her disappear, then turn back to my glass. Tap my fingers against the cool surface, though the condensation melted away awhile ago.

I stayed at McGarry's for more than one drink. And if I'm honest, I'm glad I did. I had a good time... once I got over the shock of tonight's little twist.

I never could have guessed that the woman I've been speaking to on RightMatch is none other than my little sister's best friend.

Daisy is Sisi.

And Daisy invited me—and all these guys—here tonight to meet her.

It was easy enough to brush off our messages and dismiss our conversations when I thought she was a stranger. I figured I'd never actually meet her, so it was easy to compartmentalize her, ignore what I was feeling. But now that I know that the woman on the other end of the message thread is Daisy...

Well, I don't know what to feel. I don't know how to process this.

My gut reaction was to shut down. Apologize and leave the bar. I don't know what made me stay in my seat except perhaps a desire to tell her the truth. Tell her that I'm Aaron. But I couldn't just drop it into conversation; I had to find an opening.

I never found that opening. Or maybe I couldn't bring myself to say anything. What if I have it wrong? Can there be another Aaron?

The thought prickles my skin, and I stand from the booth, grabbing my jacket. I sense Floriana trying to catch my eye, but I bow my head as I make my way to the bar to pay for our food and drinks. I don't let myself notice how my eyes scan the crowd for a particular head of light blonde hair.

When I get to the bar, I'm surprised to see that Daisy's already there. Talking to a good-looking man with coal-black hair.

My stomach does the strangest little clenching motion. I keep my pace slow as I approach, but Daisy sees me immediately. "Oh, Luke! I was just talking to Bert here. He's from France and works in Denver, but he came all the way to Mirror Valley for drinks this evening."

"Really." I glance at Bert. He barely gives me a look.

"It was simply destiny that I meet a beautiful lady here tonight." Bert kisses the top of Daisy's hand, who giggles sweetly.

My stomach clenches again, and my jaw locks. Bert has a thick, *thick* accent when he uses cheesy pickup lines.

I force a smile. "I'm gonna pay and head out."

"Oh, no." Daisy's eyes go wide. "I was hoping to pay before you could come over."

Finally, Bert looks at me. There's so much bored impatience in his eyes that I almost laugh. "Are you here together?"

"Yes we are," Daisy surprises me by saying. She grabs my arm and pulls herself towards me. "It was nice to meet you, Bert."

Bert gives a little grunt before briskly turning and walking away. I look down at Daisy, notice the way her lips are tilted up in a small grin as she looks after him. Her palm feels small and warm against my bare skin. At that moment, she drops my arm and steps away, and I'm taken aback. Having her on my arm felt...

Never mind.

"Phew." She shakes her head. "That guy was a bit much."

"What? Cheesy French guys aren't on your trope list?"

Daisy smirks at me. "Not at the moment, no. Nothing

against French guys, but Bert went a little *too* hard with the pickup lines."

Her waggling eyebrows make me laugh, and she smiles at me in a way that makes her entire face glow.

My heart does another weird skip, and I force myself to break eye contact. Whatever I seem to be feeling, whatever might be going on in my chest right now... well, it can't. I thought the Daisy-Sisi revelation wouldn't affect me that much, but that doesn't seem to be the case.

It's the shock, that's all. It's making me confused, and it's time that I head home. The last thing I need right now is to fall for anyone, let alone Daisy Griffiths. The risks immediately outweigh any possible reward.

"I'm gonna settle up," I say, turning to wave down one of the servers.

Daisy places a firm hand on my arm. "No, you don't. Don't even try to... Dee?!"

I follow her line of sight to where Dee is, indeed, striding through the bar with Noah hot on her heels. She catches sight of Daisy and changes directions to beeline our way.

"What're you doing here?" Daisy asks her.

"Isn't it obvious?" Noah knocks his shoulder with Dee's teasingly. "I finally managed to convince this one to come out tonight."

Dee sighs tiredly and rolls her eyes. "He promised to get me a slushy and one of those really good cheese scones from Morning Bell if I came to see how things went. And you should know..." She turns to him. "That I expect *two* scones because you made me change out of my sweats and into jeans. On a Saturday night. Talk about cruel and inhuman."

Noah bumps Dee again, and I catch a smile threatening to break across her lips. Her gaze barely lands on me before she turns to Daisy. "So how'd it all go? Find someone who's peaked your interest in this mess of people?"

Maybe, my brain answers. Stupidly.

My mouth presses into a stern line as I reject the thought. Unfortunately, I catch Noah watching me at that moment with an eyebrow raised. I shift slightly, not enjoying his scrutinizing look, and clear my throat. "I'm heading to the bar." Daisy opens her mouth to argue, but I hold up a hand. "You'll get it next time."

Seeming slightly appeased, Daisy nods once. But I don't miss the way Noah's eyebrow climbs even higher on his forehead. He missed his calling as a Charlie Chaplin-style face actor.

"I'm surprised to see all the people who paired up tonight," Daisy's saying as I walk away.

"I'm not," Dee replies. "And I'm not the only one. Has Mrs. Perez found you yet?"

"Gloria's here?!"

My lips slide into a grimace. Uh oh. Hope Daisy isn't in trouble for what happened here tonight.

I flag down Tony, the bar manager, to pay our bill. I know him well given that he used to cover the front desk at the Brookrose Inn if my grandparents were busy. He's a surly guy, but I have fond memories of going fishing with him as a kid. He and I would sit on the water for hours... in total and complete silence.

If I need anything right now, it's silence. Tonight has had more than enough twists and turns for my tastes.

The solution? I've got to head home, get a good night's sleep, and work this all out tomorrow at Valley Fitness or on a long run with Stella on the roads outside of town. My head will be back on straight, and it'll be like tonight never happened.

Easy.

10

DAISY

I should've seen it coming.

I should've prepared myself.

I had more than enough warning.

But when Gloria Perez ducks out from behind a row of bar stools and grabs my arm, I yelp in surprise anyway.

"Hello, Daisy," she sings, clearly not registering that she almost gave me a heart attack. To be fair, I know she wasn't intending to hide. Mrs. Perez has a tiny, waily stature, and I quite literally tower over her. Even now, I have to bend to hear what she says next. "I'm so glad I found you!"

"Here I am," I say brightly, low-key looking around for Dee and Noah. They *just* walked away—headed for the jukebox at the other end of the bar to put on a Shania Twain song for Noah. They promised they'd be right back.

I was hoping against hope that this little shindig wouldn't get back to the town council—you usually need their approval to host an event like this, intentional or not. So it would make sense that she's upset with me.

But as I try to assess her expression—pursed lips, raised eyebrows, rosy cheeks—the jury's out. She's either *really* mad, or *really* excited. The good news is that she's not wearing pajamas but a white vest over a blouse and slacks, along with a bit of lipstick and mascara, so she clearly wasn't called out of bed to be here.

Instead of giving me any indication of what she's feeling, she simply grabs my hand. "Come! I have something to show you."

She takes off across the bar, dragging me behind her—which is basically one big walking advertisement for the strength exercises in Flo's pilates class. McGarry's certainly isn't as busy as it was earlier, but there are still a good few people lingering about.

Gloria brings me all the way to the bar, where Luke is standing with the lovably grumpy manager, Tony. He used to work at the Brookrose occasionally, but his real love is McGarry's—he's been working here so long, he could do the job in his sleep. Pretty sure he has, actually.

"How're you doing, Tony?" I ask, standing at the bar a few paces away from Luke. Being in his close proximity for too long just goes to confuse me. It's like when you're watching TV and a big storm comes in and makes everything hazy and full of static. Luke Brooks is just a big ol' signal-confusing storm of nice hair, and big muscles, and manly forest smells.

"I'm great," Tony responds flatly. "It's been a doozy of a night. The bar's busy enough on Saturdays, but this was a whole 'nother ball game." He places his hands on his sizeable hips. "I don't think we've brought in this much money since that snowstorm stopped those cowboys on their way to a rodeo in Wyoming. Remember that?"

"I remember. Thank you, Tony." Gloria smiles at him, and he gives a quick nod before going off to tend to a couple customers. "Now, a few of the ladies mentioned that *you* invited them here, Daisy."

Here it comes. I wipe my palms on my dress, thankful that it's black and therefore hides all sweat stains.

"So?" Gloria's dark eyes are focused on me. "Is this some sort of special event?"

I pause for a half-second, then release an exhale. "Look, I can explain—"

"It was for the community center," Luke cuts in.

"Sorry, dear?"

"It was an idea that Daisy had for the community center." Luke's voice is steady and firm, and I look at him in surprise. "To raise money."

Wait, what?

Gloria claps. "I knew it!"

I drag my eyes away from Luke. "Knew what?"

"When Tony called to say that he needed more bar staff because McGarry's was packed, I had to see for myself. I couldn't believe the amount of people here, the amount of *couples.* And as Tony said, tonight's little gathering brought in a lot of money. I assumed that this was some sort of test— a trial, perhaps—for a fundraising event for the community center."

I open my mouth. Close it. Try again. I have so many questions, I'm not sure where to start. I pick one at random. "So you're not mad?"

"Dear girl, not at all." Gloria lays a hand on my arm. "Of course, we normally require that people notify the council when running a special event, but I understand that time is of the essence! This is one of those cases where it's better to ask for forgiveness than permission, hm?"

This conversation has gotten so far away from me, I dare not speak.

"This is exactly what Fran and I were saying—we know you have the town's best interests at heart, and we trust you completely. You clearly have a knack for this, if tonight's trial tells us anything. We've held a few matchmaking events over the years, speed dating and the like, but nothing has been so fruitful as this evening." She gazes around proudly. "Singles events are *all* the rage these days. A nice alternative to online apps like Tender, and Lunge, and that one Diandra works on."

I manage to break through my shock enough to croak, "Lunge?"

"Think she means Hinge," Luke mutters. Which surprises me all the more.

"The town council will be *thrilled*." Gloria claps again. "Wait 'til I tell Fran and Dora Mae. Organize a couple more of these with proceeds going towards the community center, and let's Hashtag Save-The-Center!"

I flounder for a long moment, seriously considering how to respond. First, I've never considered that singles events could be a form of fundraising. Second, this was a totally unintentional singles event that I'm not sure I can repeat. And third...how on earth is this all happening right now?!

For some reason, I look at Luke. He's gazing back at me with a curious but non-judgmental expression. Like he's expecting a certain answer from me, though I'm not sure what that answer would be.

Thankfully, that's enough to kickstart my brain back into gear. Obviously, I would do anything to help the community center, but organizing singles events? Purposeful, intentional singles events? I've been to my fair share of those over the years, and I joke about being a matchmaker sometimes, but those are just light-hearted quips. Never serious.

Because what sort of crazy irony would it be for me—the first-dates-only girl—to be *actively working* to find other people the loves of their lives?

But if Gloria is right and these events really could help save the center, how can I say no?

Plus, she's staring at me with so much hope in her eyes. And I *am* down a job at the vet clinic so I have extra time on my hands...

I screw up my face. Let out an exhale. "Of course. Whatever it takes."

"Wonderful! And with a smart man like Luke on your side, it shouldn't take long at all."

I physically feel Luke tense up next to me. "What was that?"

Gloria turns to him. "You'll be working together... That is what's happening here, is it not? Daisy will put together the matchmaking events, and Luke, as a representative of Argent Accounting, is going to be taking care of the finances. It's just a few events, surely you have time for such a thing. And besides, you might meet a special lady along the way."

Luke's entire mouth slides into a stern grimace. A red flush starts to crawl up his neck. "No, I don't think that's—"

"He'd love to!"

Noah pops up behind Luke, wraps an arm around his shoulders and gives a squeeze. Luke's entire body is tensed and rigid, like a panther about to pounce, so it's probably not Noah's wisest move, but he seems unfazed by Luke's glare.

"Would I," Luke says, his voice dangerously low.

"Sure! He'd be thrilled—no, *ecstatic*—to handle the finances for singles events," Noah goes on. "He's sitting around bored all day at Argent, doing tax stuff and spread-sheets. This'll liven up the workload."

With that, Noah pats Luke on the back and strides over to Dee, who's shaking her head. She gives me a shrug as if to say "whatcha gonna do?"

Even I can feel the daggers Luke is sending Noah's way. There's a chance he just lost his internship at Argent.

"Splendid!" Gloria exclaims, clearly unaware of Luke's bristling. He turns back to her, impassive. "So kind of you to help Daisy, Luke. These events could be a saving grace for the community center."

"No, I'm okay. Really," I pipe in, hoping to get Luke off the hook. For his sake, but also for mine. Being stuck matchmaking with Luke Brooks can't be good for the whole hyper-aware thing I'm experiencing tonight. Avoidance is my usual tactic, but I can't avoid him if I'm working with him.

"Are you, dear? Organizing big events is a lot of work. Ivy would be the perfect help, but she's otherwise occupied at the moment." Gloria waggles her eyebrows horrifyingly. "The other Brooks sibling is your perfect stand-in."

I don't have to look at Luke this time. I already know that we're both deeply troubled by this news.

"Now you two had better get to work," Gloria cheers. "Clock's ticking!"

She turns and waltzes over to Tony, who's unloading glasses from the dishwasher and passing them to Cindy for polishing. I'm amazed she's able to keep hold of the glasses given the way she's shamelessly staring at Luke.

The two of us stand in silence, no doubt both wondering how on earth we ended up in this ridiculous charade.

Luke and me... Me and Luke... Us helping other people find love. This has to be some vivid fever dream, and when I wake up, I'm going to have a good, long laugh.

Because I will wake up from this, right? Luke and I aren't actually going to be working together, in close proximity, talking about love and dating and all the stuff we've never even touched upon before a couple of weeks ago?

"Guess we're doing this thing," Luke eventually says. There are not enough words to describe the scowliness of his scowl. "We should probably schedule a meeting to get started."

I let out a quick laugh. "That's very Luke of you."

He actually cracks a small smile at that. "Let's meet at the community center coffee shop next Wednesday during our lunch breaks. I'll look into what sort of budget we can set."

"Great. I'll research some event ideas. What do people even *do* for matchmaking events?"

He holds up his hands. "That is out of my scope, Dais."

While Luke types away in his phone, I bite the inside of my cheek in thought.

This'll be fine. It really will be fine. Luke and I will tackle this as you would any work project—with a professional, detached sort of passion. Luke will handle the money, I'll handle the events. Easy. Boring, really.

So in typical Daisy fashion, I paste on the brightest smile I can muster. "This should be fun. Hope you're ready for some matchmaking thrills."

And, in typical Luke fashion, he shakes his head, looking thoroughly ticked off. "See you next Wednesday."

11

DAISY

"You've been WHAT?" Ivy screeches so loudly, I have to hold my phone away from my ear.

"Poltergeisted," I repeat.

"Why are you saying that like I should know what that means?"

"It's what I'm calling the next level from being ghosted," I explain. "To be ghosted, you likely have SOME idea about the person you were talking to. To be poltergeisted is to be unsure who the person on the other side of the screen even was in the first place. A more complete form of ghosting."

I smile proudly, but my smile falls as I remember why I came up with the word in the first place.

"Dais, I think you missed your calling as an Urban Dictionary wordsmith."

"Ugh, their editors are tough nuts to crack. You'd think a crowd-sourced dictionary would be more willing to accept submissions."

Ivy's silent for a moment. "What?"

Oh. She was kidding. "Never mind!!"

"Seriously, though. You've made up and blended so many words, there should be a Daisy encyclopedia."

"A Daisy-pedia…" I frown. "Erm. That sounds like an infectious illness. Why does blending my name with any other word sound like something that needs to be treated in the hospital?"

"I dunno, 'Daaron' isn't too bad." Ivy giggles. "Or 'Aarsy'… Hmm yeah, not great. But this has to be a sign. Good riddance to that one. What kinda name is Aaron anyway? Psh." Then a second later. "Now I feel mean, Aaron is actually a very nice name. But you get what I'm saying. He's clearly not worthy of you if he ghost—sorry, poltergeisted—you. You deserve much better than that. You deserve the very best with five cherries on top."

I giggle. "You have to say that, you're my best friend."

"And I thank my lucky stars every day that my parents named me after a plant and Ms. Caplan thought it would be cute to pair us up in the second grade… because you haven't been able to get rid of me since!"

Ivy and I both laugh, but in all honesty, I feel the exact same way. My parents certainly weren't the most present of adults, so while Dee and I spent a lot of time here at the community center, we were also lucky to fall in with a couple of chosen families. I was often with the Brooks family growing up, and Dee, meanwhile, fell in with Noah, his parents, and his three rowdy brothers.

I always joked that our differences started there. Noah and his brothers were sweetly inclusive of Dee, and she grew up playing baseball, hockey, volleyball, and other team sports with "the boys". I, on the other hand, developed a sunny, relatively "girly" temperament, and I absolutely suck at all sports aside from soccer.

Dee and I aren't close to our parents now. After the divorce, they moved to big cities on opposing coasts, and while they do check in a few times a year, we're happy with just each other and our chosen families. It's probably why neither of us can bring ourselves to leave Mirror Valley.

"Anyway," I say, changing the subject away from my wilting love life. "How're you doing? I'm assuming that you and James are filling your days with castle visits, crumpets and tea."

"Absolutely. We've definitely been keeping... busy."

I can almost hear the waggling eyebrows in her tone, and I wrinkle my nose. "Oh gosh, you two." Ivy giggles, and I hear her stifle a yawn. The fifth in as many minutes. "I should let you go. What time is it there?"

"10pm, but it's fine. James is downstairs chatting with the owner of the inn we're staying at. Trying to get some inspo for the Brookrose, I think."

"Without you?! Now I *really* have to let you go."

Ivy laughs. "I'll talk to you later, Dais."

"Send my best to James, and promise me you'll visit at least *one* castle while you're there."

"We'll do our very best!" Ivy cackles before she hangs up.

I smile, missing my best friend but also feeling so happy for her and her happily-ever-after. If anyone deserves it, it's Ivy.

I'm about to stash my phone in my pocket when I see the time.

Curses!

I whip open the back door of the community center and run back inside, heading straight for the coffee shop. I'm seven minutes late to meet Luke, and I already know that he's sitting waiting for me. Ivy and Luke have that whole "early bird catches the worm" thing very much in common. I veer more on the (un)fashionably late side of things.

I do feel extra bad today though, given that Luke was pretty much forced into this project for my sake.

I turn the corner towards the coffee shop and spot him immediately. He's seated at one of the tables outside, bathed in autumn sunlight and clasping a mug of black coffee with one hand while the other hand rests casually on the back of the chair next to him. He's wearing a cozy-looking wool pullover in a dark green color that I already know brings out the darker flecks in his eyes. His sunglasses are perched on his nose as he looks out, and beams of light hit the planes of his face so his jawline looks extra sharp and jawline-y.

Of course, I notice all these things because he's the only customer.

Obviously.

But before I go to join him, there's one thing I need to grab from the front desk first…

"Sorry I'm late!" I say as I collapse into the chair across from Luke.

He removes his sunglasses to look at me, and I'm very aware that he looks like a forbidden dessert incarnate, whereas I probably look more like a stressed-out carrot in my orange community center uniform. "What else is new."

I place my retrieved item on the table between us. "Cactus for your thoughts?"

Luke stares at the cactus, then raises his eyes to meet mine. "What's this about?"

I give a shrug, lightly poking at the needles. "I've had him on the front desk for about a week, but he's looking a little sad. Figured I'd bring him out for our talk so he can get some direct sunlight."

"He?"

"I figure he's a he."

Luke looks totally bemused.

"Love a good cactus."

"Right…" Luke pushes a steaming mug towards me. "Hot cocoa with extra whipped cream."

96

I'm weirdly touched that he remembered my favorite drink. "Thank you." He nods wordlessly, and I feel the need to explain why I was late. "I am sorry for being late, though. I was on the phone with Ivy. We were catching up on her honeymoon shenanigans with James."

Luke's nose wrinkles, and I laugh.

"Oh, lighten up. We both know you're a big ol' softie."

This pulls a smile out of him, and my heart warms to see it. Luke's always been a serious, stern type of guy, and he's only become more so since the broken engagement. Which is why I feel so much delight when I make him smile. Even the smallest lip-tilt feels like an Olympic-level win.

"Well. Shall we get to work?" I ask. "I shouldn't be away for too long."

"Definitely not. Especially given how... busy this place is."

I follow Luke's gaze towards the completely empty community center through the coffee shop windows. There's literally only Ricky, who's sitting behind the coffee bar and reading yet another comic book. I sigh. "At least now you can see why we need to 'Hashtag Save-The-Center."

"Gonna need to make a lot of matches to get this place going again." Luke says this seriously, but his tone is anything but defeated, and that realization cheers me a little. Maybe he sees hope in this too?

"Well, fingers crossed that there are a few people out there who are ready to fall in love," I say lightly. As if I could actually be that confident in my skills.

I grab my bag, ready to get to work, but Luke doesn't move.

"Out of curiosity, why *is* this such a big deal to you?" Luke asks. "You work here so it makes sense that you don't want the community center to scale back for that reason, but this is a lot of work to go through just to keep your job."

I shift in my chair a little, feeling weirdly exposed under his gaze. Like if I meet his eyes for too long, he might see each and every one of my secrets. Might understand all of my thoughts. "You know me and my jobs—eight isn't enough." I hazard the joke, but even before the words leave my mouth, I know it'll fall flat. Finally, I raise a shoulder. "I guess it's nostalgic for me. I spent a lot of time here as a kid."

"You and Dee?"

"Yeah. I mean, you know that I spent a lot of time with your family growing up, but this was the other place that Dee and I came to. Our parents were..." I bite my cheek, wondering how to put this. "Hard workers. Dedicated to their jobs. Or they were fighting, so it was better that we were out of the house."

I've never really talked to anyone about this. Even Ivy. She knows the basics, the surface level stuff, but I never went in-depth with her about my childhood. After what she and Luke went through losing their parents at such a young age, it felt almost selfish to complain about my own situation.

"So this was another home for you," Luke says. He's sitting up in his chair, leaning towards me, like he's really paying attention.

"It was."

"Well then, we're going to save it."

I finally find the courage to meet his eyes. "You think so?"

"Absolutely." The note of confidence in his voice lifts me up and gives me strength. It's hard *not* to believe this man. "Now, I went through the budget, and with taking the council's finances into consideration, along with expenses coming up for the holidays, I've developed a timeline for us to work towards. Mind you, it's conservative, but it's our best bet."

"Alright. Lay it on me." I cringe internally at my own phrasing. *Why am I like this?*

"We have a month."

I wait for him to say something more. To expand. When it's clear he isn't going to say anything else, my throat closes up. "A month?" I croak.

"Yup. One month to raise money for this place."

"One. Month…" I repeat dumbly. Oh, gosh, that doesn't feel like *nearly* enough time! But I can spiral later. I *will* spiral later. For now, I force a smile. "That sounds great."

Luke raises an eyebrow. "Yeah?"

"Absolutely." I feel like I've inhaled too much oxygen and can't exhale. My chest is continuously expanding. I'm going to float away like the evil aunt character in that *Harry Potter* movie.

"Dais." To my ultimate surprise, Luke places a hand on top of mine. His palm is warm and firm and slightly calloused, and my skin sparks at his touch. "We'll work it out. We'll work together to find a way to do this."

With those simple words, all at once, I can breathe again. I exhale quietly, taken off guard. His tone is warm in a way that I can feel something within myself start to melt. I steel myself against it. Because being in any way "melty" around Luke Brooks is a molten slippery slope into broken heart territory.

"Was that a dash of optimism?" I joke.

He raises a brow, shakes his head, and we're back to normal.

I take a stack of folded papers filled with scribbled notes out of my bag. "I do have a few ideas. During my research, I saw this event called—and please excuse my French—a 'Dîner en Blanc'."

"And by 'research', you mean...?"

My cheeks heat. "I binged dating shows. Anyway, it's fine. Have you heard of a Dîner en Blanc—or Dinner in White?"

"Nope, and I'm pretty happy with that state of being. I'm the money guy, remember?"

I feel a sudden pang at the term, thinking of my unanswered text thread with Aaron. The Poltergeist. I shake it off. "Well, I spoke with Dee, and she thinks she can replicate the bug that caused the accidental mass text. So we'll be able to get in touch with everyone who went to McGarry's, and they can simply reply if they're interested in doing another event. From what she said, based on the McGarry's night, there should be a fair bit of interest."

"Great."

"There is one *tiny* thing I should tell you." I shift on my seat. "A Dinner in White requires you to bring a plus one to mix and mingle with the crowd. You know, to pad numbers and all that. Obviously, don't feel you have to, but that's the idea."

Luke's expression—which had been going from uncertain to downright skeptical—brightens considerably. "A plus one?"

"Yes." I pause as my heart makes a subtle twisting motion. "Do you have someone in mind?"

"Sure do." Luke smirks, looking out again so his defined, stubbled jawline reflects sunlight my way.

I know it's wrong, I know I shouldn't care, but I'm dying to know. Who would Luke want to bring as a plus one to a matchmaking event? I have to physically hold myself back from asking the question. Because Luke and I don't talk about these things.

Correction, we *didn't* talk about these things... before my trope list. The rules seem to have changed now.

Before I can ask my burning question, Luke grumbles, "See how Noah likes it."

My lungs deflate as my brows draw together. "Wait... you want to take *Noah*?"

"Yes. He's the one who basically forced me into this matchmaking thing. We'll see how he likes being forced into it himself."

I already know the answer to that question. Noah might date a LOT, but singles events are very much not his thing. A fact that I suspect Luke knows.

"What about you?" Luke nods my way. "Gonna bring a plus one?"

I could swear I catch an undertone in his voice, but I can't identify it. I give a shrug. "I might."

Although, who that plus one would be, I have no clue. In all honesty, the only man I've flirted with recently—aside from Poltergeist Aaron—was Bert. And the thought of spending time with cheesy Bert is about as appealing as wearing jeans to bed. He's a little *too* smooth, a little *too* suave for my tastes. I prefer men who are strong, silent, stoic...

With one exception who I simply will never think of like that again. No matter how gorgeous he is. Or how he seems to see right through me sometimes in the most unnerving of ways.

"What about that French guy from the other night?" Luke asks, further confirming that he can, indeed, read my mind.

Oh goodness, the internal ramblings he must be subjected to...

"Nope. I think I'll just go solo rollo."

"Well, if you want to drive over with Noah and me, I can give you a ride."

I raise a brow. "Three people in your brand new car? That's awfully un-Luke of you."

He shrugs, but his eyes are oddly intense when they meet mine. "Guess you could say that I'm trying a few new things these days."

12

LUKE

I understand the argument.

I get why people are so obsessed with change, and why change is good, and why change means progress, etc. etc. Logically, it makes sense—change means throwing out the old and beginning fresh.

But I have to wonder if the people arguing for change would see tonight as a particularly good example of its benefits.

Because I don't.

"I couldn't believe it. You and Eleanor breaking up like that. Out of the blue. After twelve years together." Floriana pops out her bottom lip in an angelic pout, blinking her brown eyes up at me. "You're so brave, Luke. So strong."

I nod once, then remind myself to be nice. "Like I said, I'm just trying to move forward."

"You're right. *So* right," she says enthusiastically, grasping my arm and moving closer. Which makes sense given how loud the meeting room's getting. I can hardly believe the amount of people milling about, grabbing slices of pizza and tacos from the food tables, laughing in large groups, or splitting off into couples to chat.

I don't think the community center—let alone its one meeting room—has been this busy in a long time. The doors are actually propped open, with people spilling out into the lobby area. It's a testament to Daisy and her matchmaking skills, really.

"I gotta say," Floriana purrs, pulling me back to the present moment, where I'm standing in a corner of the room, trapped between the wall, a folding table, and her white-spandex-clad body. "I was surprised when I heard that you were dating again. I knew I had to talk to you."

I can't stop the frown now. "How did you know I was dating again?"

"Gemma told me. She heard something from Cam... you're on an app or something?"

Of course. One of the Dude Crew must've let it slip that I downloaded RightMatch at that barbecue. Which explains why the questions and comments about my dating life have intensified over the last couple months. "Right. The thing is—"

"And I thought maybe you'd want to talk to me, too," she speaks over me. She might be forgiven for doing so given the sheer volume in the room. It just goes to confirm how much I'd prefer to be at my condo right now, hanging out with Stella. In relative quiet. "I mean, we both go to Valley Fitness, we both like to workout, we both have dogs... I can't believe we haven't run into each other!"

"Crazy," I mumble. I work to relax my posture and drop my crossed arms. Daisy wouldn't be happy to see me alienating one of her "guests", as she jokingly called them on the drive over. A drive which I enjoyed more than I might have expected.

I look for her in the crowd again, my eyes grazing quickly over faces I recognize and others I don't. I've been catching myself doing this all night. It's like my body is tuned into her frequency, aware of the places she might be. I'm surprised at the fall in my chest when I don't see her.

"I'm sure I've asked you this before," Floriana says. "But what do you do for work?"

"I'm an accountant."

Floriana giggles sweetly. And she is a sweet girl. With spectacular lung capacity, if her ten-minute monologue on her fledgling pilates YouTube channel is anything to go by. I have to respect the woman's dedication. All the more because three of those minutes also included a pilates teaser demonstration that nearly tripped a group of people.

"Oh, wow," she says. "Accounting must be so... *boring*!"

I blink, amused by her honesty. "I like it."

"Like the job, or like the money?" Floriana gives that tinkling laugh again, and I'm sure there are many men out there who would be drawn in by the sound. It just grates my ears. "What would you do if you could be anything?"

"Anything?" I tap my chin, pretending to consider. "I'd probably be an accountant."

Floriana goes serious. A blush colors her cheeks. "Oh, yeah. That's great. I was kidding before."

She pastes on another smile, but I understand her reaction. Accounting isn't the most exciting of career prospects. I think there was a time, way back during my childhood, when I wanted to be a drummer. But after my parents died and I took on more responsibility, that dream faded fast.

Truth is, I really do like being an accountant. I like the stability, the consistency. Numbers are reliable and infallible. There's an explanation for every little thing that happens on my spreadsheets.

And to Floriana's point, it has afforded me some luxuries over the years. Allowed me to put away savings, while also providing for my family. The Inn is doing well now with Ivy's creativity and passion put to work, but my grandparents were struggling for a long time, ready and wanting to pass along the business and retire. Being able to contribute here and there to help them out made me happy.

Although it was a strain in my relationship with Eleanor at times. She didn't like the way I put my family first, though the two of us wanted for nothing. I made sure Eleanor had all the things she wanted and needed, but the house I bought for us was the one thing I wouldn't budge on. She wanted something big, flashy, and full of those state-of-the-art fixtures and appliances, but to me, those were all trends. Impermanent. I wanted a house that would last, that would be home to our children for years to come. A home in which we could grow old.

The big ranch house on the outskirts of town is currently vacant and empty. I was renting it out to a small family over the past year while they searched for their own dream house, but they moved out last month, and I haven't bothered to start looking for another tenant.

"My cousin's a CPA, but he's definitely doing it for the money," Floriana says now, letting out another laugh. "So where's the best place that you've vacationed? I once went to Paris, and I would do anything to go back..."

I let my gaze travel out over the crowd again, this time not even pretending to listen. I have a feeling that Floriana isn't going anywhere, no matter how unresponsive I become. But in the mess of people, there's only one person that I want to be speaking with right now.

And finally... I spot her.

Daisy is standing across the room, handing out nametags and looking like an absolute dream in her long, lacy white dress.

When I pulled up outside of the little mint green bungalow she shares with Dee, and Daisy walked out the door... well I can't explain what came over me. My jaw went slack, and my heart slammed. I literally couldn't tear my eyes away from her.

Until Noah reached up from the backseat to smack me on the shoulder, saying that I was drooling.

The jerk.

Speaking of Noah...

"You know what, Floriana? I gotta go," I say briskly, prying her fingers from my bicep. "My plus one has wandered off somewhere, and I should find him. He's easily lost."

Floriana blinks once, as though surprised I interrupted her. "Are you sure? I was about to tell you about my trip to Southern France."

"You know who'd love that," I say, taking a quick look around until I see him. "My buddy Bert. He's over there by the speakers, and he loves France, probably."

"Oh, okay." Floriana gives me a slightly perplexed smile. "See you at Valley Fitness?"

I give a half-hearted nod, then step away into the crowd. I tried my best not to be short with her, not to be rude to one of the dinner guests, but there's a reason I spend my days in an office by myself. And as soon as I find Noah, I'm going to make sure he knows just how much I prefer things that way.

As soon as I can get through this crowd...

There are so many people here. Too many people. Daisy is clearly too good at her job. To be fair, she's the only reason I'm here tonight—to support her—but even so... wouldn't some of these people prefer to be at home right now?

I notice that even the town councilors are in attendance, most likely to monitor the event. Though it's hard *not* to notice Fran in her all-white denim outfit. Gloria Perez, Dora Mae Movis, and the rest of the councilors almost blend in compared to her.

Aside from that group, everyone else is appears to be here in order to be paired off through this Dinner in White event. Which I reluctantly read online started in Paris as an "elegant dinner for friends". It certainly explains why the meeting room is an absolute sea of white slacks, fancy skirts, lacy tops, and dresses.

I myself drew the line at wearing all white. I settled for chinos and a white T.

Daisy didn't seem to mind, though. She barely even gave me a glance when she slid into the passenger seat and buckled in.

Maybe I'll go over to her table real quick and check in on her, make sure she's doing okay. That's what any hard-working accountant would do, right?

I ignore the little voice in my head screaming that I'm an idiot and head in her direction.

"Dude, you finally got out of there!"

A big arm falls over my shoulders, and I stop walking. Fix Noah with a glare until he removes said arm. Though that might've been a comfort choice more than anything else—the guy's tall, but I've got an inch or two on him, and he had to stretch a little to reach my shoulders. Not to mention he's still sporting a beaming grin.

"Got out of where?" I ask.

"Talking to that Flo chick. I saw her going for you through the crowd like a torpedo towards its target. It was really somethin'." He smacks his gum and fiddles with his ball cap, which is white, of course.

When I told Noah that he would be coming tonight as my plus one, the guy started cheering. Actually cheering. Like he was excited or something. And then, he went on about the "hot single babes", which just goes to show how spectacularly my plan backfired.

"Thanks so much for sticking around and helping me out," I say sourly.

"I wasn't about to mess with a torpedo." He gestures over his shoulder. "Plus, Dee called me over to help with something. Have you been over to the sandwich display yet? It's worth seeing."

Noah snickers, and I roll my eyes at the thought of whatever weird shenanigan Dee and Noah did with the sandwich arrangement. It's the sort of thing James and I used to do when we were younger, but Noah and Dee clearly still have that joking, pranking kind of friendship. It's not what you'd expect for Dee given that she has such a serious, no-nonsense way about her. Pretty sure Noah's the only one who sees her goofy side.

"You should ask her to dance," Noah says suddenly.

"Who? Flo?"

"Daisy."

I look at him in confusion. "Why would I ask Daisy to dance?"

"I dunno. Because this is a good song, and because there's a dance floor..." Noah gestures towards a large section next to the DJ booth where people are jumping, and holding hands, and knocking hips. There's even a conga line forming. "And because you can't keep your eyes off her."

My neck gets hot as I realize that I am, once again, looking at Daisy even as Noah says these words. "Am not!" I sputter.

Noah's grin only grows. "Dude. You're so obvious. I could see you looking for her across the room."

"I don't know what you're talking about."

"Sure you do. She's the one you were looking for just now, right?"

I don't answer.

Noah laughs. "Don't worry, man, I'm not gonna say

anything. And for what it's worth, I know both of you pretty well at this point, and I think you'd be good together."

I don't know about any of that. I choose to ignore that last comment. "Really? 'Obvious'?" I grumble.

"Probably only to me. I recognize a longing look when I see it."

"I'm not 'longing' for Daisy. I just..." I trail off, unsure how to vocalize exactly what I'm feeling.

I've always known that Daisy is kind, and funny, and intelligent. That she's beautiful, and quirky in a unique way that's hard to explain but is so *her*. I've also always known her as my little sister's best friend...

But since starting to fall for her alter-ego on RightMatch and discovering that I was really talking to Daisy all along, I'm having a hard time not being blisteringly aware of all the things I've never let myself notice before. I haven't been able to stop thinking about her, no matter how much I've tried not to. No matter how often I've tried to "logic" my way out of it. Because falling for Daisy Griffiths is pretty much the most nonsensical thing I could do at this point in my life.

"You're longing, my friend." Noah pats me on the shoulder, sympathetically this time. The guy clearly does not bother himself with personal boundaries.

"I mean... I don't know." I break down. "Something's different."

"So *act* on it. Take advantage. Seize the day, and carpe diem, and all that. Besides, Dee's off somewhere chatting to some guy she met by the punch bowl, so seeing you ask Daisy to dance will keep me entertained."

I roll my eyes.

"Seriously, though." He pats my shoulder again. "I think you should do it. It doesn't have to mean anything, you can even just do the robot chicken with her, if that's what feels right." I'm sure I look horrified because he laughs. "It's not like you two would stand out for dancing together. It's so low risk. What do you have to lose?"

My friendship with Daisy. My relationship with Ivy. Basically having to endure the town rumors all over again if things don't work out. Not to mention potentially hurting or breaking Daisy's heart if it turns out that I'm not ready to date again.

Then again, to Noah's point, it *is* one dance. It's not like we're committing to anything. It's simple. Low stakes.

It's a chance for me to see if something else might lie between us. To see if we're more the playful "friend" types doing the sprinkler on the edge of the crowd, or whether we're leaning more towards the "first date" side.

And in all honesty—crazy as this sounds—I actually *want* to ask Daisy to dance. Even if we do end up doing some ridiculous conga line together, I want to do it with her.

"You're a lot smarter than you look," I say to Noah before I take off through the crowd again.

"Thanks, dude!" he shouts after me.

I smirk.

13
___

DAISY

"And that's why the eagles simply could not have taken the Fellowship to Mordor," I finish my *The Lord of the Rings* rant around a mouthful of sour cream and onion chips. Bits of the seasoning flake off, and I brush the crumbs off my white dress.

"I see your point," Luke acquiesces from his side of the car. I hear the smirk in his voice. "And it's a good thing cooing as we're almost at your house."

I relax a little in my seat, holding back a relieved sigh.

Did I speak the entire drive back to my house following the Dinner in White? Yes I did.

Did I do it while also mowing through an entire bag of sour cream and onion chips? Absolutely.

Was it because being anywhere near Luke tonight is making me feel things I really can't be feeling?

No comment.

I sneak another look at him and realize quickly that it's a mistake. It's simply unfair how gorgeous he is. Luke refused to wear all white tonight (no surprise), but the alternative he chose is a big problem for me.

Chinos are my kryptonite. Most women love a guy in a

good pair of jeans, but it's the well-fitting chinos for me. And paired with a crisp, white t-shirt? Lethal.

His eyes slice my way, catching me in another sneaky look, and I turn away quickly. "Uh... thanks for letting me eat in your car," I blurt out. "Sorry, I know you prefer to keep it clean."

"Dais, stop saying thanks and stop saying you're sorry. I offered you a lift home; I knew what I was getting myself into." He cracks a small smile. "I noticed that you didn't get a chance to have dinner tonight. So please, eat as much as you'd like."

Of course he noticed. And of course he cared enough to sneak me a bag of my favorite chips, a Tupperware of chocolate-covered strawberries, and some delicious candied almonds. He must've swiped them earlier in the night, because by the time everyone left, the food was gone. It's like he was paying attention, like he wanted to make sure I was able to eat too.

Which totally justifies why I'm currently scarfing down food like a zoo animal with my hair up in a messy scrunchie-tied knot, my hoop earrings tucked away in my bag, and wearing flip-flops instead of my glittery ballet flats.

Those old feelings of mine have absolutely no business resurfacing. Not now, not ever. I'm treating them like you would a rogue black bear—no sudden movements, no surprises. So I will not be the least bit melty at the thought of Luke's thoughtfulness, and I will make sure that this car remains a completely flirt-free zone. Which means that I will make no attempts to be remotely cute—or even civilized at this point, let's be real.

Instead, I will move forward all casually, calm and steady-like. And those feelings will amble off into a deep forest never to be seen again.

"Thank—" I cut myself off as Luke gives me another

look, and I shove a chip into my mouth instead. "You really don't mind me eating in your car?"

"Nope."

"Who are you and what have you done with Luke Brooks?"

"Hey now, I was never *that* bad. I mostly enforce the no-eating-in-my-car rule with Ivy. The ice cream sundae spilled across the backseat of my truck was more than enough reason."

With a chuckle, I avert my gaze out the window at the row of darkened bungalows along my street. The one I share with Dee is in the same style as all the rest, but ours is particularly old and outdated. Ivy always jokes that she has a room at the Brookrose waiting for me whenever the house spontaneously falls in on itself.

Dee keeps insisting that she wants to renovate it, fix it up. I'm not sure what she's waiting for.

If I'm honest, I don't want this night to end. And not only because the Dinner in White was a "roaring success", as Fran and Dora Mae put it. When Luke showed me the numbers at the end of the night, I could hardly believe how much progress we'd made towards our goal. We certainly aren't there yet, but it's looking plausible that we might Hashtag Save-The-Center!

Too soon, Luke rolls to a stop in front of my house. I don't make any moves towards the door, and to my surprise, he turns off the car. Could it be that he's not ready for tonight to end either?

No, Daisy. Don't go there. We're in strict friends-only territory. He probably just wants to talk LOTR.

"Tonight was fun." My voice is uneven, and I hope he doesn't notice. I'm very, very aware of how close he is to me right now. So close that his forest scent is surrounding me, bathing my senses.

"It was," he agrees.

"So you actually had fun at a singles event?!"

Luke lets out a chuckle that makes my stomach clench into a ball of unwanted butterflies poised to take flight. "I did. Well, I didn't. But this part was fun."

"The driving me home and listening to me eat and talk about hobbits part?"

"You forgot about the choice ABBA music in the background."

"Of course. How could I forget ABBA?"

"You're right." Luke's voice goes deathly serious. "How could you?"

I prop my elbow up on the windowsill so I can look at him comfortably. He's peering back at me, his big hands on his thighs, and his lips twisted up in a little smirk. I nod towards the empty backseat. "Still can't believe your plus one abandoned you."

"Meh, I'm okay with it. Noah's not my type."

Though I know I shouldn't, I have to ask. "So who would you have gone for tonight? I saw you speaking to Flo for awhile."

And I was fine with it. Really. One hundred percent fine.

Even when she was demonstrating some fancy pilates moves with her perky, spandex-clad butt up high in the air.

"Floriana's a nice person, but she's not for me."

"So no one caught your eye?" I ask casually. Calmly. Steady-like.

Luke pauses. Tilts his head just the smallest bit. He has on the most peculiar expression, like he's working something out. I suddenly wonder if I've crossed our friendship boundary and upset him. "I didn't say that," he says.

"No, you didn't," I backtrack quickly.

Because I already know the answer to my own question —Luke *does* have a type, and that type is Eleanor Wilkes.

I am the polar opposite of Eleanor Wilkes. She's petite and delicate, while still managing to rock some curves. She has long, flowing brown hair that forms effortless beach waves no matter what she's doing that day. And she has the kind of enviable, carefree, boho style that so many Instagram and TikToks lifestyle influencers seem to have.

Meanwhile, I'm about as curvy as a North Dakota highway, and I'd probably fare better in one of those Scandinavian countries with the really tall people. My blonde hair couldn't be classed as wavy on its best day. And heaven forbid I try to wear heels—none of the stores in town carry my size, so I normally drive to the big malls in Denver to find a nice pair.

"What about you?" Luke asks. "Any guys on your radar?"

"Nope," I say, because I'm pretty sure Luke doesn't want to hear about my woes with Poltergeist Aaron. "No one at all. And I'm pretty sure I saw Bert go off with Flo at the end of the night. Which further proves my point."

"What point?"

"Couple names work. Hello. Flo and Bert? Fl-ert? They're meant to be. So it's another win for us involuntary matchmakers."

I can practically feel Luke's grimace from across the car. "Don't let that get back to the rumor mill. Left at the altar and also the town matchmaker? I'd never hear the end of it."

I let out a sudden laugh, then realize how rude that might've sounded and slap a hand over my mouth. But Luke's face shifts, and within seconds, we're both cracking up. His deep, rich laugh fills the car, and the sound is so light and easy that I'm instantly reminded of the Luke of years ago.

But speaking about Eleanor clearly shifts something within me, because the feelings bear creeps off into the sunset, and I'm at peace again. I'm reaching for the door, ready to call it a night, when Luke speaks again.

"Dais, did anyone tell you how beautiful you look tonight?"

I freeze, my hand grasping the door handle. I must've misheard. I turn back to Luke, and he's looking at me with the same sort of expression he had earlier in the night, when I saw him making his way towards me through the crowd. It's a look I've never seen on him before.

Like he's a man on a mission, and the mission is me.

My stomach clenches back into a mess of butterflies, and my skin feels flushed. "No. No one. I mean, aside from myself in the mirror before I left home."

Why am I like this?!

Luke smirks, his eyes still on mine, like he actually liked my answer. "Well, let me be the second one to say it, then. You looked beautiful tonight."

My throat is dry as the desert. Never has a compliment meant so much to me.

Because I know how carefully Luke chooses his words. He wouldn't lie, wouldn't say anything unless he truly meant it.

"Thank you, Luke. You looked beautiful, as well." I press my lips together, try to ignore the way my heart is currently zinging around my chest. "You know, in a manly way."

With that graceful response, I open the door and exit the car. But before I can head up the sidewalk, I gesture for him to put the window down. I have to ask now, before I lose my nerve. "Tonight, earlier... it seemed like you were coming over to talk to me, but then Fran pulled me away."

"I was."

"What did you want to say?"

Luke's face is impassive but open. "I was going to ask you to dance."

My heart slams, and the butterflies finally take flight. "Me? Why?"

"Because I wanted to see something." Now, he seems curious. "What would you have said?"

"If you'd asked me to dance?" I sputter. Is this really happening right now? Past Daisy is—*would be*—celebrating this so hard. I decide to be honest, like he was with me. "I would've said yes."

Luke smiles. "Good."

He starts the car, gives me a wink, and pulls away from the curb. I stare after his taillights until they disappear around the corner.

When I get back inside, my skin is warm and prickly, and my heart is beating fast. I'm the human equivalent of champagne, light and bubbly and sparkling. Luke's words echo in my head, and the fact that he wanted to ask me to dance feels like a deja vu dream come true.

But as I close the front door behind me and lean my back against the cool wood, it's like waking up from said dream. I'm being wrenched back to the real world, where Luke Brooks is still my best friend's older brother, and the man who inspired feelings in me that I very strategically and painstakingly had to get over years ago.

Yet here I am, opening the door to those old feelings all over again. And while I thought the feelings bear had crept off into the sunset, I clearly took my eyes off him a moment too long as he's done a U-turn and barged right back into my life.

Which has happened in Mirror Valley before, by the way. With a real bear, not a feelings bear, and it walked right into someone's house when they left their front door open while barbecuing.

Anyway. That is not the point.

The point is this: I'm veering dangerously close to remembering why I fell for Luke Brooks all those years ago. It's time I put some distance between us, just to make sure that I don't get any crazy ideas. Like thinking for a moment that he might feel the spark too.

14

LUKE

Something's changed.

I can't explain it, I can't understand it.

But something is definitely different.

And it's all because of Daisy Griffiths.

My fingers tighten on the steering wheel as I take a left turn away from her house. Her answer to my question rings in my ears.

No, I didn't get a chance to dance with her tonight, to test out whether there was something between us, as Noah suggested. Before I could reach her, Fran whisked her away, and we were both occupied for the rest of the night.

If I'm honest though, I didn't need to do anything else to know. Even now, I can't get her out of my head—the vision of her blonde hair hanging straight down her back like liquid sunshine, her dress cascading down her body in a way that made her seem even more ethereal. I meant what I said to her, she *was* beautiful tonight. She took my breath away.

And it was more than that. It was the way I kept looking for her through the crowd, the way her laughter seemed to reach me from across the room, the way her lengthy LOTR monologue in the car just made me smile. These are the kinds of things you hear about in passing from friends, parents, or from the happy couple at weddings. I'm sure James said the same things about Ivy during theirs.

I always thought those sentiments were blown a little out of proportion. Exaggerated. Don't get me wrong, I looked for Eleanor across a room. I paid attention to where she was, and made sure I was available if she needed anything. I enjoyed doing those things for her.

But tonight was an entirely new ballgame. There was nothing purposeful or forced in the way I looked out for Daisy. I was simply... aware of her. Like I was craving to be near her. Even when she was sitting next to me in the front seat, munching her way through the messiest bag of chips known to man.

Like I said, I can't explain it.

Once again, Daisy is breaking all my rules. Without even trying.

And she's making *me* want to try. Making me want to be the guy she deserves, the man who would be good enough for her. The person who would commit for the right reasons.

But if I'm going to try and win Daisy Griffiths's heart, I need to take the advice she may or may not have given to Ed at Ivy and James's wedding—I need to start from a place of honesty.

Minus the embarrassing public display of adoration.

15

DAISY

The day after the Dinner in White is the perfect fall day.

There's a bite in the air, a crispness that makes me want to wrap up in blankets and read a book in front of a roaring fire. The leaves have turned and are falling off the trees so that every step gives a satisfying crunch. On my way to Valley Fitness early this morning, kids were bundled up in jackets and gathering the leaves into piles.

And best of all, the smell... that earthy, dry scent that indicates summer is over and winter is on its way. It's a very close second to a certain manly forest scent.

Of course, all I can smell right now are sweaty yoga mats.

Valley Fitness's group fitness studio is empty as I hold a particularly moist mat away from my body and give it a good dousing with the cleaning spray. I try not to grimace. Hot yoga attendees are strongly encouraged to clean their own equipment after class, but there are always a couple mats left laying around.

It's fine, though, because this stinky mat is keeping me from dwelling on the whole Luke-calling-me-beautiful thing. And let's not forget about the entire Luke-saying-he-wanted-to-dance-with-me fandango.

No big deal. Nope.

If only my heart would listen. Because it's been racing around my ribcage for the past twelve hours in a way that has to be medically unhealthy.

I need to keep reminding myself that this is *Luke Brooks*. He's practically plastered in yellow tape screaming OUT OF BOUNDS. Make a U-Turn. Go back. I can't be reading into anything he said past the words themselves. Can't be placing hope on something I know will never go anywhere. I might be optimistic, but I'm not stupid.

So he called me beautiful—he'd probably say the same to a nice sunset, or a really cool lamp. So he said he wanted to dance with me—he probably would've danced with Ivy had she been there. Maybe he just wanted someone with whom to join in on the conga line before it got too raucous (which it did. Who knew such a thing was possible?).

Unfortunately, the one person who has always helped me get my heart back in line is currently overseas with her new husband. Ivy has never expressly said anything to discourage me from having feelings for Luke, but her friendship alone and how much it means to me is enough to quiet any annoying heart-skips or naughty butterflies. I never told her about my schoolgirl crush on Luke because I didn't need to. It was a stupid crush on a guy who was spoken for, and I knew it was up to me to be a big girl and get over it.

Because the truth is, Luke Brooks has not, does not, and will not ever feel anything for me past being his little sister's best friend. And his go-to for a friendly LOTR debate.

I just need to remember that.

With that resolution at the front of my mind, I give the mat a firm wipe with a clean cloth, then hang it over the barre to dry properly. I tend to earmark the weekly hot yoga class as the time to give all of the group fitness equipment a clean—from the weights and bolsters to the resistance bands and jump ropes.

I'm about to walk out of the room to grab a few more cloths when the very person who's been on my mind appears in the doorway like some conjured mirage.

"Hey, Dais." Luke's deep, rich voice is almost enough to make me forget my resolution completely. Seriously, how can he make those two words sound like some of the sexiest on the planet? He must stop.

"Hey, Luke," I say chirpily, taking a subconscious step back and away from him. "Sorry to say that you're an hour late for hot yoga. Tough luck."

Luke raises a brow. "Shucks. Have to come earlier next time."

I refuse to let my eyes travel down his body. Even still, I notice that he's not wearing workout gear but a fitted black polo and dark slacks that I already know perfectly emphasize a very firm backside.

What? I'm only human.

"What're you doing here?" I ask, hurrying to the cupboard at the side of the room in order to pull all of the bolsters and weights off the shelves for cleaning. I need something to do with my hands. My heart's being all zingy again, and it's coupled with that bizarre sort of energy I get being this close to him.

"Came to see you."

I busy myself taking the weights of the shelves and putting them in a pile on the ground. "And what can I help you with today?"

"Why do you think I need you to help me?" Luke asks, and his hand grasps my arm gently, urging me to come to a standstill. He turns me towards him. "Maybe I just wanted to see you."

"Well, here I am." I smile wide at him. Then, I make the mistake of looking into his dark hazel eyes.

Red alert! Dangerous territory.

But I can't move. I'm happy here. I might as well be one of those foolhardy moths being drawn towards a flame. Though in this case, Luke is a particularly dangerous, sexy type of flame with nice biceps.

Before I can react, Luke takes another step so that mere inches separate us. I tilt my chin up, leaning back slightly so my back meets with the cool wood of the shelves. His eyes never break from mine, and the heat between is impossible to ignore. I'm trapped here between him and the cupboard, but I can't feel my toes right now so I have no business trying to walk away.

He reaches an arm up behind me, and my breath catches. My skin feels alive at the places he might touch me —my shoulders, my back, my neck. We're practically chest to chest now, and my chin is tilting further up without permission. I'm a magnet, following his every movement.

Then, Luke pulls his hand back, and he's holding a ten-pound weight he pulled off the shelf behind me. He dips his head slightly so his mouth is closer to my ear. "Maybe I can help *you*."

And I'm not sure whether this was purposeful on his part, but his voice seems to reach new levels of huskiness. I'm aware of his warm breath on my neck. That same energy is buzzing through my veins at top speed, and my fingers tingle with a desire to run across his bare arms.

"You don't have to," I say a little breathlessly.

"I don't generally offer to do things I don't want to do."

I swallow thickly. His eyes glance down to my mouth, and for one heady millisecond, I can almost believe he's thinking about kissing me. I force out a chuckle. "Okay. I won't fight you on it."

"Good." Luke smirks and steps away, and the tension in my body releases.

But all at once, I'm missing him. Craving more, craving to be closer.

It can't only be me, right? Does he feel it, too?

Luke grabs the remaining weights off the shelf and arranges them on the ground, and I snap myself out of it, shoving the ridiculous questions away with a firm hand. I focus squarely on handing him a spray bottle and a cloth.

While Luke cleans the weights, I start wiping down the blocks and bolsters. I sneak a couple glances towards him, but his face gives nothing away. If anything, he seems totally preoccupied with the task of cleaning the weights, his brow furrowed in concentration. The energy I'm feeling must be entirely on my side, which checks out given our history.

I try to be kind to myself, remind myself that everyone slips up once or twice. It's okay that I let my imagination get the better of me for a moment. It won't happen again.

After a few moments of silence, Luke surprises me by saying, "Any thoughts on what the next matchmaking event is going to be?"

"Are you making small talk, Luke Brooks?"

"I wouldn't call it small talk. Small talk would be like 'how're you liking this beautiful fall we're having?'" He shakes his head. "Kill me now."

"Noted. And for the record, I actually do love this weather."

Luke gives me a dry smirk. "I do too."

I bite my lip to hold back a smile. "To answer your question, I'm not sure what to do for the next event. And it seems like a few people are pairing off now. For example, our friends Fl-ert." My smile fades fast. "I'm not sure any event will be quite as good as the last one. I hope we're able to find more people to attend."

"Well, that's a good thing, isn't it?"

"What is?"

"That we need to find more singles. It means that you helped a few people find someone they care about."

I blink, put down the bolster I'm cleaning in order to look at him. He's right. I was so caught up thinking of the community center, I hadn't even thought about the real-world consequences of these events. Hadn't even thought about the people who were single—just like me—finally finding the person they've been looking for.

"Thanks, Luke," I say seriously. "I didn't see it that way."

He gives me one of his rare smiles before picking up another weight and spraying it thoroughly. "I wonder if Dee can come up with something on RightMatch. Maybe create some sort of a community board to advertise local events. More interest will come. Things like this don't just die off."

The confidence in his voice makes me feel warm inside. "Mr. Positivity over here."

He elbows me gently, and I knock into him, lingering for just a moment, though I doubt he notices. He picks up a stack of clean weights from the floor, holding about eight of them like it's nothing. Then, his mouth sets in a line as he clears his throat. "Listen. I did come here today to see you, but I also have something to tell you."

"What is it?" I avert my gaze from his currently popping bicep and busy myself picking up a much smaller stack of weights. I balance them slightly precariously on my forearm as I put them away.

"It's about RightMatch."

I continue stacking weights on the shelf. "What about it?"

"I don't really know how to say this..." Luke trails off, his mouth pinched. He seems nervous, uncertain, and my mood shifts to become more serious. It's rare to see Luke like this, so whatever he has to say must be a big deal. I decide the best thing I can do is wait patiently.

"Uhm... okay." He exhales a quick breath. He doesn't look at me and instead focuses on the task of putting the rest of the weights away, one by one. "Remember that Aaron guy you were speaking to?"

I blink. Wasn't expecting that. "Yeah?"

"I'm him."

My stomach drops violently. "I'm sorry?"

"I'm Aaron B." Luke finally looks at me cautiously. "I was the one you were speaking to on RightMatch. The one you asked to meet at McGarry's that night."

My entire body freezes up as the realization hits me like a truck.

Luke Brooks... is Aaron B? Poltergeist Aaron?

The guy I texted for days on end? The one who listened, and made me laugh, and who I couldn't get off the mind? The person I was falling for, only to have him spectacularly ghost me?

My arms release a tiny fraction, but it's enough to shift the balance.

And the weights tumble directly onto my left foot.

16

LUKE

Note to self...

Telling someone a shocking piece of news while they're carrying about twenty pounds' worth of weights is *not* a good idea.

"I told you, I'm fine," Daisy says as she hobbles—yes, *hobbles*—up the sidewalk to her bungalow.

"According to the doctor, you are *not* 'fine'. A toe contusion is not 'fine', Dais," I grumble. My entire body is buzzing with a furious energy directed at myself for being so freaking stupid. Even so, I keep my grip gentle on Daisy—one arm around her waist, the other holding her elbow. If I had my way, I would've picked her up in my arms and carried her inside, but she insisted very vehemently that I would not be carrying her over any thresholds.

Which felt extreme to me, but whatever.

"That's just fancy doctor language for a bruise," Daisy goes on with a swift roll of her eyes. "And that's all this is. One tiny, insignificant bruise on my big toe—"

"And across the top of your foot."

She goes on. "I probably didn't even have to bother the doc about it."

My lips press into a firm line. We argued back and forth about this at Valley Fitness, and then again in my car. She insisted that she didn't want to take up the doctor's time with a "small injury", but there was no way I was going to allow her to go home without getting her foot checked first.

She finally caved when I promised to buy her favorite sour cream and onion chips. Plus, whenever she tried to walk, her face turned white, and she almost keeled over. So my argument seemed pretty justified.

"We've been over this," I say and there's a warning in my voice. "You were in pain. What? You don't think you should be cared for when you're hurt?"

My question is sarcastic but Daisy actually goes silent for a moment. Those two seconds of quiet say more than anything else, and I subconsciously hold onto her tighter.

"I can take care of myself, and I'm fine," she says. "The doctor said I'll be healed in no time."

"If 'no time' means three to four weeks."

Daisy ignores me. "It's barely an issue. It's actually not an issue. A non-issue." She tries to put weight on her left foot to put her keys in the door. Immediately winces and falls back into my arms. "Okay, it's still a bit painful... But I should be all set by tomorrow."

"Your capacity for denial is truly something, Dais."

"I do what I can."

I'm basically propping her up as she unlocks the front door, hobbles inside, and sets her keys in a small bowl. She turns on all the lights, then leans against the wall to hang up her purse by the door and take off her jacket. I take the opportunity to have a look around.

I've never been in Daisy's house before. The open space that apparently holds the living room, dining room, kitchen, study, yoga room, etc. is wonderfully cluttered and full. Warm light emanates from scattered ceiling lights and

130

vintage standing lamps. A huge, blue, worn couch takes up a corner of the room facing a small TV. The dining table has mismatched chairs and is topped with clean dishes that have yet to be put away. In another corner sits a group of various cactuses—cacti?—which I have to assume belong to Daisy.

It all seems so cozy. Homey.

The sort of place you could come back to after a long day and just relax.

I spy a light out above the dining table and feel a sudden impulse to fix it. I quickly tamp it down.

"You've never been in my house before." Daisy comes to the same realization I did, and her cheeks turn the slightest bit pink. "I'm sorry it's such a mess. You know Dee, she's just so..." Her voice trails off, and she snorts. "I can't even pretend. This is all me."

"Wouldn't have believed it even if you'd said it."

I hold my arm out so I can help her to the couch, and she collapses onto the cushions, sinking right down so I wonder for a minute if they might swallow her whole. She sighs and smiles contentedly, like she's been dreaming of this moment all day.

I'm unable to keep a smirk from my lips. "Happy?"

"Deliriously so."

I grab one of the chairs from the dining table—a short, rickety thing with a light wood frame and a deeply purple seat cover that would look right at home in the 70s. I pull it up close to the couch so I can sit next to Daisy, who lifts her left foot slowly and perches it on the couch's armrest, toes pointed up. We haven't talked about my big revelation at all, but that takes a backseat to making sure Daisy's okay.

"Those painkillers kicking in yet?" I ask her.

"Maybe a little. I am feeling a bit loopy." Daisy sticks

her tongue out the side of her mouth and makes a goofy face.

I shake my head, even as relief fills me up inside. She was happy to make jokes and play it all off, but I was worried about her. Am still worried. Daisy's like a power-house all her own, but everyone needs help sometimes. And I'm realizing with stark clarity that I want to be the one helping her if she needs it.

And not because I'm the reason she dropped the weights on her foot.

I have to fight an almost irrepressible urge to take her hand. "I'm sorry, Dais. I don't know what I was thinking—"

"Stop." She holds up a hand. "What did I say? Stop saying sorry. And stop saying thank you." She gives me a little smile, and I realize she's using the same words I said to her last night. "This isn't your fault. I shouldn't have been holding that many weights in the first place, and they were totally off-balance. Not to mention my arm strength is basi-cally negligible."

"Jake Fischer would disagree."

Daisy looks at me in surprise. "You remember that?"

I fix her with a look. "You punching the school's star quarterback in the face when you were just a junior? 'Course I remember that." My expression turns serious. "Don't tell me that guy is on your date list."

Daisy bursts into abrupt laughter. The sound is bubbly and light, like a cold can of Coke on a hot day. "Oh, no! He certainly is not. Not after what he said that warranted said punch. Besides, he's all grown up and married now." Daisy's mouth presses into a line. "I can't believe you remember that."

"I remember a lot of things with you, Dais."

She looks at me then, and I'm surprised I said the words myself. Surprised at the tender note in my own voice. But I mean it. No, nothing ever happened between Daisy and me, and I never once saw her as a potential *anything* when I was dating Eleanor.

But looking back, it's hard to deny that a lot of my favorite moments have somehow involved Daisy. Like when she, Ivy, and I would build blanket forts together as kids and play cards inside. Or when Daisy and I would pair up to play soccer against Ivy and James—she always was better than she thought she was. Or when I got into my CPA program, and she and Ivy surprised me with my favorite ice cream cake. Or when I proposed to Eleanor, and Ivy and Daisy threw me a small congratulations party with my closest friends and family.

It's like she's always understood me on some level. Like she's always accepted me as I am.

Daisy fiddles with the zipper on her sweater. "Erm. Would you mind grabbing me the crutches from the car? I have to get started with dinner."

"You're making dinner? Isn't Dee going to be home soon to help you?"

Daisy shrugs, keeping her eyes averted. "She's got a work thing tonight."

"So?"

Her voice drops even lower. "And she doesn't know..."

Of course she doesn't. Because of course Daisy wouldn't tell her.

I rise to a stand. "I'll get your crutches, but I'm also making you dinner."

"You don't have to—"

It's my turn to hold up a hand. "Nope. It's happening. Try to stop me."

With a final angelic smirk, which she returns with a sour glare, I head out the door. I retrieve the crutches from the trunk of my car, come back inside and prop them next to the couch. "You can only use these under extreme circumstances. If you even try to come to the kitchen, I will carry you back here."

Daisy snorts and rolls her eyes, but I keep my gaze firm so she sees I'm serious. She lets out a sigh. "Aye aye, captain."

I head into the cramped kitchen, opening cupboards and trying to orient myself. It's not that the kitchen is particularly small—well, it is—but the Griffiths sisters have clearly collected every single kitchen appliance known to man. I enjoy cooking, even took a few cooking classes with Eleanor back in the day, but some of these are downright worrying...

"Hey, Dais?"

"Yeah?"

"Why do you have a medieval torture weapon on your countertop?"

Daisy lets out another bubbly laugh, and when I look towards the couch, she's got her head thrown back so her blonde hair falls down the side of the armrest. "It's an espresso machine!"

"Don't believe you."

"Dee found it at a resale shop in Summer Lakes and got it for us. It works about 40% of the time, which I estimate to be pretty high, actually."

"If you ever come around to my house, I'll show you a proper espresso machine."

Daisy chuckles. "Sounds like a plan."

I smile, weirdly happy at the thought of Daisy in my house.

And that's when I realize that I'm not thinking about my condo but my *house*. My abandoned ranch house on the outskirts of town with the white shutters framing tall windows, and the big porch, and the full kitchen with mostly-new appliances.

I give my head a shake. Where was I even going with that?

I whip up a quick vegetarian dinner with the things I find in the kitchen. There isn't much, so I'm going to go out on a limb and say that the meal is very "creative and resourceful". Which are fantastic descriptors for any good meal, obviously. Daisy keeps offering to help, and I keep turning her down.

By the time I walk over with two steaming bowls of veggie pasta with crispy tofu, Daisy's on her phone. She puts it down as I approach and sits up on the couch, eyes bright as she takes one of the bowls.

"This looks delicious. Thank you, Luke." Her light blue eyes—the exact color of the sky right after dawn, I realize—remain on mine for a moment. Just long enough to fill my chest with warmth.

"Anytime," I tell her. And I mean it.

I'd be here to take care of Daisy every day, if she'd let me.

Maybe I will.

Right as I'm about to sit back down on my chair, I notice a ball of familiar-looking fur climbing up the stairs. I nod towards it. "So that's Bruce, huh?"

Daisy looks at me in confusion. "Yeah... how did you know that?"

"Noah's suit is always covered with cat hair."

Her brow clears, and she laughs. "That checks out. Bruce spends most of his time in Dee's room. She built a little perch above her desk for him, and he only comes out very occasionally to scope out the rest of his 'kingdom'."

We eat dinner together. Daisy's bowl is perched on the armrest, and I've got my elbows on my knees, leaning in close to her. We chat easily, and I'm reminded of how I felt when I was texting her on RightMatch. I can't believe I've never noticed before just how much I enjoy talking and laughing with her. Even about the dumbest topics.

Or the harder ones.

"So," I eventually say once our food is long gone, and I've put our dishes in the dishwasher. "How're you feeling about what I said earlier?"

"The Aaron of it all?" Daisy jokes, laughing it off. But I wait for a moment, knowing that she often deflects with humor. I want to hear her genuine thoughts, how she's feeling about it. Seeing I'm serious, she gives a shrug. "I don't know. I'm still kinda surprised, I guess."

"To be expected." A dry smirk comes to my lips. "I was surprised, too."

"When did you find out it was me?"

I hold my breath for a quick moment. "I realized that night at McGarry's."

Her eyes go wide. "You knew since *then*?"

She doesn't sound angry, which she has every right to be. Heck, *I* would be, if I was her. But I know I have to be honest, lay it all out on the table. I want her to know the truth, beginning to end. "I suspected. But the more we spoke and hung out doing the matchmaking stuff, the more I... knew."

A silence settles between us. It feels loud with the weight of my unspoken words. Words I can't even admit to myself at this point.

"I should've told you earlier." I bite the inside of my cheek. "Aaron's my middle name. I didn't piece it together until later that Sisi was a nickname of yours."

"It's what my grandmother used to call me. And it's honestly fine." Daisy shakes her head. "I probably would've done the same if I were you."

"That's the thing though, I don't think you would. You're a lot braver and stronger than you give yourself credit for, Dais. You deserve honesty, and I want to be honest with you because I like spending time with you."

Daisy smiles then, a quick smile that I might've missed had I blinked. It's one I've never seen on her before—a vulnerable, open smile that looks sweet, but almost scared at the same time. "You're not so bad yourself."

I smirk, but nothing about this moment feels funny. Daisy's leaning towards me on the couch, her perfect bow lips tilted slightly up. I'm so far forward in my chair, I'm almost out of it. And just like in the fitness center, the air between us seems to carry more weight, becomes more intense and heated. My body craves to be near her, and my fingers itch with a desire to touch her. To push her hair back from her face, to take her hand. To do something.

I'm a man of control in all things, but I'm surprised how much my control is being tested right now.

But does she feel the same way? Is she noticing the pull between us, or is it just me?

SLAM!

"Honeyyyyy, I'm home!"

Noah's shout invades the moment, and I launch away from Daisy with so much force that I almost topple out of my chair. Meanwhile, Daisy winces as her foot shifts on the armrest. "Oof," she mutters under her breath, and I'm suddenly standing to help her.

"Oh, hey boss!" Noah exclaims, finally seeing us. I throw a glare over my shoulder, and he blinks when he spots Daisy. "What's happening here? Why are you sprawled across the couch like some distressed damsel?"

"Who's on the couch?" Dee tumbles through the door, hoisting a huge black duffel bag on her shoulder, which she drops before standing beside Noah. Her gaze lands on me, and her brows furrow. "Luke? This is a surprise. What're you doing in our house?"

At that moment, her eyes fall on Daisy, and then travel to her foot, which is propped on the couch at an awkward angle.

"Ohmygosh, Dais! Are you okay?" Dee practically mows me down as she runs to her big sister.

Daisy shakes her head, waving with one hand. "I'm fine, I'm fine!"

"Again. Not fine," I say sternly. "She's got a foot contusion."

Dee's eyes go wide. "A foot *what*?!"

"A bone bruise," I explain. "On her big toe."

At this, both Dee and Noah go carefully neutral. They look at each other, and Daisy seems to sense something I don't because she rolls her eyes. The two then let out a snort at the exact same moment.

"You're saying that Daisy bruised her toe. That's what this is about?" Dee asks on an uncharacteristic giggle.

"Alright, guys, laugh it up." Daisy sighs. "It's actually pretty painful."

Dee goes serious again and takes her sister's hand with concern. "Sorry, sorry. Of course, it is."

Noah manages to get his face under control. "You got crutches?"

"Yup. Apparently I'm on couch rest for the next couple of weeks."

"*Three* weeks," I correct.

"Oh, no," Dee says. "What're you going to do? What about your jobs and—?"

Daisy cuts her off by flinging herself back on the couch. "One thing at a time, okay, Dee? I've only just had dinner after Luke so kindly *insisted* that he bring me to the doctor. I haven't even started to think about tomorrow."

Dee and Noah both look at me, but with very different

expressions. Where Dee's is one of appreciation and concern, Noah's is more along the lines of *yeah, you did!*

"It was no problem," I say quickly. "Anything to make sure Daisy's alright."

Noah's smirk grows so he looks like a particularly smug Cheshire cat. Dee nods her agreement before turning back to Daisy, and the two start conversing in quiet voices.

After a moment, Dee orders Noah to grab some ice from the freezer, and it occurs to me that I'm very much out of place here. Dee and Daisy (and Noah, apparently) have a routine together, a way of taking care of themselves and each other. And as much as I want to be the one helping Daisy right now, I know that the right thing for me to do is to give them space.

So I walk towards the door with some reluctance in my steps. "It's time I head out. I'm sure Stella's missing me." I look back at Daisy once more. "But I'll come again tomorrow; I believe I owe you chips. And text me if you need anything else."

"Anything?" Noah asks cheekily.

I ignore him. "Seriously, Dais."

Dee and Noah are both silent as they look between Daisy and me. She simply nods without a word, and I walk out the door, wishing that I didn't have to.

"What was that all about?" Dee asks the second the door shuts behind Luke.

"Shh," I mutter. "He'll hear you."

"Nah, he won't." Noah peeks out the curtain like some lurker. "He's already all the way down the path. Holy, the guy's got long legs. No wonder he was a big-time soccer dude back in school." Dee shoots him a look, and he shrugs. "What? You've got to respect the guy's athleticism. Even if he has the most boring job known to man."

"Luke doesn't think so," I say, shifting on the couch. Noah's abrupt entrance made me jump, which made my leg jump, and therefore made my foot move from its previously cozy position on the armrest.

Not to mention *my* previously cozy position. Which was very, very close to Luke's face. With his hazel eyes boring into mine so intensely...

Even now, the memory makes blood race to my cheeks. Unfortunately, Dee has eagle eyes, and a smirk grows on her lips. "So we *did* interrupt something. Was there a little hanky panky happening on the couch?"

My hands fly to my cheeks, which are, indeed, warm. "Dee!"

"How inappropriate!" Noah admonishes Dee. Like he's not the worst of the bunch when it comes to suggestive comments. He backs away from the window and heads towards the kitchen, whistling. "This all sounds like stuff I shouldn't be hearing so I'm gonna find snacks. Dee, do you have any of those ice cream bars left?"

"You're lactose intolerant."

"Only sometimes."

I fall back on the couch, and Dee pulls up the chair that Luke recently vacated, getting in real nice and close. "Daisy, seriously. What's going on? Why was Luke Brooks sitting in my living room, warming up my chair with his lovely butt?"

"Ew, Dee."

"Kidding. But not really. He does have a nice caboose."

I sigh loudly. "How old are you?"

"A hundred!" Noah shouts from the kitchen.

"Weren't you looking for those ice cream bars, creep?" Dee shouts back, then taps my knee. "Come on. Ivy isn't here so I'm all you've got. And I know you, you want to talk about this. What's going on with you two?"

She's right. Ivy isn't here, and I wish she was. But then again, maybe I don't. Because how on earth could I explain to her that I've had feelings for her older brother for years? And that, even though I tried so hard to fight them, they're now being unleashed again like a freaking flood breaking through a dam? Not to mention the moments when I've wondered if Luke might actually be feeling something too...

It all started building up while Luke was making dinner. I'll admit that maybe, potentially, sometimes, I like to keep busy with my eight to ten jobs because it keeps me occupied. Keeps me from thinking too much.

Well, I ended up doing exactly that—overthinking. And

141

I broke down and texted Ivy, telling her only that some nameless, faceless man that I'm attracted to has started being sweet with me out of nowhere, and maybe even a little flirty.

I did not mention that said nameless, faceless man was her freaking brother, of course.

It's probably like 4:30am her time so I don't expect an answer, but it felt good to type it out, put words to my feelings. And now, just knowing that text is out there, waiting to be read and answered... by my best friend while she's on her honeymoon.

What have I done?

I grab my phone and send a harried "Never mind!!!!!" text before lying back on the couch and pinching the bridge of my nose.

Dee's right though, I clearly want to spill my guts... and Dee, of all people, is guaranteed to knock some sense into me. Because here I go again, thinking that he meant something more when he said he liked spending time with me.

Um, hello, some people enjoy spending time with their pet tarantulas. There is no subtext when it comes to tarantulas.

I drop my voice so Noah can't hear. "Honestly, Dee, I might be feeling the teeniest, tiniest, most miniscule thing for Luke. It's not that I've caught feelings. At all. But I may have one small inkling of a feeling, like, hovering in the atmosphere."

"A small inkling," Dee repeats, and there's a knowing smirk on her lips that I don't appreciate.

"Tiny. Miniscule."

"So you said."

"But it needs to stop because there are literally 1,001 reasons we won't be going down this path."

"That's a lot of reasons."

"So, even if I ever *was* to catch capital-f Feelings, it's not like they can go anywhere. This is a no-go zone. A no-grow zone. A dry desert of nothingness."

Dee purses her lips. "Bit extreme, don't you think?"

"Deserts are extreme."

She chooses to ignore this very rational argument. "Give me an example of these 1001 reasons. I'm assuming you're thinking about Ivy?"

"'Course I am. I love Ivy, she's my best friend and has been for years. I would never want to complicate our friendship or cause any sort of rift between us. And even if—and this is a big if—Luke feels a tiny feeling too, I'm sure he'd also be thinking of her."

"Pretty sure that Ivy would give him a pass given that she's married to *his* best friend."

I have to give her that one, but it's not enough to appease my worries. "But Dee, imagine if we dated and then broke up, it would be so awkward. So hard. Would Ivy have to pick sides? Would we have to split all of our friends straight down the middle? You remember how things went with Mom and Dad."

Dee shows the smallest discomfort before going impassive again.

"Exactly. I can't do that to Ivy. And Luke and I are both a pretty big part of this community; I could never be the reason for any conflict or upset in this town. The people here matter too much to me. I can't be in the fray, making people pick sides..."

I don't realize my breaths are coming short and quick until Dee places a hand on my elbow. I force myself to slow down, calm my racing thoughts.

"Plus, he was with Eleanor for so long. I mean, they were engaged and—"

"If it makes you feel better, Luke doesn't seem hung up

143

on her at all," Noah cuts in as he walks back into the room, licking a spoon. "Eleanor, I mean. Or Lenore, or whatever her name was. He never mentions her. All he ever talks about is this chick he met on RightMatch..." He taps his bottom lip with the spoon. "Though now that I think about it, he hasn't talked about her in awhile either. Guess he's been too busy with your whole matchmaking business."

My cheeks turn hot, then cold, then hot again.

Dee, of course, notices this. "Daisy? What was that?"

I swallow thickly. "Remember the Aaron guy I was speaking to?"

"Poltergeist? Of course, you were all about him..." Dee trails off, and I see her making the connection. "Hang on. Wait."

"Wait what?" Noah asks.

Dee blinks slowly, ignoring him. "So you and Luke really *have* been getting cozy lately."

I swallow again, now craning my neck—totally comfortably, if a stern right angle is comfortable—to look out the window and away from Dee and Noah.

"Interesting," Dee says. Then, she slaps her hands on her knees. "Well, case closed then. You *have* to date him."

I look at her in astonishment. "What?!"

"He's clearly into you. You're clearly into him... yadda yadda yadda. Date him."

"I don't think—"

"Listen, Dais." Dee leans towards me again, and her expression is clearly *over this*. "You told me some of your concerns, you listed the reasons this won't work, you said you two are a dry desert of nothingness. But you of all people should know that there are certain things that still grow in the desert."

I frown. *Oh.*

"Exactly. Cactuses. Or cacti, whatever. And the thing

144

is, Luke Brooks wouldn't offer to make dinner, or bring chips, or hang the moon or whatever for just anyone."

I don't have a response to that. But Dee's not done.

"Have you ever considered that maybe your fears have more to do with yourself than with anything external? Maybe it's not about Luke, or Eleanor, for that matter." She pats me on the head. Like I'm Bruce after he's been particularly well-behaved. "Something to think about."

With that, Dee stands and gestures for Noah to follow her to the kitchen. She's already talking about the cat and what to feed him, and it occurs to me that he never came to check on me once this entire time I've been home. Friendly beast.

I lie still on the couch for a few long moments, letting Dee's words sink in. It was nice of Luke to offer to come back tomorrow, but I'm not holding my breath. It's not that I think he'll forget—Luke always keeps his word—but I can't go so far as to imagine that he's giving me any special treatment.

That being said, I don't know what she meant about my fear having to do more with myself. I'd say the external factors alone are more than enough to nip any hopes of dating Luke in the bud.

Or any hopes of kissing him, running my fingers across his bare skin, his strong jawline, into his dark hair...

Nope. All of those need to be nipped ASAP and STAT.

Luke isn't ready to date, he said so himself. He might be a little flirty and sweet these days, might sometimes look at me like I'm the only oasis in said desert and he's a man desperate for a drink.

But I know that even if something has changed for him, and he might be interested in dating again, I can't do casual. The gravity of my feelings and how quickly they've come out of the woodwork to haunt me again are proof of that. I can't let myself be the one he takes out simply because he's decided he's ready to re-enter the dating pool.

This is an all or nothing kind of situation. There is no glass half full or half empty for me.

And I wish Luke wasn't making it so tempting to take what I can get.

18

DAISY

As promised, Luke does come the next day.

And the day after that, and the day after that. In fact, he's come to my tiny bungalow every single day over the past week since Toe-pocalypse, as I've started calling it—to many eye rolls from both Dee and Luke.

The first day he came by, he brought me my promised chips, along with a full bag of groceries, and has been using said groceries to make us dinner every night. Meanwhile, I've been lying prostrate on the couch with ice bags on my foot looking every bit the dreaded damsel in distress. Which is not normally my vibe, believe me.

That being said, having a tall, capable, good-looking man make me dinner every night isn't all bad.

After making us food, Luke sits with me, and we talk about everything and nothing. We watch TV, play cards or board games, or sometimes read together. Just the two of us. Because Dee is a certified night-owl and prefers to work when the sun sets.

In fact, the two of them often pass each other at the front door. Have even resorted to fist-bumping in lieu of greeting each other with actual words. I've made a few jokes about the "changing of the grouchy guards", which did pull a smile out of Luke.

My toe and foot are now turning a lovely shade of greenish-yellow, which according to Luke is a good thing. And of course, he's also started helping me with the stretching and strengthening exercises the doctor prescribed that I was originally hoping I could get away with not doing. But Luke wouldn't have that, so I've been grunting and straining my way through them every night.

This has to be my peak attractiveness. How can he possibly resist?

And yet, Luke has made his way from sitting on a chair, to sitting next to me on the couch. Tonight, he happens to have my non-injured foot in his hands and is lightly massaging the arch and up my calf while he scrolls through his phone. It's definitely *not* doing weird, gooey things to my insides, even as my brain struggles to rationalize all of this.

Because truly, in what iteration of the universe would Luke Brooks be sitting on my couch massaging my feet after making me dinner?

It simply makes no sense. It's a glitch in the matrix.

That being said, I definitely missed a beat not having "foot massage romance" on my trope list. Is that a trope? It should be.

"Unnng." The guttural, completely inhuman moan escapes my lips when Luke hits a sweet spot. I slap a hand over my mouth as he looks at me in surprise. "Sorry. That was..."

Luke smirks. "Sexy."

I laugh, even as my cheeks go blistering hot. I hope the dim lighting is enough to hide it. "No. I was going to say that this is really nice of you."

"I'm not being nice, Dais. I'm just being here."

"Well, thank you." The words don't feel enough. "Did

you happen to run into Beverly today? Or Angus? How're they holding up?"

Luke shoots me a look. "You mean at Valley Fitness, the after-school program, the bike path maintenance office, and all the other jobs you're working? Well, they're falling apart without you."

I reach up and give him a swift punch in his bare, very firm bicep.

He chuckles. "Somehow, everyone's muddling through."

"That's good. I'm glad." I lie back on the couch as Luke digs into my arch again. "This is all so crazy..."

"What is?" He tilts his head. Like he doesn't know how completely bizarre and outlandish this entire situation is.

"You. Sitting on my couch right now. Massaging my foot." I spell it out for him. There's no light of recognition in his eyes, no sudden "waking up" that a part of me is constantly expecting to see in him. I'm just waiting for it— waiting for him to come to his senses and realize that there's more to life than spending every evening with his little sister's best friend and her injured toe.

"Speaking of." Luke lightly taps my ankle. "Probably time to lower this one. Shouldn't keep it elevated for too long."

"Aye aye, captain." I place both feet on the ground somewhat reluctantly, and in doing so, my eyes sweep over my cactus collection. I bite the inside of my cheek and attempt to stand up.

"What're you doing?" Luke asks, immediately standing with me and holding my elbow. Like I'm an elderly person who can't be trusted to walk by herself.

"I'm okay, Luke. I just have to water one of the cactuses."

"*Water* it?" His eyebrows raise a fraction.

"Yeah, she's in her growth stage, and she's looking a little dry. Don't you think?"

Luke looks utterly perplexed, but he doesn't fight me on it. Instead, he helps me back onto the couch. "I got it."

He heads into the kitchen, and I direct him to fill the designated jug—it has a glittery "cactus" label—and then water the plant sparingly. He kneels on the old shag carpet (yes, we still have shag carpet) in his blue jeans, and my stomach does a funny flip at the sight of him watering a plant from a sparkly mug with so much care and concern.

"What's the deal with the cactuses—cacti—anyway?" he asks as he puts the jug away.

"Both are correct," I say off-hand, and then I give a shrug. "And I don't know. They've always been my favorite plants. They live in the harshest of environments, thrive in places where nothing else could survive. And I kinda like that they're tough and spiky on the outside, but every once in awhile, they grow flowers."

Luke does a half-smile, and I realize that I might have an affinity for things that are tough and spiky on the outside.

When Luke takes a seat next to me again, he's serious. He places his elbows on his knees and clasps his hands together loosely, frowning down towards the carpet. I recognize this position—it's his thinking pose. Much better and more attractive than any *Thinker,* in my books.

"I do actually have something to talk to you about."

He shifts slightly as I sit up, tucking my good leg under me. "Is it about the games night?"

Yes, Luke and I settled on the next matchmaking event —a games night, hosted in the community center's gymnasium. The meeting room was too small last time, and the larger space should hopefully work perfectly. Per Luke's suggestion, Dee created a community board within the

RightMatch app, and we're expecting an even *bigger* turn-out than at the Dinner in White.

The games night itself was another suggestion of Luke's after I put forth a list of options involving dancing, cooking and wine/cheese/chocolate tasting. He was adamant that we'd have a hard time getting a group of single guys on a dating app to come to a "classy wine tasting".

Which, I have to say, does make sense in retrospect.

"It's about the community center," he says now, running a hand through his hair and shaking out the ends. My heart drops a little at the serious note in his voice. "We've been doing more digging into Mirror Valley's finances, and things are worse than expected."

I swallow. "How do you mean?"

"Whatever's causing these discrepancies... well, it's not good. If things continue, Mirror Valley will be in huge amounts of debt and could eventually, in an extreme case, become insolvent. The Mayor has put out orders to halt new construction, cut back on landscaping costs, and pause all upcoming projects. It's a mess."

"But how is this happening?"

"We're not sure yet. A ton of people have been looped into this; even Mr. Argent is involved. It doesn't add up."

I give my head a shake. "I had no idea Mirror Valley was having financial issues."

"It never has before. Every town has some debt, but this is new." His frown deepens, and he looks at me. "And that's what I have to tell you about the community center. They're talking about closing some public buildings next, starting with the ones that aren't particularly... well-patronized. The community center falls under that category. Even with the money made on the last event, and with the money we're projected to make next week, it won't be enough."

My stomach sinks all the way to the ground. So much

for scaling back. It feels like I've been running a marathon, and the starting line's been moved behind me. "So there's nothing we can do?"

I expect Luke to shake his head. To dole out the clichéd "we did everything we could", "it's already too late", and "let's just wrap this thing up and call it quits on the games night".

What I don't expect is the unexpected beam of hope in his next words. "I wouldn't say that; the decision's not final yet. Closing the center is up for discussion, but I'm not ready to throw in the towel if you're not."

I give my head a shake. "I'm not."

Luke nods once in response, and I can't help but notice the way that he manages to be upfront and honest, and yet gentle at the same time. It's certainly bad news, and I feel discouraged after the relative high of the Dinner in White, but Luke's got a special, unique way of making things seem like they might still turn out okay. He can appear grumpy on the surface, but the man's got layers. Layers on layers. I'm enjoying getting to see past them way too much.

But what's important right now is the community center, and what else we can do to make sure that those discussions don't turn into action. "Guess we better make sure the games night goes off without a hitch."

"I feel pretty confident about it. It was my idea, after all."

I give him another playful punch, and he chuckles, catching my fist and holding on for a moment.

He sits back on the couch with my hand in his, and turns it gently palm up. My insides turn to jelly as he starts to trace my skin, running the calloused tip of his index finger along the tender swells and dips of my palm lines. His fingers alight on a scar on the side of my ring finger. "What's this?" he asks.

"Had it since I was a kid." My voice is more uneven than I'd like. "Got it when I was helping some baby ducks."

Luke looks at me then, and I realize how close we are. His face is mere inches from mine, his eyes drawing me in like warm, forbidden caramel. They spark and dance in that way that makes my heartbeat spike. "Baby ducks, huh?"

"They were trapped on one side of a fence away from their mama, chirping away. There must've been about six of them, they were adorable." I'm rambling. I lost my brain somewhere around the time Luke took my hand, and I am now putty. "So I made them a little hole in the fence, but a piece of metal jabbed into my finger." I smile dryly. "Mom had to run me to the hospital for a tetanus shot, but as you can see, I survived."

"Thank goodness for that."

I chuckle, but the sound is breathless. Here we are again, face to face, leaning so far towards each other, we're practically glued together. And once again, I could *swear* that Luke wants to kiss me. His eyes are even glancing down to my lips right now...

I must be loopy. Too many painkillers, despite not taking any for the past couple days.

But this can't be happening, right?

"What're you doing?" I ask, my voice a whisper. A plea for him to stop, to release me, to quit toying with me.

"I'm thinking about trying something new."

"What kind of something new?"

Luke's eyes return to mine for one long, intense moment. "What it'd be like to kiss you."

Those words. His breath on my lips. That warm forest scent.

It's enough to send all of my blood racing through my body. I can no longer control my mouth. "You don't have to think about it."

Luke's pupils darken in a way that I've never seen them, and it sets my entire body alight. He slowly lifts his left hand, his fingers grazing my arm and creating electric shocks that feel like snowflakes hitting bare skin. I'm sitting upright, my spine ramrod straight. I'm ready for whatever comes next.

My mind goes hazy as his fingers trail up over my shoulder and across my collarbone, traveling with so much purpose, it's like he's thought about this. They finish their journey on my cheek, and he lightly traces my jawline, the shell of my ear. Shivers erupt on my skin, and I close my eyes.

"Dais, do you want me to kiss you?" he asks quietly. "Because I want to kiss you. But I won't do it unless you want it."

I can barely manage a response past the blaring YES in my head. I've never wanted anything so badly.

"I do." My words are a whisper. And then, through some inhuman display of self-control that I didn't know I had, I place a hand on his firm chest, keeping him at bay. "But I don't know if it's a good idea."

Ohmygosh. How am I doing this right now?

I finally understand the whole "Mom lifting a car off her baby" surge of strength thing.

Luke sits back a little. He doesn't seem angry or upset, just contemplative. "Because of Ivy," he guesses. "I get it. I'm sorry, Dais. I just can't stop thinking about you."

My brain wants to press pause on this whole moment. Immortalize it forever. *Luke Brooks wants to kiss me? He can't stop thinking about me? What?!*

But I push on. I need to say this now, or I might not ever. "Yes, Ivy. But also because what you said a few weeks ago."

He looks genuinely confused. "What did I say?"

"That you didn't want to date, that you were taking some time after Eleanor." I take a breath, and Luke opens his mouth to speak, but I hold up a hand. "The thing is, I'm worried that you're doing this now because we've been spending so much time together. Because you're thinking that you might want to try dating again, and you only want to be with me because we're both single and it's convenient."

Luke's mouth actually tilts up in an amused smirk. "That is not at all—"

"I can't be your convenient choice, Luke," I cut him off. "I just can't. So maybe it's best if you get out there. Date a little. Meet other fish in the sea."

Luke somehow looks *more* amused than before, which is not at all the reaction I expected from him. But then again, I never know what to expect with this man. "You're saying that you want me to date other people."

Am I saying that? Really?

If there were classes on self-destructive behavior, I should be teaching them. But I also don't think I'm wrong. There's a reason that "romance of convenience" isn't on my trope list.

"Yes I am," I say with more confidence than I feel.

"Okay. I'll find another date for the games night."

"And it has to be someone you would *seriously* want to date. I need you take this seriously."

"And who would I *seriously* want to take?"

With that question, everything comes full circle.

Because here I am, rejecting the only man I've ever loved after he said he wants to kiss me. And instead, I'm offering to play matchmaker to him.

This might be why you're single, Dais.

"Okay." My mouth feels full of cotton balls. "It needs to be someone you have lots in common with. Someone who shares your values and interests, who likes the same activities. Someone who has the same temperament as you."

Something flashes in Luke's eyes. A spark of a challenge. "Someone like... Dee?"

I blink, hardly believing what I just heard. "You want to date Dee?!"

"No. I want to date *you*. But if you want me to go to this games night with someone with my same temperament, it should probably be your sister. You always say we're both grouchy."

The challenge is alive and well in Luke's expression. Meanwhile, I feel like I've fallen down six flights of stairs into an entirely new dimension. Forget about a glitch in the matrix. We're no longer anywhere near the matrix.

But in some weird, backwards way, this almost makes sense. I know I can't be Luke's convenient choice, so games night is his chance to really consider who else he might want to date. Right now, he's joking about Dee, but the event is a week away, so that's plenty of time for him to consider his options, change his mind, and bring someone else.

And even if he *does* decide to bring Dee, I guess the good news is that I'd have the inside scoop on their relationship.

If they have one.

In the unlikely case that she says yes.

Okay, maybe I'm not completely cool with Luke dating her. I'm only human.

"Fine. Dee, it is."

"Fantastic." Luke smiles that full smile of his and extends his hand. I place mine in his and give it a firm shake, not allowing myself to remember the way he was tracing my palm mere moments ago.

19

LUKE

"All good?" I ask Dee as she settles into the passenger seat of my car.

"Yup."

I start the engine and pull away from the curb. Dee looks out the window towards her office on Main Street.

We both sit in silence. A comfortable, if a little strained, silence.

Which normally wouldn't bother me; I wouldn't think anything of it. But now, I'm remembering the last person to sit in that seat. I'm remembering the night of the Dinner in White, when Daisy started speaking from the minute she clipped into her seatbelt until I turned off the car. I'm remembering the day I brought her to the doctor so she could get her toe checked, and she kept insisting over and over that she was "fine".

I loved having Daisy in the passenger seat next to me. Loved the way her voice and laughter filled the car even as she munched through various messy food items. Which normally would bother me.

But once again, Daisy is the exception to anything "normal" in my life.

"Music?" Dee asks, and before I can stop her, she cranks up the volume.

"Super Trouper" blares through the speakers.

I clear my throat and switch off the cassette player. *Note to self: stop playing ABBA before someone gets into your car.* "Sorry. Don't know what that's about."

"I do." Dee smirks. "You're listening to ABBA. Tell me, do you often sing along?"

I press my lips into a line. "No." Then, under my breath. "Not often."

Dee didn't seem to catch that last part, and she looks out the window again as I switch to a country station. The strums of a guitar fill the car, and I lean my left elbow on the windowsill, biting my pinky nail.

In all honesty, I can't believe I'm here right now, picking up Dee.

Because when I asked her to come to the games night with me... she said *yes*.

I was teasing Daisy when I pitched Dee to be my date. Truth is, I already know how I feel, and there are no other fish in the sea for me. I want to be with Daisy. I want to win her heart. And if she wants me to go on a date with someone else to do so, I'll play by her rules. I'll do what makes her feel comfortable.

So I did what I could over the last week to convince her, pretended to really consider who else I might want to take to the games night, when really, it could only be her. At the last minute, I finally asked Dee, fully expecting her to say no.

The look on Daisy's face when she heard Dee's actual answer confirmed that neither of us were expecting it.

"You can relax."

Dee's voice startles me, and I release my pinky to look her way. "What?"

158

"Relax. I know this isn't a serious thing tonight."

I return my left hand to the steering wheel. "What do you mean?"

"I know you have no intention of taking this seriously. You're into Daisy. Anyone with an eyeball and half a brain can see that. So take it easy, I'm not expecting you to sweep me off my feet, or make grand gestures, or even flirt with me." Then, she adds. "You should know I'd shut you down *so hard* if you tried."

I snort. Shake my head. "I don't doubt that you would."

Dee gives a smirk and looks out the window again.

My brow furrows as something occurs to me. "Is that why you said yes?"

"To what?"

"Going out with me tonight. You knew it was a low risk option. You knew nothing would come of it." I frown, recognizing this behavior pattern in myself and my own recent past.

"I guess that's part of it," she says lightly. "It's about time Daisy gets her head on straight, and I figured seeing you on a date with someone else might push her in the right direction."

"And the other part of it?"

"That, my friend, is none of your beeswax."

I smirk. "So there *is* something else going on."

"No, nothing. There's just... well, I..."

She trails off, and I stay quiet, don't prompt her to go on. I don't want to pry, and if Dee doesn't want to tell me the truth, all the power to her. I certainly understand wanting to keep your life private.

"I might be a little interested in someone, and I'm curious to see if he shows up tonight."

She says the words on a quick exhale, one word tumbling over another. I keep my gaze focused on the road.

I doubt that Daisy knows about this—she always says that Dee is proudly and happily single. That she's completely independent with no need or desire for a relationship.

"Now before you go off and tell my sister that I have a crush," Dee adds, apparently reading my mind. "You should know that I have friends in high places. And Noah can seriously make your life difficult at Argent."

"Are you threatening me?" I ask, amused more than anything.

"Never." Her voice is sweet as sugar. "Consider it a friendly warning. A preview of pranks to come, if you will."

I chuckle. The Griffiths sisters could not be more different, and yet some similarities do shine through... Like their penchant for upsetting my daily routines.

"Anyway." Dee lets out a sigh. "I figured I'd come out with you tonight. See if a bit of old-fashioned jealousy might do the trick."

"You've thought about this."

"Not at all," she says too quickly. "These are just things that I've picked up in movies and books. You know, while doing research for my role at RightMatch, of course."

"Of course." I glance at Dee, and she's fiddling with the ends of her hair. She doesn't know that I'm looking, and her expression is one I've never seen on her before—unguarded and almost vulnerable. I look away before she can catch me.

But my thoughts churn. Dee has her eye on someone who might be at the games night tonight, same as I do. Because Daisy will be there, and I'm sure she'll be watching. Her doctor gave her the all-clear to come to the event with a couple of stipulations: One, that she takes it easy and takes frequent breaks. And two, that she wear a moon boot.

Yup. Like one of those clunky casts.

Daisy seemed less than thrilled with the idea, but she insisted on being at the event herself given that the games require some coordination. She drove over to the community center earlier this evening with Fran, Mrs. Perez, and all of the materials.

Up to this point, I figured that Dee and I would go our separate ways at the event, or at the very least, that we'd all hang out together.

But hearing Dee's news gives me an idea.

"Dee, what if we play into this tonight?" I suggest. "What if we make it seem like we're having a good time together, like we're actually going all-in on this date thing?"

She lifts a brow. "Are you suggesting that we do a fake dating scheme?"

My nose crinkles. "If it has to have a term, I guess it could be that."

Dee pauses for a moment. Smiles. "I'm in."

20

DAISY

Well, I've done it.

I, Daisy Elena Faith Griffiths, have reached my full potential. Gone to entirely new heights, in fact. I am at my peak level of attractiveness. Right here, right now.

I made it to the games night, so there's a plus, and the gymnasium in the community center is full to bursting. Fran's actually standing at the door with a clicker thing counting newcomers to make sure we don't commit any fire code violations.

But while everyone mills around in their cute date-night outfits, looking all sporty and flirty, I'm wearing a calf-length, striped, flannel dress with long sleeves that I had stowed away at the back of my closet from the Halloween party I went to as Ebenezer Scrooge (Ivy went as the Ghost of Christmas Future, so our costumes together actually made sense).

This glorified nightgown was my only option for tonight. I couldn't wear pants or shorts, I don't have a long skirt, and all of my other dresses are short and summery.

As in, not suited to the cold snap blowing through Mirror Valley.

So here I am, dressed as Scrooge and hobbling around in the world's most awkward moon boot. The doctor suggested I wear one tonight "as a precaution", and I might precaution him that I will be kicking his butt the next time I see him. All the more because they didn't have any boots in my size (of course) except for this hulking blue one for men.

The cherry on top of the attractiveness cake is the way I'm currently shoveling pretzels into my mouth like I don't have a care in the world.

Except that I do have a care. One very big care.

And that is Luke Brooks mingling his way through the crowd with my little sister on his arm.

Yes. Dee has her arm linked through Luke's, and they're laughing together. *Laughing.*

What was I thinking, okaying this date of theirs? Never in a million years did I think Dee would say yes. Not only is the girl not interested in dating point-blank, but she's never shown even a shadow of interest in Luke.

Why *did* she say yes?

In any case, I know that, logically, I have no reason to be freaking out right now. I told Luke that he should find other fish. But unfortunately, I'm only now realizing that I want to be his one and only fish. Or if we're going with underwater creatures, his lobster—per Phoebe Buffay.

I've been scared of Luke realizing that he could have anyone else, so I pushed him away. Pushed him to do the very thing I was most afraid of. And clearly, I'm an idiot because if it wasn't obvious before, it is now...

I've fallen for Luke Brooks all over again. Fallen so deep, I'm not even sure which way is up. The thought of him making dinner for someone else, reading on the couch next to someone else, getting all sweet and vulnerable with someone else...

It makes my toes curl. If my toes could curl.

"You should be kissed, and often."

I startle. The words, so tender and romantic, are said so...

Flatly.

"Hello, Ed." I sigh, turning around.

Eddie gives me a pressed-lip smile as he points to the piece of paper taped to my dress. "'And by someone who knows how'," he reads. "*Gone with the Wind.*"

I smirk. "You know your romance movies."

"Used to watch a lot of them before..." He trails off, and his mouth slides into a grimace. "Looks like we're matched up, huh?"

I look between our sheets of paper, which together create the entire quote from *Gone with the Wind*. Of course I'd be matched with Eddie, of all people. "Looks like it."

This game is one of the many activities we've organized as part of tonight's festivities. Luke and I wanted to make the singles event as fun and low-pressure as possible (yes, Luke even said the word "fun"!), so we organized a mix of activities for everyone, from ping pong tables and a mini-golf course, to speed dating and musical chairs. "Competitive socializing" is what Luke called it.

This movie quote game is a classic Meet your Match icebreaker. On arrival, everyone receives half of a movie quote instead of a nametag, and the goal is to mix and mingle in order to find the other half of your quote by the end of the night.

Clearly, Eddie didn't want to wait that long.

"So do I get, like, a prize or something?" he asks. "And don't say that my name will be put into a raffle. I always lose raffles. One time..."

Eddie goes on, but I've stopped listening. Behind his head, Fran is approaching Luke and Dee. She kisses them

164

both on the cheeks and shakes their hands excitedly. Luke and Dee lean close together, laughing along with her.

They *look* like a happy couple.

"That's why I'll never trust another one of those swan floaties," Eddie finishes. He snaps his fingers in front of my eyes. "Daisy? Hello? That's nice, zoning out in the middle of a conversation."

I give my head a shake. "I'm so sorry, Eddie. You're right, that was very rude of me. I just…" At that exact moment, Luke looks over and catches me blatantly staring. "Eek!"

On instinct, I duck down behind Eddie, grab his shoulders, and re-position him so he's blocking me from Luke's view. I vaguely remember Ivy joking about doing this sort of thing around her old crush, Cam, and her now husband, James. I finally understand it.

Eddie does not.

"What're you doing?" he squawks.

"Can you stand on your toes?" I whisper. He's a little shorter than me at the best of times, and the dreaded moon boot gives me another inch or two.

"You're being weird."

I refrain from pointing out that the last time we saw each other, he spent the evening hiding in rosebushes.

I peek out from behind Eddie's shoulder and see that Luke and Dee have disappeared. "Phew, I think we're good." I finally give him my full attention. "To answer your question, there is no prize, but there's a goodie bag for everyone at the back of the gym."

His eyes light up. "Great!"

But he doesn't walk away, and it occurs to me how odd it is that Eddie's at this games night in the first place. "What're you doing here, anyway? Did you hear about this on RightMatch?"

"What's RightMatch?" He frowns. "I was at McGarry's and overheard that there was an event tonight, and I thought I'd come by in case... you know..."

He trails off, and I follow his gaze to the other end of the gymnasium, where Courtney is laughing with a group of women.

My eyes widen. "Ed, have you not talked to her?"

"No way. Not after I completely embarrassed both myself and her at the wedding. I don't know how she could ever forgive me. I just... miss her."

I follow his gaze back to Courtney, then get an idea.

"Wait here," I tell Eddie.

I hobble all the way across the gymnasium as fast as I possibly can. Luckily, people seem to be aware of the Scrooge look-a-like on a mission, and so I'm able to get through the crowd pretty quickly. By the time I reach Courtney, I'm panting a little.

"Sorry to interrupt, ladies." I give the group a quick smile and place a hand on Courtney's arm. "Can I speak with you?"

She looks a little alarmed—which is understandable—but agrees. I pull her aside, towards a quiet corner where we're half-hidden behind an old football whiteboard that's been refitted as a makeshift "pin the ponytail on the celebrity".

"What's up?" she asks, her eyes blinking slowly behind her glasses.

I hesitate for a moment. Courtney and I know each other in passing and have spoken only a handful of times. I would call us friendly acquaintances, so I don't know that she's going to appreciate me prying into her love life. "I'm going to apologize in advance for being nosy, and you should absolutely feel free to ignore me, but tonight's event is kind of perfect for this sort of thing, so I wanted to give it a shot."

"Okay..."

"You remember Ivy and James's wedding?"

She beams. "Of course, I do."

"And you remember the speech Eddie gave?"

At this, her cheeks turn bright red. She nods.

"Here's the thing. Eddie's clearly into you—some might say that he's crazy about you. I mean, the guy gave a drunken speech at someone else's wedding... for you. So, if you don't mind my asking, how do you feel about him?"

Courtney pauses for a long moment, and I wonder if she might tell me to get lost—which she has every right to do. I don't want to poke my nose where it doesn't belong or offend anyone, but in this case, I do think some mild meddling might be helpful.

Finally, she exhales. "I miss him," she says tearfully. "Jeff misses him, too. He wails through the evenings, which is when he used to play with Eddie's feet. I'm still crazy about him, but how can I go back to him? I can't just strike up a conversation and say that I miss him."

Ding ding ding!

A smile breaks across my lips. "Well... why not start with something a little easier?"

I unpin the sheet of paper from my dress and hand it to Courtney.

"Go get him." I wink.

Courtney reads the half-line and beams. She tacks the paper onto her blouse and disappears into the crowd. I watch her go, feeling happy that something good came out of tonight despite the fact that I stupidly sent my crush on a date with my little sister.

Speaking of... I can't see either of them anywhere. Though I do see a crowd gathering around Noah by one of the basketball shooting machines, cheering him on. What is Noah doing here anyway?

"Anyone ever tell you that you make a beautiful Grinch?"

I would jump in surprise, but my moon boot holds me in place. "Argh!" I grunt instead. Which only adds to the Bah Humbug vibe of the evening. I half-turn to see Luke standing next to me, smirking down at me. "The Grinch is green and hairy, thank you very much. I'm pretty sure you mean Scrooge."

"That's the one."

His eyes still on mine, he reaches an arm out beside me just in time for a guy who isn't paying attention to stumble and knock right into it. It's like instinct, like he knew without looking that the guy was coming our way and that he could take me down.

But instead of acknowledging this very smooth move, Luke looks out towards the crowd. Did he even register what just happened? "Nice thing you did for Courtney and Ed."

I clear my throat, altogether a bit ruffled. "Yeah. It was the perfect opportunity to get those two talking. To break the ice, if you will."

"This is the night for it."

"That's what I said!"

Luke smirks at my enthusiasm, and I have to giggle.

And there is it again—the skipping heartbeat, the butterflies in my stomach, the warm, bubbly feeling spreading out through my limbs like after a relaxing bubble bath... My body clearly isn't aware that Luke is on a date with my sister. It's skipping entirely past that small detail and going straight for the, "oh wow, his eyes are gorgeous" part of the evening.

Luckily, my brain is still online and functional, and I

lean away from him slightly. "What're you doing all the way over here? Where's Dee?"

"I lost her somewhere around the mini-golf. There's someone she wanted to talk to over there."

My eyebrows shoot up. "Like a guy?!"

Luke mimes locking his lips with a key.

"That's entirely unhelpful."

He purses his lips with amusement and seems to consider something. Then, he shrugs. "I don't want to get in the middle of this, but suffice it to say that Dee isn't here for *me* tonight."

I blink, trying to process this. Because if Dee didn't say yes because she's actually interested in Luke—if Dee is interested in someone else instead—well, that means...

This isn't a real date, after all.

Play it cool, Dais.

"So Dee *is* into someone!" I cheer. "I need details! Who is he? Where is he? What's the story?"

Luke shakes his head and raises his hands in surrender. "You'll have to go to Dee for the details."

"Wow, that was some disappointing gossip." I tut. "You're gonna have to up your game to be part of the Mirror Valley rumor mill, Luke Brooks."

At my teasing tone, he smiles, and it turns into a laugh. The light, carefree, entirely rare laugh of his that makes my already racing heart pick up more speed. And it's now coupled with a heavy dose of weak knees. I shouldn't be this happy to hear that Luke and Dee's date was a sham. I shouldn't be so happy that Luke came to find me as soon as he could, and yet...

I really, really am.

Luke looks at me, and I look at him, and I remember having his face so close to mine the other night. The way his eyes darkened, his breath brushing my lips when he asked if I wanted to kiss him...

The answer is yes. An unabashed, unashamed, totally sincere Yes.

He could kiss me right here if he wanted to.

"You okay, Dais?" Luke's voice has gone deep and husky. He's standing so close, I can physically feel the pull between our bodies.

"I'm fine," I manage.

"You're blushing."

"Am not."

He chuckles and raises a hand towards my face. Tucks my hair behind my ear. "You really do look beautiful tonight, even as a limping Scrooge."

"You're just saying that to be nice."

"How many times do I have to say it?" His words are said on a low growl that makes my heart rate spike. "I'm not that nice."

"You're always nice to me."

"I'm *only* nice to you."

His fingers trace my cheek, and it's weird to me that anyone seeing this right now might think this is a sweet moment. Might think nothing of it. But being this close to Luke with his hands on my face feels like the opposite of nothing.

The gymnasium just got a whole lot warmer, and I'm regretting my flannel Scrooge dress for an entirely different reason now.

"So, do you believe me now?" he asks.

"Believe what?"

"That the only person I want to date here is you." He gives his head a little shake. "Daisy, don't you know that you're the exception to everything I've ever thought to be true about myself? You steal my cookies, and you poke fun at me, and you have ridiculous opinions about my favorite movies. If it was anyone else, I don't know what I'd do, but it could never *be* anyone else because they're not you."

My breath catches. His right hand returns to my face and travels behind my neck. His touch is so gentle yet firm.

"I might've said once that I didn't want to date," he says quietly. "But once again, you're breaking that rule, too. The exception is you."

I can hardly breathe. My chest is aching. Those words... those sweet words are somehow exactly what I needed to hear. An echo from my own heart.

"You can kiss me now," I say, because what else could I possibly say? Maybe this way, I can show him what his words mean to me.

But Luke shakes his head. "I'm going to take you on a date first. I want to do this right."

I nod jerkily, my body buzzing. I've never wanted anything so badly, and here Luke is being the perfect gentleman. No surprises there. "We should wait until Ivy's back."

"Yup." Luke's eyes are on my lips again. "She's coming back tonight?"

"In a few hours."

He steps away slightly, and I step away, too. The air feels cooler away from him, and everyone in the gymnasium is going about their conversations like nothing happened. But something definitely happened. Because Luke Brooks wants to ask me out, and I'm going to say yes.

And then, I'm going to kiss the face off him.

"Well," he says. "If I can't ask you on a date yet, can I at least ask you to dance?"

I screw up my face. "Two problems... No dance floor, and I have a massive boot that prevents most graceful movement."

Luke takes my hand. "Minor issues."

He leads me slowly just a few paces away, close to the DJ booth. There's a tiny square of floor that isn't occupied, so he turns to me, takes one of my hands in his, and places the other around my waist, drawing me close.

We begin to sway together. One by one, I feel my defenses release, and I let myself relax into his arms. I lean my head on his chest and revel in this moment. His forest scent is all around me, his body firm against mine, and there's a steady vibration in his chest as he hums along quietly. What the song is, I can't tell, but it feels like we're hitting the beats just right.

I close my eyes and let myself be lead. And it occurs to me that we're doing it—Luke and I are dancing together. It feels like a stupid teenage dream coming true, but also so much more than that. I'm Luke's exception, but he's also mine.

My state of inner bliss is so complete that, when the voice calls my name, I don't even register it at first. Can't even fully comprehend what's happening.

Until it speaks again, and I realize that I know said voice very, very well.

"Isn't this a surprise?"

Daisy's gone still in my arms.

And I'm frozen, my heart on pause, as I stare in shock at the two people I least expected to see here.

"Ivy, James." My voice is robotic. "You're back."

My little sister has her hands on her hips. She's wearing the glasses that magnify her eyes by a factor of a hundred, black leggings, and a gray soccer hoodie that's way too big. James towers next to her, dressed in black track pants and a zip-up. His hair's ruffled, and he looks more than a little groggy.

Not to mention more than a little *smug*.

"Surprise," Ivy says dryly. She's usually easy to read, but I can't tell what she's thinking right now.

"Our flight came in early," James explains. "Ivy was missing you guys, and my parents mentioned that there some big event happening tonight, so we decided to drop by on the way home." He shrugs, a wicked smirk on his lips. "Glad we did."

I shoot my best friend a glare as Daisy steps out of my arms. "Iv, I don't know what you're thinking right now, but—"

At that moment, Ivy spots Daisy's hobbling, and her expression finally changes. She runs forward to grab Daisy's elbow. "Your foot! What happened?! And why are you wearing your old Halloween costume?"

I raise a hand sheepishly. "That was my bad. She dropped some weights on her foot at the fitness center, and..."

Daisy holds up a hand to shush me—yes, *shush* me. "Not his fault. I was carrying too many weights at once, and they weren't well balanced. Anyway. It's just a toe bruise, I'll be fine." Daisy pastes on a winning grin. "Enough about us. You're back! How was the honeymoon and how was England? I missed you!"

Daisy throws her arms around my sister, and Ivy giggles for a second before apparently coming to her senses. "No, you don't. I need to know what's happening..." She gestures between the two of us. "*Here*."

"Well, it's a games night," Daisy replies innocently, blinking her blue eyes. Ivy raises a brow, clearly not having it, and Daisy exhales. "Oh, you mean the whole Luke and I dancing together thing?"

She meets my eyes, her lips pressed in a line, and I give a shrug. We've been caught, and we both know it. And though this isn't the ideal way for Ivy to find out, I'm obviously eager to tell her about Daisy and me.

"Luke and I are..." Daisy's lips form a small smile. "I don't know what to call it."

I step forward and take her hand, and she leans instinctively into me. "We are in the pre-date phase."

"Romantic," James says.

"We want to date," Daisy clarifies. "But we wanted to speak with you first. Ideally not at a matchmaking event with all these people around and me dressed as Scrooge."

She closes her eyes for a brief moment, seems to collect herself. "I would like to date your brother."

Daisy's hand is squeezing mine, and I feel the nervous energy coming off her in waves. Ivy's been her best friend for years; is basically her family. I understand why she's stressed and anxious right now. How risky this might feel.

As for me, this doesn't feel like a risk anymore. Or at the very least, the potential reward of being with Daisy feels very much worth any risks. I hold tight onto Daisy, bringing her closer, as I give a smirk. "And I fully intend to date your best friend."

Ivy shoots me a quizzical look. "I thought you said that you had no interest in dating."

I catch Daisy's eyes. "I'm making an exception."

Daisy grins, and my heart beats extra hard. I have a strong sense memory of having her in my arms just moments ago, the smell of her sweet shampoo calming me. I meant what I said earlier—she's the most beautiful woman in the room, even in her Christmas grouch outfit.

Everything about standing up next to her like this feels right.

"Are you guys serious about this?" Ivy's voice is so stern that I barely recognize it. Her face could be carved of stone —flat eyes, pinched mouth, chin tilted up. "This isn't, like, one of Daisy's listicles?" Daisy shoots Ivy a surprised look. "Luke, you're not rebounding?"

I give a very solid shake of my head. "Absolutely not. This is real, Iv."

I feel more than see Daisy nod. She grips onto my hand even tighter, leaning further into me. It's a reflexive movement, and I probably shouldn't feel so happy in this tense moment... but I'm the one she's leaning on for support. I release her hand to put my arm around her waist.

Then, Ivy cracks. "Finally!"

Before Daisy or I can react, Ivy lunges forward and throws her arms around us.

"Took you guys long enough," she trills. "I was hoping this would happen while we were away!"

"She really was," James mutters. "It became a central topic of conversation at breakfast."

Ivy releases us with glistening eyes and skips back to James, and they share a fist bump before she wraps her arms around his waist. He places a kiss on her head, and they both stare at us with matching smug expressions.

"What're you talking about?" Daisy asks.

"My goodness, I saw this coming ever since we got engaged last year. I was just waiting for you two to come around. I thought setting Daisy up with Edgar at our wedding might be enough to push you in the right direction."

Daisy's jaw drops further. "You did *what*?!"

"Well, it worked didn't it?" Ivy cackles maniacally. "A little taste of your own medicine, Dais. We even had a bet going."

"You had a bet," I repeat, looking at James.

"Sure did. And you were right, Brooks. Looks like I'll be making you iced chais for the next week."

Ivy giggles, and I shake my head at my best friend. "So you bet against us getting together."

"I bet against the timeline." James chuckles. "I thought it would take you a heck of a lot longer to get your head out of your a—"

"But now that you *have*," Ivy interrupts. "We're so happy for you two! How did it happen? Luke, when did you fall for Daisy? And Daisy, what made you fall for Luke? And what's this whole matchmaking thing about? I want details!"

Daisy and I share another look, and I reach for her hand. It fits within mine so comfortably, her palm soft and warm, and our fingers interlace. "It's a long story," Daisy says. "I'll tell you later. I'm sure you and James want to get home."

"I do," James says swiftly, as Ivy stifles a yawn. "It's 4am our time, and we could use some sleep. My wife here was talking my ear off the entire flight about her plans for the Brookrose."

Ivy smacks his arm. "Don't pretend you weren't just as bad with the World Cup coming up."

He meets her teasing glare and then gives her a quick kiss. "Meet you in the car."

James gives us a wave goodbye, then saunters off into the crowd. The gazes of more than a few women trail after him, but I know Ivy's is the only one that counts.

She turns back to Daisy and me. "I'll see you both tomorrow, and we can talk about whatever this is. But know that I'm very happy for you. I'm loving everything about Duke. Or Laisy."

Daisy's lips tilt in a smile. "Let's say Duke."

"Perfect. And that barely sounds like an infectious disease."

What?

Ivy winks, hugs us both once more, and then disappears.

Daisy shyly reaches for my hand again, and I pull her towards me, lacing my arms behind her back as she lets out a giggle. "Where were we," I say.

She places her palms on my chest, but something's different now. People are looking our way, no doubt curious about Ivy and James's sudden appearance and disappearance. I could swear that I'm hearing little mutters and whispers, and I can imagine the rumor mill starting up again, taking this private moment and making it theirs.

177

Judging by the way Daisy isn't fully relaxed in my arms, she feels it too.

"I have an idea," I mutter.

I take her hand and lead her around behind the DJ booth to an even quieter area by the gym's bleachers. It's a small, cramped space with not much light and the faint smell of disinfectant, but at least no one else is around.

Daisy lets out a giggle. "Might be hard to dance here."

"That's true." For some reason, we're both whispering.

We're pressed together in the small space, and Daisy leans her head onto my chest once again. I place my chin lightly on top of her head, happy enough to be simply standing here with her for the moment.

"So Ivy knows."

"She does," I reply.

"And the world didn't explode."

"It did not." I shake my head. "I can't believe they made a bet on us."

I feel Daisy's smile against my chest, right above where my heart is beating. "I can."

Her fingers trail up my arms absentmindedly, making gooseflesh rise on my skin. She tangles her fingers in the hair at the nape of my neck. I vowed I wouldn't kiss her before our date, but there are a few things that are still fair game. I push her hair to the side and place a soft kiss on her neck.

"Luke, you said you make exceptions for me, right?"

"I do."

She pulls back to meet my gaze, and there's an intensity swirling in her eyes. My heart slams in my chest, and my arms tighten around her. I know what she's really asking, and I feel an inner fight between following the rules—following a plan—and doing what feels right. What feels perfect now, in this moment. But if Daisy's taught me anything, it's that sometimes it's worth throwing out the rulebook.

So I gently place one hand on her cheek, and the other behind her back. I lead her backwards so she's pressed against the wall, and she winds her hands behind my neck.

Then, I kiss her. It's a soft kiss at first, gentle and tender, but it becomes something else entirely. There's no gymnasium full of people a few steps away. No crash and clatter as someone in the distance wins a game.

It's just me and Daisy and this moment. This culmination of something big and indescribable.

Time warps so I can't say whether we're moving quickly or slowly. My hands graze her cheeks, tangle into her hair, trail down her arms. She moves her fingers across my shoulders with so much purpose and intent, like she's thought about doing this before.

The same way I've been unable to stop thinking about my lips on hers, just like this.

This kiss is the sweetest surrender. The laying down of every weapon I've ever had at her feet. Every wall I might've built around my heart crumbles, and any notion I might have had to fight against falling for her disappears with it.

Daisy has me. Whether she wants to or not.

I'm tuned in to everything about this moment. Everything about her. I feel every brush of her fingers on my skin, the tickle of her hair as I release her mouth to kiss down her neck, the heat where our bodies meet. She smells like a calm meadow and soap and the slightest hint of perfume. It's my favorite scent.

When we break apart, her cheeks are flushed pink. She has this hazy, starry look in her eyes that I'm sure I'm mirroring. Her breaths are coming in small gasps, matching mine and the beat of my racing heart.

I have no words. So I press my forehead to hers.

"Wow," is all I can say.

"Wow," is all she says back.

22

DAISY

When Luke Brooks kissed me, it was nothing like I imagined.

Because I never could've predicted how his hands would feel—one on my cheek, the other locked around me as he slowly backed me up against the wall. The way his mouth would so easily claim mine with no resistance on my part. The way the world slowed down for us so that I could relish every single second.

No. It was better than anything I could've dreamed.

And maybe that's why I left him standing by the DJ booth while I hobbled off to deal with a "games issue". Maybe that's why I caught a ride home with Fran before I could see him or talk to him. And maybe that's why I haven't answered any of his texts since last night.

Knock knock.

The sound startles me, and I sit up so abruptly, the papers, pencils, and yarn spread across my lap fall to the floor. I was meant to be disassembling some of the materials from last night, but who am I kidding? I was lost in daydream-land.

Knock Knock!

What if it's Luke?

The sound's more insistent now, and I can't ignore it. Even if it is Luke, I'm still technically couch-bound, so he'll know I'm home.

Knock knock knock.

It's probably Noah. Dee's upstairs watching YouTube or something, and Noah isn't exactly the most patient of beings. With that thought, I rise from the couch.

"Coming," I mutter under my breath. But when I get to the door, I pause for a moment, just in case. "Who is it?" I holler.

"You know who!"

Warmth spreads through my body, and a smile breaks across my face as I throw open the door. Ivy practically flattens me with a hug, giggling maniacally as she does. "What? No *Harry Potter* jokes?!"

"You didn't let me get to it," I retort with a laugh.

We finally release each other, and Ivy hands me a square tin with the Union Jack on it. "Present for you, all the way from England."

"Ooh! Iv, you shouldn't have... But what is it?" I go to shake the tin, and Ivy places a hand on my arm. "Shortbread biscuits and tea, but don't move them around too much or the cookies will crumble! You have no idea the lengths I went to just to make sure that these got to you safe and sound." Ivy shivers. "James got hungry when we were on the train, and I had to sit on these to make sure he didn't get to them."

"Well, I appreciate your seat-cookies." I laugh, hugging my friend again, and then wobbling towards the kitchen to make up a plate of snacks for us.

"Let me help you!" Ivy goes to follow me, but I raise a hand.

"I got it."

She hesitates for a moment before perching on the edge of the couch. "Looks like you're getting around better than you did last night," she says.

"I'm getting used to this thing." I gesture to my boot. "Plus, if it means that I can exit damsel-in-distress territory and be a regular, old run-of-the-mill damsel with a limp, all the better. Guess you could say I'm *over the moon* for the moon boot."

"How long have you been waiting to use that on someone?"

"Pretty much the whole morning. Thought Dee would be the one to hear it first."

"Aren't I lucky."

I chuckle as I place a few cookies on a plate, along with some fudge and other sweets left over from one of Dee and Noah's volleyball meets. I make my way back into the living room and place the plate on the coffee table before collapsing next to her.

She stares at me quizzically for a few long moments.

"What?" I ask.

"You know what." Ivy tucks a leg up under her, eyes sparkling with excitement. "I've been up since 5am wanting to hear about what *you've* been up to since I've been on my honeymoon. And yes, part of that was jetlag, but the other part was seeing you and my brother dancing together all cozy-like. So, spill!"

"Are we talking about Daisy and Luke?"

Of course. Dee is skipping downstairs holding an empty bowl from her breakfast.

"We are!" Ivy waves for her to join us.

Just what I need. Tweedle Dee and Tweedle Ivy quizzing me.

I roll my eyes sarcastically. "Join us. The more the merrier."

Dee apparently didn't pick up on my tone, or she didn't care, because she pulls up a chair. "Don't mind if I do."

She places the chair next to the couch and leans forward so that both she and Ivy are staring at me like curious owls. I grimace. "I feel like I'm being interrogated."

"You are. So how long has this been going on?"

"I can answer that," Dee pipes up before I can say anything. "At least a couple of weeks. Maybe three. Luke's been over here, like, every day taking care of Daisy and her toe."

Ivy's eyes are practically bugging out of her head. "He *has*?"

I shift on the couch a little. "He's been great. Making me dinner and keeping me company."

"That's nice of him," Ivy says with this smirking, knowing tone.

"Yeah. He was just... here." I smile.

"And?" Dee leans forward all the more. "Are you gonna talk about the kiss?"

My cheeks flare red. At the same moment, Ivy and I both shout, "What?!" with a special chorus of "How did you know that?!" on my part.

Dee rolls her eyes tiredly. "Please, you two are so obvious. You came out from behind the bleachers last night all starry-eyed and red-faced. Obviously, you kissed."

Ivy's eyes might actually pop out of her head. "The bleachers? Starry-eyed? What?!"

I give my head a shake, trying to catch up. It isn't that I intended to keep the kiss a secret, but I'm still trying to wrap my own head around it and what it means.

"Have you kissed before?" Ivy asks.

"No. We wanted to keep things friendly until we could talk to you. Neither of us wanted to do anything that would hurt you."

Ivy half-smiles and places a hand on my wrist. "That was stupid. Kind, but stupid."

I roll my eyes.

"I'm not buying it." Dee snorts.

"Buying what?" I ask.

"This whole thing." Dee waves towards me. "I get that you were worried about Ivy and yadda yadda yadda, but there's something else up with you, Dais. I can feel it."

I open my mouth to defend myself, but no words come out. Because the truth is, Dee's right. Not in the words she used and in the way she put them, obviously. But in a broader sense, she made a good point all those days ago. A point I've been finding it progressively harder to ignore...

And just like that, all the doubts and fears that have been nagging at me come to a head like shadows gathering to form darkness.

"Dais?" Ivy asks me imploringly.

At some point, I started holding my breath, and now my lungs ache. My thoughts are churning and racing and spilling over, and I have to let go. My words come out on a long exhale. "I don't know if I can do this..."

"Do what?" Ivy asks. "Be with Luke?"

"No, I can definitely be with Luke. I want to be with Luke," I say, and I almost start laughing. "I've wanted to be with Luke."

Ivy frowns in confusion. "What're you saying?"

I exhale a long breath. It's time for me to be honest with my best friend.

I pick up my scrunchie from the side table and fiddle with it. "Look, Iv, there's something I've never told you. I had a crush on Luke a long time ago."

Ivy's eyebrows pop up. "You did?"

Next to me, Dee looks smug. I can almost hear her *I knew it!*

"Yeah, I fell for him back in high school. You know the deal—he was the hot, smart soccer player who was nice to everyone." I laugh dryly. "But I don't know, there was something about him, something else... He was different, and interesting, and he made me laugh." I shake my head. "But of course, he started dating Eleanor, and so I tamped all of those feelings down. Rejected them. He was the one person I couldn't fall for. The one person who was totally off-limits."

I watch Ivy's face carefully, and she just looks surprised. Which is fair. It feels like a hollow win that I managed to keep my feelings a secret over the years. "Why didn't you tell me?" she asks.

"Your family meant a lot to me when we were growing up. I didn't want to rock the boat, didn't want to cause any problems or rifts. And it felt like such a minor issue. You were—you *are*—my best friend, and so you came first. I knew you were having a hard time without your parents, and then there was the James drama, so my little crush felt like such a blip."

Ivy shakes her head adamantly. "Daisy, how you feel is *never* just a blip to me. You're my best friend, too. I'm sorry you felt you couldn't talk to me, but I'm here now, and I want to listen. I want to be there for you."

Her voice is filled with this genuine passion, and my heart twists to hear it. I pull my best friend into a hug. "Thank you, Ivy."

"So why are you saying you can't do this?" Dee asks.

"I always believed that there was no possibility of Luke and me. I was dating, trying to find someone else, someone new. I made it my mission to find another man who inspired those feelings in me. I had so many hopes." I smile feebly. "And how insane is it that I *did* finally find someone on a dating app, and—"

Ivy's eyes go wide. "Wait. Dating app? Are you talking about Aaron?"

Dee mutters out the side of her mouth, "Aaron is Luke."

Ivy looks even more stunned.

I'm fidgeting with the scrunchie, twisting it around my fingers. "Yup. Well, things are actually happening between us now, and it feels too good to be true, you know? It feels like my teenage dreams are becoming reality, like I'm having my happily-ever-after, but all I can think is... what happens after?"

"After what?"

"After the happily-ever-after. After you fall for someone, and they fall for you, and have the most amazing kiss of your life. After you have everything you want. How can you not be terrified of losing it all?"

Dee and Ivy share a quick glance, and Ivy places a hand on my knee. "Daisy. You *know* the happily-ever-after isn't the end of the story. It never is. Relationships take work, and they can be messy and difficult, and they're going to pull stuff out of you that you wished you'd never have to show anyone. But honestly? All those tough moments make life even sweeter. Because someone else sees and loves that most honest, raw, vulnerable side of you."

"But how can you know that things won't fall apart?"

"You don't and can't know. You just have to have faith and believe in your own love story. Believe that everything will work out in the end."

I twist my lips. "That sounds risky."

Dee laughs a short and sudden laugh. "Daisy, your entire life is believing the best of situations. So why not believe the best in this one?"

My mouth screws up even more. My scrunchie is tied in a knot that I don't think I'll ever be able to undo. "It doesn't feel so simple, not after training myself to think and feel a

187

certain way for years. And I know, I *know*, it isn't fair to Luke. He's gone above and beyond, he's shown me how much he cares at every turn. But I can't help but wonder when the other shoe's going to drop."

There's a moment of silence, and Ivy and Dee look as lost as I do. My heartbeat's so loud, I barely hear Dee's inhale. "Do you know why Luke invited me to the games night?"

"Because I told him to."

"No, silly. It's because he's crazy about you. He probably thought I'd say no, but I said yes, and you know why? Because I knew that he could never take it seriously with anyone but you. You can sense how he feels in the way he talks to you, or looks at you, or cares for you. Luke isn't going to just disappear."

Ivy nods her agreement. "That's why I've been shipping you two so hard. When you sent me that text while I was in England about the man who'd started being flirty and sweet, I was hoping against hope that it was Luke. You two are a good match, you balance each other out. So it seems to me that the answer really is simple. Stop fighting. Stop thinking about the end."

I bite my lip, thinking it over.

Past Daisy would've found some excuse to give up. To find someone else. Someone new.

I reflexively pick up my phone and click into my Right-Match app. There are dozens of unread messages, dozens of potential matches. How easy it would be to find someone less complicated, a man with whom to start fresh...

But life doesn't work that way. Maybe you have to let the difficult stuff in so that your love can truly grow.

So I swallow thickly, and delete the app.

Give myself one second, and then I click into my message thread with Luke.

Daisy: Hey, sorry for not responding earlier... Would you like to go on a date?

The response is almost immediate.

Luke: Thought you'd never ask. And I know the perfect place to take you.

23

DAISY

The week after the games night feels as close to a happily-ever-after as could be.

First, my moon boot comes off, and the doctor says I'm able to start resuming my day-to-day activities—which means that I'm back at Valley Fitness and my myriad of jobs. Plus, Ivy's at home, and my life's brighter for having my best friend around.

And then... Luke.

He's everywhere and everything all at once. He's making my days infinitely better, filling them with laughter and conversation and witty, teasing arguments. We had our official first date the same day my moon boot came off, and it was perfect in every way. Luke was right about that.

He was also right that I'd never gone to a rooftop movie in mid-November.

I wasn't sure what to expect when he parked the car in the community center parking lot. He brought me inside, and we climbed the stairs to the roof, where he'd set up a projector and a screen. There were bean bag chairs, and plush cushions, and the warmest, coziest blankets ever. Not to mention the best snacks.

We were up there for hours, snuggled up beneath the blankets and watching movies—all of our favorites. Sometimes we talked, sometimes we didn't. But I loved being curled up against Luke, his fingers playing with my hair or drawing lazy loops on my shoulders and back.

At the end of the night, we kissed beneath the blinking stars. We were both wrapped up in blankets and jackets, but I loved the way his mouth was warm on mine while his cheeks and nose offered a snap of contrasting cold whenever he kissed down my neck. The kiss was tender and slow at first, but still possessed the fire we had beneath the bleachers.

And this time, I let myself enjoy it. Let myself sink into the moment. Time slowed and I noticed every delicious detail about the way he held me—gently but firmly, like I was something precious, but not delicate. The way his fingers traced across my skin, leaving trails of sparks in their path. The way he tasted like mint and pretzels and all of the best things in life.

That kiss competed with our first kiss for the title of "Best Kiss Ever".

There have since been many, many contenders. I still don't know which one would win.

Miraculously, nothing has changed yet. The other shoe hasn't dropped, there haven't been any surprises or sudden reversals. Luke is still falling for me. I'm still falling for him. And little by little, I'm trying to follow Dee and Ivy's advice. I'm letting those emotions back in and allowing myself to hope for the best.

It's a strange feeling, but more than that, it's just... relief.

"What do you think, Dais?"

Luke's voice startles me out of my thoughts, and I peek up at him. I'm laying on top of him on my couch, my back to his front and our legs tangled together.

"Hm?" I mumble because I was *not* being lulled into some dreamy comatose place by the timbre of his voice and his heartbeat against my cheek.

"About the carnival?" He drops his hand to his side so the papers he's holding ruffle loudly. His abs flex as he strains to look at me. "Please tell me you're paying attention, and I'm not planning a *Mirror Valley snow carnival thing by myself.*"

The last part is said in a thunderous grumble that vibrates my upper body. I have to giggle as I look up at him. "'Course not. I'm locked in and focused. My eyes are strictly on the prize."

"Why do I doubt that?" Now his growl is a whisper in my ear, and his breath on my neck makes my skin flush.

"You're hogging the couch *again*?"

Luke and I look over to the kitchen, where Noah's standing with a bowl of cereal, staring at us flatly. He came in the door a few minutes ago saying that he needed to speak with Dee... then took a detour to the kitchen because "volleyball tired him out, and he might faint if he doesn't ingest carbs ASAP."

"Maybe you shouldn't be lurking in the kitchen," I suggest helpfully.

He ignores me. "Have you guys even moved since yesterday?"

It's a fair question. Luke and I have fallen effortlessly into this comfortable, effortless state of being together. We eat dinner side by side most nights, go for dog walks with Stella... we even had brunch at Ivy and Luke's grandparents' place one morning. It's all been surprisingly easy. So easy that anytime I think about it too long, I feel that gut instinct to shut down again. Instead, I'm reminding myself to stop fighting it, stop doubting it.

Now, Luke looks down at me and places a quick kiss on

my head. He sighs loudly. "None of your business, Noah. Aren't you meant to be working on those numbers for Mr. Argent?"

Noah swears under his breath, then takes off towards the stairs with his bowl. "I'll get those done first thing tomorrow morning. I swear it!"

I feel Luke shaking his head. "Noah's smart enough to be an accountant, but his motivation leaves something to be desired."

"At least he keeps Dee appeased."

Luke chuckles. "At least there's that."

I close my eyes against the sound of his laugh, feeling completely happy and at home.

Until he speaks again. "How're you feeling about the carnival given the news from the community center?"

And there it is.

My smile disappears.

It's the one very rainy, stormy cloud on my otherwise sunny horizon.

Luke broke the news to me a couple days ago. The council made their decision—they're going to cut back on staff at a ton of public buildings in Mirror Valley and have decided to shut the community center altogether.

Normally, I would have forced myself to look at the bright side, then almost kill myself trying to save it. Luke and I did try... we approached the council together, but there was no budging. And after sitting through a very long and tedious—though informative—council meeting, I can see, financially, why this makes sense.

It was a tough pill to swallow, but Luke's been right there with me, and he's reminded me that it's okay to be sad. It's okay to grieve the place where I spent so much of my childhood.

Which is why I volunteered to plan the Mirror Valley

Winter Carnival this year. Usually, a team on the town council puts it together, but I offered to do it given that the council is already so preoccupied with the financial drama.

Plus, I figured it would be a good opportunity to raise money for the people who have lost their jobs, and to put towards maintaining the shuttered buildings. Which is appropriate given that the carnival always takes place on the grounds of the community center.

Luke's offered to help plan the carnival with me, so we're tackling this together, just as we did the matchmaking events.

I shake my head against his chest. Splay a palm on top of his heartbeat and let the steady rhythm ground me. "I'm glad we're doing this. And what a fun way to celebrate the community center and all it's done for Mirror Valley." I pause for a moment. "It's going to be fun, right?"

"It will be fun. Very fun, some might say."

I let out a chuckle, but close my eyes against the disappointment once again. I had so many hopes, so many plans for the community center once we got it up and running again. I may have a lot of jobs, but this one felt the closest to my heart.

Something tugs at me, and I sit up abruptly.

"Gloria!" I shriek as I grab my computer.

"Name's Luke but okay."

I shoot him a glare, and he smirks. "I promised I'd walk Gloria Perez's bulldogs tomorrow."

I log into my email and type up a quick response to Gloria saying that I'd be there in the morning. I press send and look up to see Luke peering at me with an eyebrow raised.

"What?" I ask.

He shakes his head. "Just you and all your jobs."

"What about them?" I push a finger into his chest, forcing him to lay back down on the couch so I can return to my position on top of him.

"Are you happy?"

His question stumps me for a moment. "Of course, I am."

"Really. You're happy when you're running around all the time, stressed and constantly thinking about others."

I pause, and the silence seems to speak volumes. Luke doesn't say anything though, just waits. "I am..." I say slowly. "I'm happy to be helping people."

He shakes his head, and the movement makes me shift, so he reflexively loops his arms around me again. "You've got the biggest heart of anyone I know, Dais. It's not something I always understand, but it's one of my favorite things about you. And it's because I care about you that I want to make sure you're happy." He pauses and his arms stiffen slightly around my waist. "Hang on, is this what it feels like for you? Caring about other people's happiness?"

He sounds so flabbergasted that I have to laugh. "Pretty much."

"The time. The energy. And for people who aren't even your close friends or family." He exhales dramatically. "You must be exhausted."

I bite my lip, and my gaze travels down to my foot. I remember how it felt to be off for a few days while my toe healed. It was probably my first major break in a long, long time. "Sometimes," I reply faintly.

"All I'm saying is, don't forget to consider your own happiness. Follow your own heart."

He kisses me on the head again and picks up his papers, but now I've stopped paying attention for an entirely different reason.

I've never really considered the jobs that came my way. For some of them, I simply heard that someone needed a hand, and I hopped on the bandwagon. Other times, I noticed an area that could be improved and took on the responsibility myself, like I did with the community center.

I find joy in helping others, in being a support. I always have. But Luke might have a point. I *am* exhausted a lot of the time—Toe-pocalypse showed me that, if nothing else. Maybe there's a chance for me to figure out what I really want, see where my heart is leading me. Maybe I can be more intentional about where I go from here.

Luke checks his watch and sighs. "I've gotta run, there's something I have to do at work. But can you meet me later?"

"Sure." I get up with more than a little reluctance, and Luke heads towards the door. I follow him, standing next to him as he puts on his shoes. "Where should I meet you?"

"My house."

"Like your apartment?"

He shakes his head. "My house." He takes my hands in his. "I've started moving back in, and I want you to come see it."

His offer sounds simple enough, but there's something so sweetly vulnerable in his voice that my heart does a little squeeze. "Let me guess, you want to show me your coffee machine?"

Luke laughs, and the sound washes over me like a warm spring rain. "Something like that."

He puts a finger under my chin and tilts my head up, then places the softest kiss on my lips. Just a brush, really. But it's enough to make my brain fall out of my head like it does every time he kisses me.

And then he's gone, and I'm filled with this over-whelming sense of peace and calm. For the first time since we've been together, my happiness isn't tinged with nerves or anxiety. For the first time, I really believe that things might work out. That I could have my very own happily-ever-after with Luke Brooks.

24

LUKE

Want to know the best way to tell if you're really into a girl?

If, after a full day of work, you take a detour to visit the most gossipy, eccentric lady in your town in order to pick up an item that would've made you scowl to new levels of intensity in the past, all so you can see her smile.

Or that's what I'm telling myself as I pile heavy, maroon, velvet curtains into the backseat of my car, along with a box full of gothic melted wax candles and a crystal ball.

Yes, you read that correctly.

I, Luke Brooks, have a freaking crystal ball rolling around my backseat.

"Thanks again, Fran." I give a wave as I pull away from the curb. Fran waves back from the front door of her multi-colored townhouse with a wide, beaming grin. As I'm driving away, I spot her good friend Raymond coming up behind her from inside the house, still wearing Fran's purple apron.

I lower my window, enjoying the breeze after the heat in Fran's house. The woman radiates charming warmth herself, but I think she'd be better suited to a life in the

Bahamas than mountainous Colorado. Raymond doesn't seem to mind the pseudo-sauna that is her house though— he puttered around the kitchen the entire time I was there, making falafels in her purple floral apron. Like the oven wasn't adding another sweaty twenty degrees.

But it's fine. Because Daisy asked me to pick up Fran's stuff for the carnival, and of course I would do it for her.

The mere thought of Daisy brings a smile to my face. The past week has been... indescribable. I'm a man of numbers, not a man of words, but if there was any way to communicate how I'm feeling, it's 100 percent. Across the board, every day. I can't believe how different my life feels with her in it. How she makes every day brighter, and fills it with a new sort of meaning I've never experienced before.

I'd do anything for her. My after-work errand today is proof of that.

On cue, the crystal ball rolls across the seat and thwacks into the door.

What is my life right now?

I turn up the volume on my Bruce Springsteen cassette as I take a turn down a familiar country road. My stomach fills with anticipation as I think of seeing Daisy again. Earlier today, I asked her to meet me at my house after work. Knowing her, she'll most likely be late, but I'll wait. I'd wait for her for as long as it takes.

My ringtone goes off, interrupting the uptempo beats of "Dancing in the Dark".

"Luke Brooks," I answer the phone handsfree. Formally, in case it's Mr. Argent. Despite the closure of the community center, our team is still conducting an audit of the town council's finances to see how else we might be able to relieve some of the financial stress.

"Sounds like you mean business." James laughs on the other end of the line.

"Hey, man." A smile breaks across my lips. James and I haven't had a chance to catch up since he's been back from his honeymoon. I may be partly to blame for that with the time I've been spending with Daisy. "How're you doing?"

"I'm good, but it sounds like *you've* got some news. Ivy and I were at the Brookrose with your grandparents this afternoon, and Tony mentioned that he heard from someone in your building that you moved out."

I curse under my breath. The gossip in this town! "Yeah. It's a work in progress." I exhale. "I've started moving my things back to my house. It's time."

"Is it?" I hear the smirk in James's voice. He and Ivy are so much smirkier now that they've gotten together. Like they've joined forces to be that smirky, all-knowing couple.

The most annoying part is that they're often right.

"I've been in that condo for over a year now, and I need more space."

"I hear ya."

"Besides, Stella's too big for an apartment. She deserves a backyard, and tons of room to explore."

"She does."

I purse my lips. "You sound smug."

James laughs. "I just know you, Luke. Have you told Daisy that you're moving back to the house?"

Ugh. Of course, he's onto me. James and I were best friends all through our childhoods and high school, and even though we parted ways in college and James went on to work in Denver, it often feels like he never left.

I clear my throat. "I'm on my way to meet her there now."

"'Course you are."

"You need to stop, or I'm going to take back my blessing of you dating my little sister."

James cackles. "Too late now, dude."

I roll my eyes. But the truth is, meeting Daisy at the house today matters a lot to me. Though she's never been there before, I can picture her in every room so vividly. Picture her making the place hers—making it ours someday, if that's what she wants.

I see her walking the hallways, laying across the couch in a living room crowded with her cacti, cooking meals with me in the kitchen. I wonder how she'd decorate the spare room she can make into her own personal yoga studio, or gym, or office, or whatever else she'd like. I imagine what bedspread she'd choose for the bed, or how she'd look waking up in the morning with her blonde hair across said bedspread...

Good grief. Getting ahead of myself.

Thing is, I'm already picturing a future with this woman. Literally picturing us being married and living together someday.

"Luke?"

James's voice pulls me back to the moment. "Sorry, what?"

"I was just saying... things are going well with Daisy, huh?"

I pause for a moment, then smile. "Yeah, they're going good. Really good. We've only been officially dating, like, a couple of weeks, but it doesn't feel like that."

"I get it. It was the same with Ivy. The timeline felt completely skewed."

He's right about that. In the past, I would've wanted to do everything by the book, but with Daisy, there is no book to follow. Part of me feels reckless, like we're breaking the rules. But another, bigger part knows that we're not breaking rules but making them together. And I know she feels the same.

No, we haven't had any big four-letter-word conversations, but I know she's falling for me too. I can tell in the way she's vulnerable with me and lets herself be sad with me. Daisy is a force to be reckoned with—powerful and strong and full of positive energy. But I get to see past that, get to be her safe space when she needs it. It's an honor I don't take lightly.

"I'm kind of crazy about her." I mean every word.

"You don't say." I hear James's smile through the phone. "You two seem pretty solid, like you ground her, and she lifts you up. So don't mess it up. I'd hate to see Ivy cry if things don't work out between you two." He chuckles dryly. "But as your best friend, I know you're not stupid."

I'm warmed by his words... even if they were almost an insult. "Thanks. I think. But I gotta go, I'm almost at the house."

"Have fun giving her the *grand tour*."

I grimace. "Why'd you say it like that?"

James laughs. "Say hi for me."

We hang up right as I take the final turn onto my street, and that's when I spot her. Seated on the front steps of my house with her red winter jacket bundled tightly around her and a fuzzy white beanie on her head. And as is the case every time I see her, she takes my breath away.

"You're early," I call as I step out of the car. I hesitate for a moment, then walk down the path. The crystal ball, etc. can wait.

She hops to a stand. I love the way her blue eyes crinkle at the sides when she smiles like that. "You wanted to surprise me, so I thought I'd surprise you back!"

I jog up the sidewalk and take her hand, pulling her close to kiss her. Her lips are a shock of cold, and she tastes like bubblegum, and I can't wait to get her inside so I can kiss her properly.

I place my hands on her cheeks to warm them up. "Come on."

We walk up the steps together, hand in hand, and I reach for my keys.

I barely register the slamming of a car door behind us.

"Lukey?"

25

LUKE

I had a pretty clear expectation of how tonight would go.

I thought I'd show Daisy around the house, we'd take Stella for a walk together before it got too dark, and then we'd have takeout while watching a movie. I figured we'd talk about her work, or my work, or the carnival, or whatever else was on our minds, and it would be like any of the other wonderful evenings we've had together lately.

I thought it would be just another normal night—our normal.

But this is the opposite of normal. This is the last thing I could've expected.

Because my ex-fiancée—the one I haven't seen since she ran out on our wedding day a year and a half ago—is currently standing at the end of my walkway.

"Eleanor." I say the name on a croak that sounds strangled.

"Hi, Luke," she replies, coupled with that wry smile of hers. "It's been awhile."

I'm frozen, I can't move. I don't know how to process what I'm seeing right now, don't know how to take this shock. My mind is a fuzzy mess of confusion and questions. What is she...? How is she...? *Why* is she...?

There's a sudden movement by my left shoulder.

Daisy.

My hand is grasping hers tightly, and my body kicks itself into gear enough for me to let go. "I'm sorry, Dais."

"It's okay." Her voice is as uneven as mine, and I wonder if she, too, feels like she's been gut-punched by a WWE wrestler.

But her words trigger something in me, and I have to look at her. Her face is white, her lips pale. She's clearly as surprised as I am. I grasp her hand again, more gently this time, and place myself instinctively just ahead of her.

Eleanor registers this entire exchange, and her brown eyes zero in on Daisy. She raises one perfectly groomed brow. "Daisy, right?"

At this, Daisy reacts in only the way she could. She starts a little, and then giggles awkwardly. "That's me! Daisy, here."

And maybe it's because of the absurdity of the moment, or maybe because Daisy is so wonderfully herself, but I actually crack a smile. Despite this *very* unfunny situation. When Daisy's blue eyes rise to meet mine, the shock that's been paralyzing my body tapers down, and I find strength in her gaze to look back at my ex-fiancée.

"What're you doing here, Eleanor?" My voice isn't gruff, but it isn't kind either. It just sounds cautious, wary, which is pretty accurate to how I'm feeling right now.

Eleanor opens her mouth, and I can feel it; sense her wanting to correct me. She shortened her name to "Lenore" during our relationship as she thought this would boost her "unique, boho persona" on social media. But the name change came with a personality that shifted, little by little, until I couldn't even recognize who she was anymore.

Now, instead of correcting me, she simply pushes her long hair behind her shoulder in that practiced casual way she has. "I wanted to talk to you."

"Me," I repeat, though it very clearly could only be me.

"I think we have a few matters to discuss." She pauses. "Preferably alone?"

Eleanor's eyes drop to Daisy again just once, just quickly enough to be pointed and obvious. I keep Daisy's hand in mine. "Anything you have to say to me, you can say to Daisy."

Eleanor looks almost amused. Like I told a joke. "Pretty sure she won't mind giving us a bit of privacy given our history. Wouldn't you say, Daisy?"

I very much dislike her tone of voice, and I bristle. "I don't think—"

"It's okay, Luke." A gentle hand rests on my upper arm. "It's fine, I can go."

I look at Daisy again, and she's grinning up at me. Like this is no problem at all, like everything's fine. Everything is most definitely not fine. Five minutes ago, I couldn't wait to show her the house, couldn't wait to spend the evening with her. And now...

Well, there's no roadmap on how to behave at a time like this. There are no books titled: "How to react when your ex-fiancée comes back to town and you're with someone else". For dummies.

"Besides." Daisy shrugs a shoulder. "I should probably get home anyway. If Dee and Noah are left alone too long and start feeling pranky, who knows what state the house will be in when I'm back."

I place my hand on top of hers on my arm. "Are you sure?" I ask her.

"Definitely."

"I'll come by later."

"I'll wait up."

With that, she steps away, and her hand drops from my arm. She strides back down the walkway to her bike, and I look after her, missing her presence already.

She doesn't look at us as she clips into her helmet, but she gives me a wave before taking off. As soon as she rounds the corner, Eleanor climbs the steps to my house. "Shall we?"

26

DAISY

If I could make a list of things I thought would never happen today, having Eleanor Wilkes show up on Luke's doorstep would fall somewhere among the following:

1. Bruce growing wings and flying around the bungalow like some sort of Batcat
2. Sid deciding not to post on social media for one day
3. Waking up with a complete and thorough knowledge of Romanian

Needless to say, it feels like some sort of backwards miracle that Eleanor is here right now. In Mirror Valley. At Luke's house.

Talk about ghosting... That's one ghost I never thought I'd see again.

And, as is always the way, she looked as beautiful as she did the last time I saw her—the day before her wedding. Her hair was still long, streaked with gold, and slightly curled. Her face was perfectly made-up in that way that makes you want to hop on YouTube and perfect your own beauty routine STAT. And she was wearing knee-high boots beneath a cream sweater-dress and a fluffy winter jacket. I bet she smelled of sugar and cinnamon and a hint of pumpkin-spice.

Though I can't speak to that because I hopped on my bike and rode away before I could get anywhere near smelling territory.

Yes. My bike. Because of course I chose today, of all days, to take a chance on the weather and ride my bike.

Do you know how long it takes to clip into your pink sparkly helmet when your boyfriend's super gorgeous, put-together ex is staring at you? About five years.

I left them at Luke's house a couple of hours ago now, and I'd be lying if I said I wasn't constantly about *just one second* away from hopping right back on my bike and going over there. Bless them, Dee and Noah have been trying to keep me entertained with a ping-pong competition.

Between the two of them.

I get to be the referee.

"Well done, woo!" I cheer for either of them (or both of them) as I pick up my phone once more. No texts.

"Daisy, pay attention," Dee tuts, setting herself up at one end of our dining table, which is currently serving as the ping-pong table. She crosses one arm over the other to stretch her shoulders, and leans into a squat. Her baseball cap is turned backwards on her head in a way that says she means business. "That's another point for me, which puts us at 5-4, and—"

"Excuse me, Dee, I think you've got that wrong." Noah interrupts, swinging his paddle around like he's an old-timey sheriff and this town is too small for the both of them. "Last I checked, that shot you made didn't count and it was..."

I tune out their bickering and roll my eyes with a sigh.

Then, a car door slams outside.

I jump to my feet. "Be right back!"

Dee and Noah don't even spare me a glance. I run to the front door, throw it open, and see Luke helping Stella out the backseat. My heart feels full to see him. When he looks over at me, he smiles and the two lumber up the sidewalk together.

Well, Stella lumbers. Luke has that confident, swaggy way of walking that you see with glamorous Hollywood stars. And over-confident men in the sauna.

Why am I like this.

"Hi, girl," I greet Stella, petting her shaggy brown coat. She snuffles and leans into my legs, and I look up at Luke somewhat shyly. "Hi."

"Hey." He immediately wraps his arms around me, and I relax against his chest. "Want to go for a walk? Stella hasn't been out all day."

"Do I ever. Dee and Noah are bickering again, so let's get out of the house."

I bound back up the steps and open the door just long enough to grab my winter jacket and shout, "Be back soon!"

They both holler a quick "bye!" before returning to their heated debate about goodness knows what now.

I return to Luke's side, pulling on my winter jacket and beanie. It's not quite sunset yet, but the sky is turning a nice shade of faded yellow behind the clouds. Luke takes Stella's leash in one hand, and my hand in the other, and we start walking, making our way along our usual route. We walk in silence for awhile as I try to gauge what he's thinking.

Eventually, he blows out an exhale that sounds suspiciously like a grunt. "Big day, huh?"

"Sure was. How're you doing?"

"I'm okay. Still processing."

"Makes sense."

Luke goes quiet again. He takes a breath in, holds it, and then releases. "She wants to come back to Mirror Valley."

My heart does a weird, uneasy little squeeze. "Like she wants to move back?"

"Yup. She's been in San Francisco this whole time by herself. She wanted to start fresh, wanted to do something new and get away somewhere no one knew her. She's been focusing on growing her social media thing and apparently, it's going really well. But she misses home, misses her parents. They haven't spoken to her since the wedding last year."

My stomach now joins in on the uneasy party by tying into a knot. "So, she's coming back here. For good."

"I don't know. I don't know what her plan is. She's staying at a motel in Summer Lakes at the moment and only came into town to ask me if I could help her get in touch with her parents."

I bite my tongue, unsure how to respond to that. "Huh..."

"I said I'd try, but I don't know what she wants me to do."

I nod slowly. I can't imagine how Luke must be feeling right now, what must be running through his mind. He and Eleanor were in a loving, committed relationship for twelve years before she broke off their engagement. I can't wrap my head around the levels of shock and hurt that he must be experiencing.

And that's when I realize where my own uneasiness is coming from. Eleanor was right earlier—she and Luke have a history I'll never understand. In the past, whenever I was around the two of them, it was always them plus me. Or them, plus Ivy and me. If Eleanor is thinking of moving back to Mirror Valley, there would be a serious change in our dynamics. And I can't help but wonder if this is the change I've been dreading, the beginning of the end...

Really, Dais?

I snap myself out of that line of thought immediately, slightly disgusted that I could be thinking about myself right now. That I could be making anything in this situation about me.

There's a tug on my hand, and I realize that Luke and Stella have come to a stop. We're standing by the high school now, and Stella's off her leash, trotting through the fallen leaves. The air is crisp and cool, and the smell of autumn intermingles with Luke's forest scent as he pulls me gently towards him. "You okay?"

I swallow, getting rid of those selfish thoughts once and for all, and pasting on a bright smile. "Absolutely. Just a little cold."

Luke wraps both arms tight around me, locking his hands like he'll never let me go. He's wearing this big, cozy jacket, and I nuzzle my face into his neck, inhaling. He laughs, and his chest moves beneath my palms. "You smelling me, Dais?"

"Yeah, you smell like manly forest."

"What exactly is a manly forest?"

I smile against his chest. "You'll know it when you smell it."

Luke presses a kiss to my forehead. "You're amazing, and I—"

"Woohoo!! Luke, Daisy? Is that you?"

Luke releases me, and we swivel around to see Dora Mae jogging towards us in stylish athletic gear. Her short hair is gathered back in a low ponytail, and it looks like she's barely breaking a sweat. She is in pretty incredible shape, though. She's even wearing makeup, but that shouldn't be a surprise. Dora Mae's hair and nails are always perfectly done, and her clothes beyond fashionable for little Mirror Valley.

"Hey, Dora Mae. A little late for a jog, isn't it?"

"Only if you're lazy," she replies. "Which I pride myself on never being."

She laughs this short, breathy laugh and then places her hands on her hips. "My, my, I wasn't expecting to see you two out and about this evening. Are you working on the Winter Carnival?"

"Not at this moment, no."

"Oh." Dora Mae's brow furrows a little more. "So, what brings you two here looking so... cozy?"

I glance up at Luke, choosing to defer to him. Given past experiences with his love life and the town gossips, we've been trying to keep our relationship mostly under the radar when we're in public. So as expected, his face gives nothing away. "We're out walking Stella together."

"Ah, yes." Dora Mae's gaze swings to me. "I heard that you are the town's top dogwalker, Daisy."

I give a little smile. "That's me."

"You certainly have a lot going on these days." Dora Mae tuts. "Though I was so sorry to hear about the community center. What a shame. In all my years in public service, I've never seen such a mismanaged council. Financially speaking, of course. I'm sure you've been seeing this in your audit, Luke."

Luke furrows his brow slightly. "Actually, the finances thus far have been more or less what you'd expect. Though we'll be conducting a deeper dive over the next week or so."

"A deeper dive?"

"Yes, we'll start by gathering the councilors' financial statements and going from there."

I could swear that Dora Mae's mouth twitches slightly.

"I see. Yes, that does sound like a worthy avenue to pursue. I'll let the council know to expect this."

Is it just me or is Dora Mae being a little shifty all of a sudden? Luke and I exchange a brief glance, but Dora Mae speaks again.

"Now." She leans forward conspiratorially. "What's this I heard about a long-lost fiancée returning from the coast?"

Luke and I both freeze right up. "Excuse me?" he asks.

"Franny was saying earlier that she saw a familiar face wandering around town. And she heard from the Wilkes's that their daughter has been in touch. I figured that, if she *has* returned, surely she'd go straight to her ex-beau."

Luke clenches his fists by his side. Unclenches them. "Honestly, I don't think that's any of your business, Dora Mae."

She doesn't seem particularly phased by Luke's discomfort. She simply shrugs. "I understand, and I'm sorry if I've crossed a line, dear. I, too, have had to contend with spurned ex-partners in the past." She tuts again, and I have to grimace. Sure, the people of Mirror Valley can be a bit nosy, but this feels like something else entirely.

"We should probably head off," Luke says curtly, turning away from Dora Mae. "You ready, Dais? Stella's getting cold."

The big dog is lying across the grass snoozing away and presently looks the opposite of cold, but I understand Luke's desire to get out of here.

"Sure thing. Bye, Dora Mae." I give her a wave as Luke and I walk away.

This time, he doesn't reach for my hand.

27

DAISY

My shift at Valley Fitness the next day should feel like any other shift. I take a seat at the front desk right in time for Sid Rossleigh to sign in for his daily workout. The upbeat tunes and shouted commands from Flo's lunchtime pilates class mostly drown out the techno playlist that's on repeat through the main workout area.

And Mr. Wilhelm is here with Gloria Perez. They're lifting weights in the corner, and I could almost swear that they're being a little flirty.

Which is normally something I'd want to pay attention to, but today, I only give them both a small wave before getting lost in my thoughts all over again. I keep going back to what happened yesterday—learning that Eleanor wants to return to Mirror Valley, questions about how Luke is handling this crazy change, and selfishly, worry over how or if this might affect our relationship.

Everything just feels very up in the air, which wouldn't usually be a problem for me. But I will say that this is a pretty unusual situation.

After all, what are the chances that your boyfriend's

runaway bride comes barging back into his life? Outside of movies and reality shows, I'm gonna guess not high.

With a sigh, I pick up a pile of towels strewn on the floor to put them in the laundry.

"Hey!"

The squawk surprises me, and I turn to see Sid glaring at me from a bicep curl machine. "Sorry, Sid. These yours?"

"They were!" he exclaims, sounding more than a little disgusted. He swipes the towels from my arms. "Now I don't know which is my face towel or my arm towel!"

I press my lips into a smile. "I'll get you some new ones."

"Psh. Okay." He returns to the machine, places his hands around the handles, then proceeds to snap a photo in the mirror instead of doing a bicep curl.

I roll my eyes, remembering the good ol' days when he was on my trope list. So much for enemies-to-more. Who would've thought that "best friend's grumpy older brother/co-matchmaker/online date mistaken identity" would be the trope(s) for me?

I return to the front desk and nod at Benji, a kid fresh out of high school who helps out at Valley Fitness part-time. "Hey Benj, just gonna grab some towels for Sid."

"That guy?" He sighs. "I used to follow him on Insta, but he kept posting, like, every five minutes. He even used to do lives when he was making dinner. Not even talking, just had his phone on while he made food for, like, an hour. It was so boring."

I stifle a snort at the thought of Sid puttering around his kitchen making carb-less burgers or whatever. I grab a couple towels, fold them neatly, then return to place them on the machine next to Sid's. He's too busy on TikTok to notice.

I'm walking back to the desk when the front door opens and Luke walks into the fitness center. It's not his usual workout time, and he's wearing a polo and slacks instead of athletic gear. My heart squeezes a little to see him, and I have to fight an urge to run over and hug him. With everything that went on yesterday, I'm not exactly sure how he's feeling. Probably best to play it cool for now.

But as soon as he spots me, he smiles and closes the distance between us in two seconds. He takes my hand and pulls me close. "Thought I'd find you here."

I give a little laugh. "What gave me away?"

"Had a feeling you'd be making yourself useful. Want to go somewhere and talk?"

I grin, even as my back goes ramrod straight. I'm not sure what to expect with this, what Luke might want to talk about. He was obviously annoyed after our conversation with Dora Mae last night, but we didn't get a chance to talk then. Now, his expression is composed—no surprises there —and I still can't tell what he's thinking. But I suppose the best way to find out is to talk about it. "Sure," I say.

A few minutes later, Luke's parking in the deserted lot in front of the community center. The windows are dark, some of them even literally shuttered. Tables and chairs are stacked at one corner of the coffee shop's outdoor seating area.

"What're we doing here?" I ask.

"I wanted to take you somewhere quiet. I know the community center is closed right now, but I think I know where Fran stashed the keys."

We get out of the car and walk up the path. Luke stops at a bush right next to the front door and picks up a garden gnome painted a rainbow of colors. Fran once had a hobby of painting these little guys and selling them on Etsy. She had to stop when the high school seniors decided their school prank would involve filling the principal's office with her gnomes.

217

Yup. Gnomes covered the desk, the chairs, the file cabinets... Some even teetered on the principal's ship-in-a-bottle display. Gave him quite a fright when he came in the next morning and found hundreds of little eyes staring at him.

Now, Luke picks up the garden gnome and turns it over. Lo and behold, there's a single metallic key right underneath. "Found it."

"What does it say about you that you knew where Fran hid it?"

"Let's just try very, very hard not to go down that line of thought, shall we?"

I smile as he unlocks the door. He doesn't have to know that I never gave my key back, and it's on the key ring in my jacket pocket right now.

We walk into the lobby, and it's surprisingly warm despite the community center being shut for the past week. We head to the coffee shop and take a seat at one of the tables by the window. I have a brief memory of the last time we sat at one of these tables to plan our first matchmaking event, and I brought over the little potted cactus. Said cactus is now at home with the others. Dee often jokes that I'm trying to build a cactus collection, which actually seems like an alright idea to me. Until it's time to vacuum.

Luke goes behind the coffee bar and puts the kettle on. "Hot cocoa?" he asks, even as he's getting mugs for us. The man knows me so well.

When Luke returns to the table, he sets down our mugs and sits in the chair across from me. "Careful, it's hot," he says off-hand.

I keep my eyes on him, monitoring his face carefully. He looks as neutral, calm and collected as can be, but now, I can see the dark circles beneath his eyes, the way his mouth is slightly curved down at the corners. His hair's a little wild, like he's been running his fingers through it. At the moment, none of my own fears or anxieties matter. Above all, I feel worried for him.

Before I can say anything, he takes my hand. "I'm sorry I left so abruptly last night."

I give my head a shake. "It's okay."

"No, it's just been a lot to take in." He runs his fingers through his hair. "And today, Mr. Argent was pushing us to get started with these financial statements... there's a lot going on."

"Really, Luke, it's okay. I'm more concerned about you and how you're doing. Especially with Eleanor being back."

His nose crinkles a little. "She messaged me about getting lunch today, but I declined."

"You don't want to talk to her?"

"I don't know what I'd say. There's not much for us to talk about, honestly. What happened happened."

I register the clicking of his jaw, and I suddenly realize something.

Luke's always been the strong one, the reliable one. He was Ivy's biggest support when their parents died, and he helped their grandparents when they were managing the Brookrose and it hit upon hard times. He's always confident and collected, and I've only very rarely seen him hesitate, seen his lesser-known uncertain side.

But if he's always being strong for everyone else, who's being strong for him?

Maybe I can do that. I *want* to do that.

So I come around to his side of the table and pull up a chair next to him. "It's okay not to be okay," I repeat the words he's said to me so many times.

And now, his face changes. Now, his lips twitch, and he leans his head on the wall behind him. Closes his eyes.

"I thought I'd never see her again," he says quietly. "Dais, that was the worst day of my life. Not only because she ran out, but because of everything that went along with it. Having to cancel the wedding, send our guests home, return the gifts. And then the months of gossip and rumors and pity..."

He rolls his head back against the wall. He doesn't sound sad or mournful, but exhausted. The voice of a man who's had to take on way more than he should, and had to bear the burden alone. No wonder he's become all the more stern and surly over the last year. I place a hand on his arm, wishing I could take some of his pain for myself. "She shouldn't have done that to you, Luke. You didn't deserve to be treated that way."

His lips press into a grim line, and he looks down at his hands. "For months, I wanted everything to go back to how it was. I wanted things to fall back in line, go back to normal. You know I hate change, but eventually, I had to get over it. And I moved on—moved on from her, moved on from what my life used to be, and what I thought the rest of it would look like. I rented out my house, got Stella..." He smiles a little at the thought of his dog, softening. "And I started falling for you."

He looks at me then, and his expression is totally unguarded. So genuine and vulnerable and open with what he's feeling. My heart bursts with affection for him, and I almost wish that I could wrap him up and take away his pain. Show him how wonderful and incredible he is.

I remember what Ivy and Dee said about relationships being messy and difficult sometimes, that you have to be vulnerable. And I know that it's time I speak my truth, too—that even though things feel up in the air right now, I know exactly where I stand when it comes to him.

I swallow thickly. *Just one second...*

"What was that?" Luke asks, and only then do I realize that I spoke my mantra out loud.

I clear my throat. "Sorry. I said, just one second."

"One second for what?"

"It's this stupid thing I do whenever I'm scared or worried of what comes next, I tell myself that I just need one second of bravery. One second to start saying or doing what needs to be said or done, and after that one second, well, the ball's rolling anyway. It's too late to turn back."

Luke's lips tilt in a lopsided smirk. "I like that. So, what's the one second for this time?"

I bite the inside of my cheek, then go for it. "I'm falling for you, too. Actually, I've already fallen. Have been falling for a long time."

"What do you mean?"

"I had a crush on you back when we were in school. Actually, I have a vivid memory of you accidentally kicking a soccer ball into my face during practice. My nose was bleeding, and I was crying, but I remember the way you rushed over to me and wouldn't leave my side until I was feeling better. No matter that your coach was angry with you and wanted to get back to the game..."

I trail off, laughing at the memory. It was probably the first time I really got to see Luke's sweet and caring side.

I get back on track. "Obviously, I never would've done anything about it because you were with Eleanor, but yeah, needless to say that I've fallen for you all over again." I look down at my fingers now, feeling weirdly nervous. "And I also think that's been weighing on my mind lately. It still seems surreal that you could have fallen for me after years of my feelings being unrequited. It feels like a dream, and I'm waiting to wake up."

Luke is silent for a long moment. Then, he puts his fingers under my chin and tilts my head up to look at him. Facing those hazel eyes when I'm so vulnerable feels like it should be the hardest thing, and yet the minute our gazes meet, I know that he's got me. We've got each other.

"Dais, this isn't a dream," he says and his voice is rough as sandpaper. "If I'm honest, I feel the opposite way. I feel like I've been in a dream, and I've only just woken up. You woke me up." He shakes his head. "I've been moving through life always following the rules, always wanting to do everything right. You break all my rules, and I love it. I can fully say that I've never felt this way before. *You* are it for me."

His words are everything. The feeling of warm sun on your bare skin after winter, the soothing of cold water on a sunburn, the creamy foam on a good cup of hot cocoa. So, I do the only thing I can do: I circle my hands behind Luke's neck and kiss him.

And this kiss is nothing like the other ones.

When our lips meet, it's the spark and crackle of fire. The crash of lightning. Urgent and passionate and necessary. So necessary.

The space between us closes as Luke pulls me towards him and locks his arms tight around my body. My hands are in his hair, my fingers tangled, and I'm breathing him in. I can't get enough. His lips meet mine, over and over, and at some point, I move from my chair so I'm sitting in his lap.

My mind goes hazy, and I almost wish it wouldn't because I want to remember every second of this. Want to feel every second of this.

Until there's a knock at the window that makes us both jump.

In fact, if Luke wasn't holding onto me so tight, there's a chance I might've toppled right onto the floor.

And there, beyond the glass is Fran Bellamy, smirking with so much prideful excitement, she might as well have a flashing neon sign that says "YOU'RE NOT FOOLING ANYONE!"

My breath catches, and I wonder what Luke might do next. Fran is the worst (or the best, depending on your perspective) of the bunch when it comes to gossip, and she's very clearly caught us red-handed, mid-makeout.

It would make sense for him to put some space between us, to backtrack or make an excuse to keep the rumors at bay.

Instead, he simply smirks back at her, turns to me and lowers his mouth to mine once more. He kisses me sweetly. Chastely. But with the kind of tenderness that says I'm all his.

And he's all mine.

28

LUKE

"Hey, dude. I'm heading out for lunch, want anything?"

I look up to see Noah standing in the door to my office. Miraculously, he's still working at Argent all these weeks later, and Daisy was right, he's been a nice addition to our team. Smart, if not a little jokey. And he's found a good compromise with his attire—pairing suits with a "formal" black ball cap. Whatever that means.

"I'm good," I reply. "Already had lunch."

He raises a brow. "A strawberry banana protein shake doesn't count as lunch. And you should probably get out anyway, you're starting to look like a troll all bent over your desk like that."

I shoot him a tired glare which, as usual, doesn't faze him. "I'll have a big dinner. Tons to do today."

Noah shrugs, then spins his ball cap so it's facing forward. "Suit yourself."

He gives me a peace sign, then walks off down the hallway, whistling something that sounds suspiciously like a Katy Perry song.

Not that I listen to Katy Perry. I have a younger sister, and that should explain that.

I check my watch and give my neck a stretch. Noah's right—I've been bent over my desk all morning, poring through the last of the financial statements sent in by the town councilors. I've been working through these nonstop the last few days, hoping that something would come to light... a clue or indication of what might be causing some of these financial irregularities. But our team has been working hard with no results.

Now, even Mr. Argent is starting to divert his attention. Focusing on patching over small leaks rather than finding out why the ship is leaking in the first place, so to speak.

But I can't let this go. Not when our town is downspiraling in this way. After I've finished this audit of the councilors, I'll be moving onto examining the financials of every department with a fine-toothed comb. It's going to be a long, tedious task, but if I find an answer, it'll be worth it in the end.

For our town but also, hopefully, for Daisy and the community center.

The thought of Daisy fills me with warmth. The conversation we had the other day at the community center has been swirling through my head. She was there for me in a way no one else ever was, and her support and kindness were unwavering when I told her about how difficult things were after Eleanor left. Then, to find out that she had feelings for me all the way back then...

Things are serious between us now, and I'm remembering how I felt a few weeks ago when I was dead-set against dating. Against bringing anyone into the mess that is my relationship history.

But I can say with certainty that the thought of committing to Daisy isn't at all what I was afraid of. It isn't a commitment for duty or loyalty, but for something deeper.

Something real. And I hope she knows how serious I am about her.

I turn to my computer and click to open the last set of financial statements. I glance across the screen, only half paying attention.

Until my eyes catch on a line and I sit up.

Hm. Interesting.

Very interesting.

Could this be—

Knock knock. "Hello!"

The cheery greeting makes me jump, and I utter an automatic, "Noah!"

But when I look up, bewildered, it's definitely not Noah.

Eleanor giggles lightly. "Noah who?"

Before I can say anything, she swishes into the room. Literally. She's wearing a short coffee-colored dress in a noisy fabric that floats around her as she moves. With her knitted cream beanie—clearly for style more than warmth— black boots, and shiny necklace, I already know that she spent a good half-hour taking photos before leaving the house.

"What're you doing here?" I ask warily, trying to wrap my head around the surprise of her sudden appearance. Not to mention the discovery I may have just made.

She places a huge wicker basket on top of my desk. "Time for lunch."

I give my head a shake. Eleanor's been reaching out lately, but I've told her that I'm busy and unavailable. Which are both true, but I also had no intention of seeing her again after the day she came by my house. I certainly didn't expect her to show up here. "Now's not a good time."

"Don't be silly. I made you your favorite lunch, and I

was hoping we could have a little picnic on your break. Just like old times."

My lips press into a line. "We never had a picnic here."

"No, but we did in high school. Remember when we'd sit out on the quad together and have food before your big games? There were always people wanting to talk to you. It was the best."

I run my fingers through my hair. "Look, Eleanor..." I correct myself. "*Lenore*, I—"

She lets out a short, breathy laugh. "You can call me Eleanor, Luke. It's fine."

"Well, I'm sorry, but I'm right in the middle of something. I can't do lunch today."

She stops. Looks at me with genuine surprise. "Are you serious?"

I nod, finding it hard to believe that she's surprised in the first place. She should know how seriously I take my job —it wasn't like we never talked about it when we were together. But she seems thrown by my comment, like it never occurred to her that I might say no.

"Oh." She collapses into the chair across from my desk, not looking sad so much as uncomfortable.

It briefly occurs to me that I would've once acquiesced, dropped everything for her because it was the right thing to do.

Those feelings are almost alien to me now. I don't really care what Eleanor does anymore. "You can stay and have lunch, if you'd like. But I'm going to get back to work."

"Fine." She grabs a small pot of hummus and some crackers, and digs in. I turn to my computer screen, ready to dive back in, when she speaks again. "What're you working on?"

Her voice is slightly petulant, but I decide to ignore it. "Something for the town council."

"I don't know how you do it. I'd be so bored all the time."

I smile dryly at that, flashing back to what that spandexy Floriana woman said at the matchmaking night. "I've heard that before."

"Yeah, but I guess it works for you. Accounting is stable, reliable, consistent. Just like you are."

I have nothing to say to that. The office goes silent for a long moment, but I'm finding it hard to concentrate. Eleanor's staring at me, and her gaze prickles my skin.

"Luke?" she finally says on an exhale. "I want you to know that I really am sorry for that day. For what I did. I shouldn't have left like that. I should have talked to you instead of leaving a note."

I tense up for a moment and sit back in my seat, lips pressed in a line. I can honestly say that I never thought we'd be having this conversation. What I said to Daisy at the community center is true—I moved on from Eleanor, whatever we once had is over, and I can definitively say that any romantic feelings are long gone. I simply figured I'd never get answers for what happened that day, never get total closure.

But we did have twelve years together, and I did once love Eleanor. Maybe we owe it to ourselves to talk about what happened—if only so that we have that total closure, once and for all. Although how to start this conversation, I have no idea.

Thinking of Daisy gives me strength, and I suddenly remember her little mantra.

Just one second...

"'I can't do this. I have to go.' That's all you wrote," I say the words without emotion, my voice detached. Because this is simply a fact.

"I was scared. I didn't know what to do, or what I

wanted. I didn't know how to face it. Face you." Eleanor gives her head a shake. "Lukey, I loved you, I really did. But I wasn't happy, and I knew that I had to try and go for what I wanted."

There's a brief silence as I consider her words, consider her point of view. And then, it all clicks into place. "I think I get it," I say.

"You do?"

"I mean, I don't get running out like you did, but I think I understand how you felt. I was ready to follow all the next steps—settle down, get married, be happy here, or in San Francisco, or wherever. But you wanted something else, and that's okay."

"I did..." she says. "Back then, I did..."

"I'm genuinely happy that you got what you wanted when you left town, that you became successful and found a good life. We weren't right for each other, Eleanor." As I say the words, I realize how much I mean each and every one of them. I consider the pain of that day, and the months following, and then the stark contrast to how things have been over the last month and a half. "You leaving that day was one of the worst things that ever happened to me. But also one of the best. I think it was for both of us."

My words hang in the air. I don't feel angry towards her, or upset. We're simply different people, and we weren't meant to be. Our paths were meant to separate eventually.

And in all honesty, a part of me is grateful now for how everything played out. Grateful that we broke up and my life seemingly fell apart.

Because it brought me to Daisy. Brought me to a life better than I could've imagined.

"I think you might be right." She pauses again. Swallows. "But can I ask one favor? For old times' sake?"

"Shoot."

229

"Can you tell my parents what you just told me? They still won't see me, but if they hear it from you, they might agree to talk to me." She smirks. "Then I can move back in with them and get out of that motel."

My lips pull up at the corners as I nod, feeling totally safe in the knowledge of where my heart truly lies. And for the first time, feeling grateful for the journey that brought me here. "I'll give it a try."

29

DAISY

"How do I look?"

I glance over my shoulder and burst into laughter. "Like the mankiest pirate I've ever seen."

Ivy smiles, revealing a false black tooth to complete her ill-fated seafarer costume. "Arr."

We both crack up laughing. Ivy has donned a misshapen pirate hat—bent from one too many days spent in Fran's costume closet—along with a moth-bitten black jacket, and a rounded hook to boot.

"What do pirates have to do with the Winter Carnival again?" Ivy asks.

"Beats me. But knowing Fran, there's a story."

Ivy removes the costume, puts it on the dining table, and returns to her place across from me on the living room floor. We've taken over my bungalow to make glittery signs and banners for the carnival. I can already imagine Dee's reaction when she comes home tonight and sees the state of the house. But maybe it'll push her towards making those renovations she's always talking about.

It's hard to believe that the Winter Carnival is kicking off tomorrow. The carnival is one of Mirror Valley's biggest events of the year, and I'm honored to be the one organizing it.

With Luke. Mostly.

I check my phone again, but the screen is blank. I chew the inside of my cheek, preoccupied as I put it down again.

"You okay?" Ivy asks.

"Yeah, totally fine." I offer a smile. "I just haven't heard from Luke since this morning. Barely heard from him the last couple days, either. He said he's got a lot going on at work these days, so I hope he's doing okay."

"I'm sure he's fine. Luke's nothing if not totally on top of things. It's almost annoying at times."

Ivy chuckles to herself, and I refrain from telling her that that's exactly what I'm worried about. I just hope that Luke's taking care of himself with being so busy.

"If I were you, I'd be more upset that he's basically abandoned you to finish this carnival planning by yourself." Ivy tuts, shaking her head teasingly. "The nerve of the guy. Good thing he has a wonderful, eternally helpful sister to help you out."

I laugh at her joke, appreciating the way she's lightening the mood. Luke was meant to be helping me today, and I'll admit that I'm a little disappointed he's not here. He's actually dropped off from planning almost completely over the last few days, which I do understand given his work, but I do still wish he was doing this with me.

Today, we were going to push this whole Winter Carnival business over the finish line together, but he messaged early this morning to say that he wouldn't be able to make it and that Ivy would come in his place.

The minute I read that, I popped out of bed right in time for the doorbell to ring downstairs.

On the bright side, extra quality time with my best friend is a pretty great trade-off. Especially given how little I see Ivy these days between her work at the Brookrose, her blissful married life, and my scrambling around like Bugs Bunny for the carnival.

As I get back to glittering a large plastic banner, my thoughts wander to that conversation Luke and I had at the community center. I was happy to be Luke's support in that moment, to be the strong one for him. The way he came apart and was so vulnerable with me made him even more precious in my eyes. Made me care for him all the more.

I still can't quite believe that I spilled my guts about my long-held feelings. But really... when *is* the best time to tell your best friend's older brother that you've had unrequited feelings for him since he basically disfigured you with a soccer ball?

It felt right to tell him the truth, though; to share some of my anxieties since we've been together and now that Eleanor's back.

"Dais, you're gluing glitter onto your pants."

I startle out of my thoughts. Remove the banner from my lap to see that Ivy's right.

"Curses," I mutter. "This is never gonna come out."

Ivy laughs. "It's quite the fashion statement. Glitter jeans might be the next big thing."

"Glitter jeans sound too messy to be anything." I purse my lips. "I was distracted."

"With what? Thinking about your *dreamy* new boyfriend?" Ivy immediately grimaces. "Who is my older brother. Ew. I don't want to know actually."

I chuckle. "Kind of, I guess... Luke and I had a pretty big conversation the other day, and I took your advice. I spilled my guts about a few things."

Ivy looks utterly triumphant, all smug and smirky. "See? Aren't I the best best friend ever?"

I roll my eyes. "No competition."

"So, what happened?"

"We just talked. And it was a really good talk. I told him how I'd been feeling, and he told me about Eleanor and—"

"Oh, good. I was wondering about that."

"About Eleanor being back?"

"Yeah. When I heard that they had lunch together yesterday, I wasn't sure what to make of it."

Ivy's finished glittering one poster board and is grabbing another so she doesn't see my expression. Which is probably a good thing as I'm pretty sure my entire face falls when she says those words.

"They had lunch?" I eventually manage.

"Yeah, at his office. She brought him a picnic."

My heart does the strangest little movement then. Like a drop straight through to the glitter-strewn shag carpet. My hands freeze on the banner, and only then does Ivy look up. Her face drops to match mine. "You didn't know?"

I give my head a jerky shake.

"Oh, Dais. I thought that's what you were talking about."

"Nope. We definitely haven't talked about that."

Ivy's brow crinkles as she thinks it over. "That is weird. Luke is usually pretty forthcoming with the things he thinks you need to know."

I give a shrug. "Maybe he thought I didn't need to know. For some reason."

Ivy's mouth presses into a line as she cracks her knuckles. Normally, I'd be giggling at the thought of tiny Ivy taking on her huge older brother, but I feel a little winded right now. I don't want to read into this, I really don't. But hearing that he had lunch with Eleanor, combined with the way he's essentially disappeared over the last few days, I feel myself giving in. Feel my mind surrendering to the doubts.

And then, I remember something Luke said when we spoke at the community center—that he wanted for so long for things to go back to normal. Go back to the way they were.

Is Eleanor being back making those old feelings resurface? Even a little bit?

Does *she* want to get back together with him?

I reject the questions, reject the way my body and mind are quick to jump to those conclusions.

Meanwhile, Ivy places a comforting palm on my leg. "Daisy, I can promise you right here and now that that lunch, whatever it was about, didn't mean anything."

"Yeah," I agree though my voice sounds far away. "They were probably talking about the wedding. Maybe he was getting answers. Getting closure."

How easy it is to say the words, even though I'm not sure I fully believe them at this moment.

"Exactly. It would legitimately be crazy to think that Luke would give up what he has with you to pursue anything with Eleanor. I'm sure he's going to tell you all about it as soon as he can."

Ivy smiles reassuringly, and I match it with my own smile. Logically, I know that she's right. Logically, I know that I should talk to Luke about this, or trust that he'll talk to me when he can.

But then again, since when is falling for someone in any way logical?

Luke: Hey Dais, I'm so sorry I haven't messaged you today. Been in and out of meetings, but I've just stepped out to text you. I miss you. How was your day? How was glittering with Ivy?

Daisy: Hey stranger, I miss you too. My day was good, but there's a small chance Dee might murder me when she gets home and sees the state of our living room.

Luke: Well if I can have a say, I'd rather she not murder you.

Daisy: So sweet of you to say.

Luke: She's been wanting to renovate forever though. Maybe a glitter-bombed living room will get her started.

Daisy: That's exactly what I'm thinking. And that's exactly what I'll tell her when she sees the sparkling pink walls.

Luke: I have some news. Really big news. It's kind of what these meetings have been about... I want to tell you now but I think this is more of an in-person thing.

Daisy: Color me intrigued.

Luke: I'll see you at the carnival tomorrow? Fran's somehow convinced me to act as security outside of her

237

tent. Why she needs security, I have no idea, but that's where I'll be.

Daisy: Standing guard outside of a fortune teller tent at a winter carnival? Color me even *more* intrigued.

Luke: I'm a man of many surprises, but there is apparently no limit to the things I'll do to make you smile, Dais.

Daisy: I'm definitely smiling. I'll see you tomorrow.

30

DAISY

Mirror Valley's Winter Carnival kicks off with a bang.

Literally.

The Morning Bell food truck, driven by the owner, Ethan Holmes, hit a patch of ice early this morning while he was trying to park, and the truck skidded directly into a decorative haybale by the entrance. Luckily, Ethan was driving slowly at the time, so the only damage done was to the haybale.

On the bright side, the hay adds a certain flair. To every single surface.

A group of us helped Ethan pluck hay off his truck, and then park in his designated spot, all while blowing warm air into our mitts and pulling our beanies low over our ears. We had our first significant dump of snow last night, and the temperatures seriously dropped. It's safe to say that winter has arrived for the Winter Carnival.

As is the case every year, it's being held on the grounds of the community center, with extra booths and activities scattered down Main Street. But it feels especially poignant this year as the center is closed. I know I'm not the only one who's looking at the quiet building with a certain amount of nostalgia.

What I wouldn't do to see it open again. To see it busy and bustling and full of life.

Like the Carnival is right now.

There's always a good turnout, but this year feels especially busy. I could almost believe that all of Mirror Valley is here, laughing and talking above the sounds of the crackling wood in the fire pits, the clomp of horses going out on sleigh rides, and the live band playing on the makeshift stage.

I wonder if people are feeling the desire to come together because of what's been happening with the town council. Mirrorites—as I like to call them—might have their individual squabbles and differences, but they always pitch in to help and contribute whenever needed.

I myself spend the morning puttering around to assist the staff and volunteers. I help vendors set up their booths, take their places if they need to use the restroom, and help with crowd control where needed. I serve hot cocoa and tea when there's a long lineup outside of a food truck, and I'm around when the petting zoo needs someone to feed the lambs.

The excited, bubbly atmosphere automatically boosts my mood, and I'm filled with happiness to see how everything's going. When I have a spare moment, I relish the smells of warm cinnamon and sugar, of hot cocoa and mint candy canes, of fresh baking. *This* is what a mountain winter feels like.

I also discover that the pirate costume belongs to a scarecrow that stands at the center of the festivities to scare birds away from the Christmas tree decorating contest.

So that's one mystery solved.

By the time afternoon rolls around, the crowds have

calmed down a little and everything is flowing smoothly. Which means that I'm finally able to find Luke.

I meander around the various activities and food stalls until I see it—the huge, maroon fortune teller tent on the outskirts of the carnival. And Luke is standing dutifully outside, looking somehow both bored and determined. I almost want to laugh. He's wearing a dark peacoat and black slacks, and even from here, I can see that his cheeks are tinted pink from the cool air.

I beeline towards him, excited to talk to him. Excited to hear his news.

But before I can reach him—before he sees me—Eleanor comes around the corner of the tent with two steaming takeout cups. She, of course, looks like the winter carnival queen in her fluffy white hat and matching white jacket. How she manages to look fresh and sun-kissed even in this cold weather is beyond me.

She says something to Luke, and he gives a polite smile before taking a sip of the cup she hands him. I pause for a moment, momentarily thrown off by the scene. But I take my hair out of my white scrunchie so it falls down my back, square my shoulders, and walk up to them.

"Hey," I say.

When Luke sees me, his eyes light up. He reaches out and pulls me into a hug. "You're here."

I chuckle into his shoulder and hug him back. When I step away, I smile at Eleanor. She seems mildly surprised, but is grinning. "Hi, Daisy. You're looking well."

"As are you."

"Luke mentioned that you took on most of the organization of the carnival this year." She lightly touches his arm when she says his name. "You did a great job."

This conversation feels like the most stilted, unnatural small talk I've ever had. Eleanor and I weren't close, and I do remember that she never seemed particularly genuine in her words. Right now though, she seems to mean what she says, and I decide to take the compliment. "Thank you, but I can't take all the credit. Luke was a big help."

Luke gives his head an adamant shake. "Nope. This is all Daisy. She's the one who made the carnival the success that it is today." He looks at me, his face serious. "I wasn't as involved as I should have been the last few days, but you'll understand why—"

At that moment, the flap of the maroon tent bursts open, and Dee storms out, followed by Noah.

"She's nutty!" Dee exclaims with a shake of her head. "Completely nutty."

"Certified oddball, but that's Fran," Noah agrees. Then, he spots our little group and gestures towards Luke. "Hey, bodyguard. Fran wants something."

"You couldn't help her?"

Noah points towards Dee's quickly retreating back. "I have more pressing matters to attend to."

Luke bites the inside of his cheek and looks at me for a long moment, seemingly debating what to do. I squeeze his arm. "Go ahead. I'll wait here."

He gives a nod before disappearing inside the tent, leaving me and Eleanor standing outside. Alone.

Hm. Maybe not my brightest idea.

There are not enough words to describe the awkward silence that hangs between us. I fiddle with my scrunchie, lost for any sort of topic. I can't exactly be like "how's it going?" or "what've you been up to lately?" or "how was that months-long trip you took to San Francisco?"

But for better or worse, Eleanor doesn't seem to notice the awkwardness. Instead, she's peering at me, a peculiar look on her face.

"You and Luke seem to be... friendly," she says lightly. I,

meanwhile, feel the opposite of light. I am a heavy weight of restless fidgeting looking everywhere but at her. An anvil of awkwardness. How do I talk to the woman who was engaged to my current boyfriend about the fact that we are, indeed, friendly?

I shift on my feet. "We've been spending a lot of time together."

All at once, her eyes clear. "You like him."

Well, yeah...

But before I can formulate a more delicate response, she continues. "And he likes you, I can tell."

I'm thrown off by her words, so I decide to play it off with a joke. "I would hope so given that we're dating."

She doesn't laugh, doesn't even crack a smile. Instead, her already huge eyes grow wide. "I didn't know."

"Luke didn't tell you?" My stomach twists uncomfortably. Those doubts are trying awfully hard to peek their heads out.

"I just assumed... well, I mean, I came back and I thought things might... we might..."

I press my lips together. "Oh."

I can confirm that we have reached new levels of awkwardness.

On the bright side, I wasn't completely crazy for wondering if Eleanor might want to get back together with Luke.

Is that a bright side? Maybe that's the wrong word for it.

At that moment, we're saved by a horrendous ripping sound, followed by a screech.

I whirl around to see that the huge plastic banner I was working on yesterday has fallen from the wooden archway near the stage and right onto Gloria Perez. Who is now flailing wildly beneath it looking like a Halloween ghoul who missed spooky season.

"Oh my gosh, I've got to go!" I exclaim as alarm floods my body. "I'll be back."

Eleanor puts a hand on my arm for a second, and I freeze. When I look back at her, her smile is kind. Genuinely kind. "I'll let Luke know."

I give a smile in return, then take off towards the stage.

31

LUKE

I now know way too much about what a dangling fake diamond earring looks like.

"You're a doll. A DOLL!" Fran exclaims as she clips the earring onto her ear. "You kids have such good vision. I never could've found this on my own."

I give a smirk. "You sure you don't want me to turn on any lights for you, Fran? The candles aren't very bright."

Her ruby red lips form a perfect O. "And lose the ambiance?! Absolutely not. We will continue as we mean to go on." She tuts, turning with a dramatic swish of her velvet cape thing. "Of course, Raymond would choose this precise moment to check out the petting zoo. That man's love for baby goats is truly unparalleled. But alas, thank goodness I have you."

She collapses into her plush rocking chair and takes off her red glasses, wiping the lenses. Meanwhile, I head towards the exit. "I'll be outside if you need anything else."

I hold the tent flap open to let in the next set of people wanting to get their fortunes read by the great Fran Bellamy, and then I walk back to where I left Daisy and

Eleanor. I feel like I'm bursting at the seams with the news I have for Daisy.

She is going to flip. I can't wait to see her face.

But only Eleanor is waiting outside. She's leaning against a haybale, holding up her phone and checking her reflection.

"Where's Daisy?" I ask with a frown.

She straightens, but doesn't put her phone away. "She had to go."

A heavy weight of disappointment hits my chest. I know I've let her down the past few days—I haven't been the most responsive, and I canceled on our plans yesterday morning without much of an explanation. I told Daisy that I wanted to be there for her, but I know that my actions haven't corresponded with my words.

I was stupid not to tell her this news right away, but I didn't want to say anything until everything was set in stone. Until I knew for sure what was happening, and that it was good news.

"Where?" I ask.

Eleanor tilts her head. "You've fallen for her."

Her words aren't accusatory, and she doesn't sound upset. She states this like she's telling me the daily temperature, and I answer her the same way. "Yes."

"I didn't realize that."

Now my brows raise in surprise. "You didn't know that Daisy and I were together?"

Eleanor shakes her head. "In retrospect, you guys *did* seem pretty cozy outside your house the other day, but I didn't put two and two together. And you never mentioned anything so..."

This might sound insane, but this has to be one of the biggest shocks since Eleanor showed up outside my house. Things with Daisy have been so good, and we've fallen into each other so easily, I assumed that everyone knew by now. Ivy and James, my grandparents, Dee and Noah, and then Fran. I was sure that our relationship was public knowledge the very same day that Fran caught us at the community center.

But then again, I suppose that Eleanor is out of the loop these days.

"Yes, I'm dating Daisy," I confirm. "And I'm crazy about her."

Eleanor shakes her head, seeming shaken but not saddened. "Wow. I came back here, and I guess I thought we'd come back to each other. I assumed that you and I would pick up where we left off, just like old times. Just like how things used to be." She opens her mouth and closes it again. "But I don't want to step on your toes, Luke. Or on hers."

I nod, unsure what to say to all that. There was a time where I would've done anything to go back to how things were, but I love this present moment infinitely more.

"I'm happy for you both," she continues. "And I can't say that I haven't noticed differences in you since I've been back." She gives me a small smile. "She's good for you. And when I told her that I thought you and I might get back together, she—"

I startle. "Wait, you said what?"

Eleanor bites her lip, and for the first time in awhile, she looks genuinely unsure of herself. "I kind of said that I had certain expectations when I got back here. But then Daisy said you two were together and..."

A cool discomfort licks at my stomach, and I swing my head around looking for Daisy once more. This time, with just a *smidge* more urgency.

Eleanor seems to sense this because she nods to a spot over my shoulder. "She's by the stage helping with some signage issue. But can I give you a word of advice, Luke? Don't be afraid to show her how much she means to you."

I'm about to stride over to Daisy and talk to her. Put my arms around my girlfriend and tell her how much I care about her. But Eleanor's words give me an idea.

A stupid, ridiculous, completely nonsensical idea. But one that I think Daisy will love.

She wanted to find her perfect romance trope, and while I may not know much about romance tropes, I do know that every great love story has a grand gesture.

"You're right," I mutter in reply. "Thanks."

Then, I grit my teeth, curse under my breath, and take off into the crowd before I can come to my senses.

32

DAISY

"Are you sure you're okay?" I ask Gloria, brushing at a cluster of glitter on the sleeve of her fleece jacket.

"I'm fine, my girl. Just a small shock."

I smile ruefully. "That banner almost took you out."

"It was only a piece of plastic. Nothing to fuss about. The glitter is more worrisome—you can *never* get rid of the stuff." She pats her hair. A few sparkling flecks fall out. "This was part of the job when I was a teacher. Seems you can take the teacher out of the glitter, but you can't take the glitter out of the teacher."

We both laugh, and I'm grateful for Gloria's positive attitude. And she makes a good point—I vacuumed the living room for an hour last night and still found the odd fleck of glitter this morning. As predicted, Dee was less than enthused when she got home, and mildly, lovingly—or so I'm telling myself—joked that I had to move out STAT.

The good news is that the band is on their break, so Gloria was the only one around for the great Banner-Fall.

After apologizing another few times, I bend to pick up her purse for her. And that's when the most awful, metallic screech comes from behind me.

This time from a machine, not a person.

"My goodness!" Gloria exclaims, clapping her hands over her ears. She looks behind me towards the stage, and her face goes slack.

"Sorry, everyone."

The voice over the microphone feedback is rich and smooth. Like dark chocolate.

But it couldn't be. It simply cannot be...

I turn around, and Luke Brooks is standing on the stage holding a microphone.

At once, the entire carnival seems to freeze. People stop talking and milling around, children stop squealing and laughing. Even the horses stop their clomping. And instead, hundreds of pairs of eyes turn towards the stage.

Towards Luke. Who's looking right at me.

"If I can have everyone's attention for a brief moment, I have something I'd like to say."

I manage to move my jaw from its position of being totally ajar. "What are you doing?!" I mouth.

Luke simply smirks in response, and then, I know. I know exactly what he's doing. The very thing I discouraged Eddie from doing a few weeks ago. And while I said then that it was a bad move, my skin erupts in goosebumps, and my lips break into a smile.

Luke seems to gain courage from my expression, and he continues. "Y'all might know I'm not great with words, so I'll keep this short. A lot has happened over the past year and a half, a lot has changed. But the biggest change came about because of one very special person. She completely turned my world upside down, and I couldn't be more grateful. But I won't ask her up here because we've already seen what she can do when she's in the spotlight."

There's a ripple of laughter through the crowd, and I snort, remembering being up on the gazebo at Ivy and

James's wedding. My eyes are on Luke's, and I can't move, can't even blink. My cheeks feel warm, and somehow, in some way, it feels like it's just the two of us here right now.

"The key point in all this is that I am here, and I am making a stupid declaration of love speech..." He grimaces a little, and I have to laugh. "Because I am completely and totally in love with Daisy Griffiths. And I think she feels the same way."

I'm nodding, a big, stupid, enthusiastic movement. I'm aware of the whispers and mutters, the stares in my direction, but only barely. They're ripples beneath the waves of ocean water.

"Daisy, I want you to know—want *everyone* to know—that I'm crazy about you. Always will be. You've changed my life for the better in so many ways, but how I feel about you will never change."

Ohmygosh, am I floating up to heaven right now?

There's one clap, and then another, and suddenly the entire crowd is clapping and someone is cheering and another is singing some cheesy song. Luke leaves the mic onstage and walks into the crowd towards me. I meet him halfway and lace my arms behind his neck.

"So? Wrong move?" he asks teasingly.

"I will say that I never expected anything like that from you."

"Public speaking is not my strong suit."

"Well, it was great. It was definitely the right move." I smile. "But it was also completely unnecessary."

Luke's expression shifts towards surprise. "Really."

I give a nod. "My whole life, I think I had these hopes and expectations of the perfect ending, a fairytale happily-ever-after. But the thing is, that's still an ending. The story is finished. And relationships don't just end after the happily-ever-after. They require hard work and messiness some-

251

times. But you know what? It means that we don't get just one happily-ever-after, we get many."

He smiles softly, his eyes intent on my face, and I have to hold back my own grin so I can continue.

"I want you to know, Luke Brooks, that I want to be with you for all of it. For the happily-ever-afters, and also for the hard times and difficult moments. I think we can do it together."

"I know we can." Luke tucks my hair behind my ear, as confident and unwavering as ever.

"You sound so sure."

Luke is quiet for a long moment. "Actually, I'm not." His words threaten to tear a hole through me, until he speaks again. "There's a ton I'm not sure about. I'm not sure if I want to wear green or gray pants tomorrow, if I'll want eggs or granola for breakfast. I'm unsure what the color of our mailbox will be, and what we might call our kids if we have them. But you, Dais? It's not a question in my mind. I've never been so sure of anything like I want you."

He presses a kiss to the top of my head, and I close my eyes, relishing being in his arms. When I open them again, I spot Eleanor watching us with a small smile. She sees me looking and bows her head before turning away.

And with that movement, I feel completely at peace. Not because the entire town now knows, for sure, that Luke and I are together. Not because Eleanor is apparently giving us the go ahead. Not even because I know that Luke and I are meant to be together...

It's because I know that I didn't really need any of it. Life is complex, has the good with the bad, and there are going to be times in our story that aren't happily-ever-after perfect. But there's a comfort, a sweet surrender, in knowing that I really would do anything for this man to make him happy. Just as he would do for me.

The carnival has started back up again, people are returning to their activities, but even so, there are more than a few people smiling at us and pointing our way. I lean back a little to meet Luke's eyes, and he gazes at me tenderly. "Maybe Ed wasn't so off base after all," he says.

"Maybe not. I'm sure Courtney would be happy for a declaration of love speech when he isn't drunk, though." I mean this as a joke, but I bite my lip, feeling very serious. "Speaking of and just to be clear... you know I love you too, right?"

Luke lets out a dry chuckle. "I had a feeling."

I stand on my tiptoes and press a gentle kiss to his lips. "So, now what?"

"Now we start our future together. Right after I thank your sister."

"You want to thank Dee? Why?"

"For her app. RightMatch is the reason we got together. If I hadn't tried it, I might still be wandering around aimlessly when the person I'm meant to be with has been right in front of me all along." He shakes his head, seeming upset with himself.

I laugh, press my forehead to his. "I did have *quite* the crush on Aaron B."

"Nothing compared to how I felt for Sisi."

"We had that fake identity thing going for awhile."

"Guess you were my right wrong match."

I smile at the expression, and Luke bends his head to claim my lips with his once again. Just a light brush, but he pulls me close and holds me against him. I let myself fall into the kiss as this one, once again, knocks all our previous ones out of the park.

Luke is my person, my right match. The man I'll always be lucky to love, and the one who is my forever happily-ever-after.

33

DAISY

"Friends, first date, or married?" Luke asks.

I take a look at the couple he's referring to—currently having a picnic on the grass a few paces away. They're young, no more than 18, and sitting close together on a blanket. The girl is giggling and knocking her shoulder against the guy's shoulder, while his hand creeps closer towards hers.

"First date," I say with a smile. "Might be a little young to be married."

Luke chuckles. "Agree. Give them a few years."

"Mr. Positivity over here."

"You're definitely rubbing off on me."

I laugh and gaze at my boyfriend as he takes another drink of his coffee. The summer sun illuminates his face in such a way that he looks almost god-like. He's wearing aviator glasses, and he's grown out his scruff a little over the last couple months. I often joke that he looks like a younger, more country version of Chris Hemsworth—a comparison that always makes him scowl.

Luke catches me staring, and his brow raises behind his sunglasses. He takes my hand and electric sparks race up my arm, filling my body with warmth. Even nine months later, those sparks, that excitement, haven't faded one bit. The pull and fire between us is as strong as it's ever been.

In fact, over the past few months, we've only gotten closer, only gotten stronger as a couple. As much as I love Ivy and my sister, Luke's my best friend, my confidant, the person I rely on and love above everything else. He is it for me, and I'm it for him. We've talked about marriage, talked about the kids we'll have one day, and I've wondered when he might propose. He's told me he fully intends to.

But I'm in no rush. I don't want to rush a single second with him.

With Luke's hand warm around mine, I turn my face up towards the sky and close my eyes against the sun. I take a deep breath of the fresh air.

All around me is noise. Laughter and conversation. Children screeching and the splashes of water. A gentle coffee shop playlist.

Luke and I are sitting at a table on the patio of the community center coffee shop. The center reopened last week after a months-long renovation, and the interior is modern and functional now. There's an updated and expanded gymnasium, a refurbished meeting room, new equipment in the small workout studio, and a revamped library section. And there are new spaces too—a games room with ping-pong tables and basketball shooting machines, a small arcade, and of course, a jacuzzi and outdoor splash pool.

The grand opening was a huge affair, and the entire town came out to celebrate. Reopening the community center really was a joint effort though, and it was the last major change to come out of last fall's drama when we discovered the issue with the town finances.

Well, when Luke discovered it.

Turns out that Dora Mae Movis was misappropriating public funds. Had been for months. She'd been taking advantage of one of Mirror Valley's reimbursement programs to make personal purchases that ended up being in the tens of thousands of dollars. She managed to cover it all up and keep it quiet for awhile, but the problem eventually showed up in the council's finances.

Dora Mae is now banned from Mirror Valley—in that if she ever tries to come back, she will be quite shunned—and is awaiting trial.

Needless to say, after the whole ordeal, Mirror Valley did its best to get back to normal. And that meant working together to bring back staff and reopen public buildings.

Unbelievably, even Eleanor has played a part. She used her social media platforms to promote Mirror Valley and fundraise for the community center. Bit by bit, she's making amends. She finally made up with her parents, and the town is slowly but surely accepting her back. And while I certainly don't think we'll be friends anytime soon, it's good to see how much she's grown as a person. Well, that she's *growing* as a person.

There's a loud clatter at the table next to me, and I jump, my eyes slicing open.

"Daisy, Lukey," Noah greets us cheerfully, tipping his ball cap towards us. "Are we interrupting a nap?"

"Noah, you're so annoying," Dee teases him as she sits across from him. She looks over at me and Luke. "Excuse him, he's not at his best first thing in the morning."

"Now, that's rude. I personally think I'm a joy at any hour of the day." Noah pauses. "Or night."

He waggles his eyebrows, and Dee sighs. I have to hold

back a snort. I'm not sure of the truth behind Noah's words, but he so clearly loves getting a rise out of Dee.

"You working today, Dais?" Dee asks, taking a drink of her large coffee.

Meanwhile, I swirl the remnants of my iced chocolate. I'm still debating if I want to order another one from Ricky. "I worked early this morning, and I'm heading back to City Hall this afternoon as well."

"Councilor Daisy Griffiths." Noah smiles. "Does this mean you can get me out of speeding tickets?"

He sips at his iced tea with large, imploring eyes as Dee punches him in the shoulder. Of course, he has a snappy response and, within minutes, the two of them are bickering away again like an old married couple.

I turn back to Luke. "Here we go again."

He chuckles but doesn't have anything to say, which is a little out of character for him. But before I can call him out on it, I spot Ivy and James, of all people, walking up the lawn towards us.

I blink in confusion and give them a wave. "Hey, guys!"

Ivy glances at James for the briefest moment before waving back. "Mind if we join you?"

The two of them take a table on the other side of Luke and me. As James sits across from Ivy, I could swear he shares a look with Luke.

Ivy grasps my arm like we haven't seen each other in years. "Dais, you look like a dream! It's been ages!"

I have to laugh at that. I'm only wearing jeans and a white top; nothing special. "Ivy, we saw each other, like, two days ago."

"Really?" she grimaces. "Mags has been so fussy lately, it makes me lose track of time."

She tucks her hair behind her ears, laughing. If anything, Ivy's the one who looks a dream—she's got this glow about her, this aura of worldliness and maturity. Which makes sense given that she's a brand-new mom to baby Maggie, named after Ivy and Luke's beloved grandmother.

"Where is Mags anyway?" I ask with a frown.

"She's with her great-grandparents. They insisted that James and I take a break, grab a coffee with you guys."

"With us? I mean, I'm very glad to see you, but I thought I was only meeting Luke here..." I trail off as I glance at Luke, but he just calmly sips his drink with this butter-won't-melt expression.

Ivy waves her hand distractedly, and then busies herself giving James her drink order. Behind me, Dee and Noah are still chatting about goodness knows what.

It does feel a little odd that we're all here together right now, and I look at Luke with my eyes narrowed. "Is something going on?"

He simply grins, puts down his coffee and leans towards me. "We're celebrating your first few months as a town councilor, and all the good you've been doing."

"Yes," Ivy says triumphantly. "Here's to Daisy!"

"Cheers!" Noah clacks his glass of iced tea with Dee's cup as she says, "Hear, hear!"

With all the celebrations, I have to smile, my cheeks warm and my insides gooey. I never, ever envisioned myself working on a town council. Heck, I didn't even think our community would be interested in electing someone like me.

Last winter, I did a lot of thinking about what I wanted and what felt right for me as a job. And I always came back to my two biggest loves—helping people, and my hometown of Mirror Valley. With Dora Mae Movis leaving the council, there was a spot open, and Luke encouraged me to run, to put my name in.

The amount of votes for me to join council was truly touching. I cried, and let me tell you, this was the ugliest of cries—red nose, splotchy skin, swollen mole eyes. But Luke kissed me anyway and said he was proud of me, and everything... clicked.

As soon as I joined the council, I pushed for our public buildings to reopen, and they did, one by one. The community center was the last building we considered, and with Luke's financial guidance, I proposed that we do a full-scale renovation before re-opening.

Seeing the joy on everyone's faces today, hearing the buzz around the coffee shop and the lobby, I'm so grateful I fought for it.

James returns with a tray of drinks, and he, Ivy, Dee and Noah burst into conversation about the upcoming Mirror Valley Music Festival. This was a suggestion put forth by Fran to celebrate the end of summer by inviting musicians to perform in Mirror Valley. It was a bit of a debate amongst us councilors as Fran only pitched her friend Raymond playing piano, along with a random troupe of circus performers. But eventually, we found a few buskers from our county and invited them to play.

It should be a fun couple of weeks to round off an excellent summer.

"Hey." Luke's voice is low, and I turn to face him. He removes his sunglasses so I get the full force of his gorgeous hazel eyes, and he leans in closer. I lean towards him too, closing the distance between us. "I have one more for you."

I tilt my head, momentarily distracted by the half-smirk on his lips. "One more what?"

"One more couple."

I should look away, should look out for the couple he's talking about, but I can't bring myself to move. His forest scent feels like home to me now—home mixed with some special pheromone mixture that makes me want to crawl into his lap and kiss him passionately. Which might be inappropriate at this moment.

"So, Dais," he says quietly. "Which one is it? Friends, first date, or married?"

And before I can say anything, he pushes a small, square box across the table.

Goosebumps race across my skin, and time slows. "What is that?" I ask in an uneven whisper.

Luke gives me that smirk of his. He appears as unflappable as ever, but I see the small click in his jaw, the passion in his eyes. He's as tuned into this moment as I am. "What do you think it is?"

Then, quickly and smoothly in a way that I don't think I could manage on my most graceful day, he drops to one knee in front of our friends. He opens the box, and there, on a bed of white satin fabric, lies a beautiful emerald ring.

My heart rate spikes. My mouth has gone completely dry.

"Ohmygosh," I whisper. My eyes are darting between the ring and Luke's handsome, smiling face.

And that's when I realize that I haven't actually said the word out loud. Haven't actually answered past the overwhelming YES in my head.

"Married! Definitely married!" I stutter, and without even taking the ring, I fall on Luke, almost knocking him over. He laughs as he stands with me in his arms, and finally, he kisses me. I feel his smile against mine.

Time speeds up again, and I hear Ivy and Dee cheering for us. James is whooping and whistling. In the far distance, Noah mutters, "Get a room".

I'm sure we're making an absolute spectacle of the coffee shop right now. But I don't care.

Luke and I separate, and our friends surround us in a

group hug. He presses his forehead to mine and utters words only I can hear. "For all the years we've known each other, and all the years we have ahead, I'll always love you, Daisy Griffiths."

"Forever with you, Luke Brooks."

❦

Dee

"Well, that was awfully romantic," Noah says as we walk down Main Street towards my office.

"Luke did tell us to expect a proposal."

"I love the way he did it. That guy might just have a soft side after all."

"For my sister, he definitely does." I insert my keys into the small glass door next to the entrance to Ria's Salon. I rent out a small space upstairs to do my work, just to change it up from my bedroom and study at home. With the money I make at RightMatch, it hasn't been an issue to get a workspace in town.

Noah follows me up the narrow staircase. "He definitely didn't show that soft side when I was working at Argent. The guy is, like, a brick wall of seriousness."

"Compared to you, *anyone* is a brick wall of seriousness."

"Still..." Noah heads into the tiny kitchen and opens the minifridge to pull out a lemonade. "I guess you know him better than I do. You know, given that you dated him."

I give my head a shake. "You've got to stop teasing me about that. We went to *one* games night together. And the whole thing was fake because Luke was obviously into my sister at the time, and I figured that was the best way to get Daisy to come to terms with her own feelings."

"Really? So there wasn't any other reason that you went along with the fake dating thing except to bring those two together?"

"Nope. No reason. At all," I say angelically.

Noah might be my best friend in the entire world, but he doesn't need to know that I *did* actually have an ulterior motive when I said yes to Luke all those months ago. It would only complicate matters.

There are certain things that Noah and I don't talk about. Like, he doesn't ask me why I rarely date, and I don't ask him about his gallivanting with every girl in our county. We also don't talk about what happened when we went into Fran's fortune teller tent last fall. Of all the things she could've predicted for us, the words "destined for marriage" were at the bottom of my list of expectations.

Noah laughed it all off, because of course he did, and now, we simply never bring it up.

"Anyway." I change the subject. "How're your brothers? You said Sam's thinking of moving back."

"He is. Would that be weird for you, given your whole high school crush thing?"

I purse my lips. "Over it."

Noah saunters over to the plushy red couch in the corner of my office and splays himself across it. It's too short for him so his long limbs hang over the sides.

Don't look at me, *I* certainly didn't want a couch in my office. Such a thing simply dilutes the working environment and mixes business with cozy. I arrived one day, discovered my office door was unlocked, and when I got upstairs, the couch was just... here.

I still don't know how Noah got a copy of my keys.

I sit at my desk and start up my computer. Knowing

Noah, he's going to hang out here for awhile then head out to softball practice or whatever he's got going on tonight.

"How's that whole management thing going at work?" Noah asks lazily, and my back stiffens. Sometimes, I forget how good a listener he is. He actually pays attention when I tell him what's happening at work.

"It's okay," I say swiftly. "There are some shifts happening, but I don't think they'll affect me or my team."

"That's good. Because you're my sugar mama, and if you're out of a job, that means I might actually have to work."

I sigh deeply as Noah chuckles. We both know the guy certainly doesn't need money. "So, do you think you might actually get a real job sometime soon?" I ask.

"The accounting thing was alright, but boring. I enjoyed working with Ethan at Morning Bell, and helping out at the garage, but none of those things really spoke to me. I haven't found my online dating app dream job like *some* people in this room."

I stifle a chuckle. Working for a dating app was *not* my dream job. In fact, it couldn't be more ironic given how little I date, myself. "Yeah, right."

"We'll see. It would be nice to find something that clicks for me."

I have to press my lips together to hold back the words that threaten to leave my mouth. "*Are you going to look for a job away from here?*"

But Noah's never talked about leaving Mirror Valley, and I'm certainly not going to be the one to put that idea in his head.

"You'll find somewhere that can tolerate you, I'm sure," I joke so the other words can't escape my mouth.

"Love the vote of confidence, Dee-bug." Then, as predicted, he stands, presses a friendly kiss to the top of my head, and heads towards the stairs. "I'm off. Dylan wanted to work on his pitching before practice today. See you later?"

"As always," I reply.

And with that, Noah's gone, and I can finally get back to work.

Thank you so much for reading!

If you enjoyed this book, please leave me a review. As a new author, reviews mean everything to me. I appreciate each and every one of them.

Daisy's Romance Trope List

♥ ~~Enemies to lovers~~

♥ ~~Best friends to lovers~~

♥ Childhood friends to lovers

♥ Gym Crush

♥ Work Hubby

♥ ~~Fake Boyfriend~~

♥ ~~Blind Date~~

♥ Online Date

♥ Star Quarterback? Athlete?

♥ ~~Kindergarten Husband~~

++ Foot massager... romance?

THANK YOU FROM SJ

If you've made it to this point, I want to say THANK YOU!! Thank you for picking up a copy of Luke and Daisy's story. Thank you for joining me on their match-making adventures and ridiculous mishaps. Thank you for taking a chance on these two very opposite characters and their love story <3

I also want to extend a very special thanks to my incredible ARC team. This book would look very, very different without their careful, helpful feedback. And also to my exceptional beta readers... KB, you were a rockstar and this book would NEVER have come together if it wasn't for you!!

And to you, reader. I had the best time writing about Luke and Daisy, and I hope you enjoyed reading it just as much.

Now, back to the next draft, a pile of snacks, and much happy dancing.

Sending all the hugs your way.

XX SJ

Printed in Great Britain
by Amazon

46766354R00153